Andrei Livadny

Servo Battalion

Thank you FOR your support and inspiration! They mean so much to me,

Andrei Livadny.

The History of the Galaxy
Book#3

Magic Dome Books

Servobattalion
The History of the Galaxy, Book # 3
Copyright © Andrei Livadny 2018
Cover Art © Vladimir Manyukhin 2018
English Translation Copyright ©
Sofia Gutkin 2018
Published by Magic Dome Books, 2018
All Rights Reserved
ISBN: 978-80-7619-006-1

TABLE OF CONTENTS:

Prologue

THE SULTRY, OVERCAST MIDDAY on Vesuvius was lit up by a multitude of eruptions.

The air was unbreathable, poisoned by the volcanic emissions, and the sky, like a gray sheet, hung low and reflected the crimson of the fiery chaos below.

The world laid out below the oppressive sky appeared unfit for human life but the war had changed many of the suitability criteria.

Vesuvius was not just colonized but densely

populated with the industrial bases of the Terran Alliance located here, which repaired the technology damaged in the fighting. Through an anomaly in space, damaged spaceships were towed from sites of battle into orbit around the planet, and were then brought down to the surface using special technical carriers. There were also plenty of transports carrying broken servomachines, with some to be repaired and some intended for disassembly into spare parts.

Vesuvius hosted not only repair docks for large ships but also factories for restoring planetary technology. The harsh conditions of the hot young planet, whose volcanic activity meant that additional camouflage was unnecessary, and where natural resources lay practically on the surface, had another advantage: its training grounds for testing repaired servomachines ideally met the criteria for "close to combat" conditions.

DONALD CROWE had an easy attitude to life.

Serving on the testing grounds of Vesuvius would not seem like a cushy job at other times, but with a war raging across the entirety of colonized space and claiming huge numbers of victims, life under a low, leaden sky seemed like paradise if the alternative was almost certain death.

So he didn't complain about his fate.

Today did not promise any trouble and hardly

differed from Donald's hundreds of other days, bland and boring, filled with difficult but not dangerous work.

Today he had to run through tests for three Hoplites repaired after fierce fighting. It was nothing complicated or unusual — a walk through the broken and treacherous terrain with poor visibility due to the volcanic ash constantly falling from the sky, a couple of jumps using the jet accelerators over the narrow rivers of lava crossing the plain, and some target shooting.

Apart from having to spend several hours in an old combat suit with a faulty thermoregulation system, Donald did not anticipate any issues.

Leaving the hangar, Crowe strode confidently over to the last mechanism in the line. Hoplite2M was a new model that promised to become the real paratrooper 'workhorse' in the near future.

APPROACHING the forty-five-tonne giant, Donald couldn't help but note the mechanism's appearance: both guns had been replaced, the weapon pylons on the right had newly assembled missile tubes, and the anti-aircraft turret was completely absent with two medium-powered lasers installed instead.

'Interesting configuration.' Crowe thought as he circled around the servomachine. Beneath a coat of fresh 'chameleon' coating (currently deactivated), some of the armor plates showed numerous pitting. 'It really got hit hard,' Donald thought with surprise, noting that all the armored covers protecting the servomotor nodes looked factory-fresh and glossy — they had been replaced like most of the ceramlite segments. It appeared that the servomechanism hadn't just sustained critical damage but had been literally riddled with bullets...

It was difficult to imagine the slaughter that the Hoplite had been in to sustain *such* damage.

Fine. My job is to test the machine.

Donald, in an excellent mood, opened the protective screen and touched the technical access sensor into the cabin.

The hatch opened obediently and the lift segment slid down from above.

Whistling a cheerful tune, Donald ascended to the cabin, crossed the airlock and found himself inside the servomachine.

The overview screens switched on when he appeared and the mobile control panels surrounding the pilot cradle moved aside, providing access to the chair.

He switched on telecommunication through the implant — this didn't initiate the full-scale neurosensory contact of a person with the Maverick system but rather enabled third-level mental commands, which were quite sufficient for technical testing, especially since the machine would perform most of the operations itself. Donald's role was to throw it sudden curve balls, which the cyber system had to respond to quickly and appropriately.

Well, baby, shall we begin?

The communication channel responded with a ringing silence. The control panels automatically returned to their places, the autopilot lights switched on — the machine indicated its full readiness to undergo testing, but the Maverick module was refusing to talk to the human.

Donald got angry.

He was normally quite easy-going, even a bit cowardly, and it was only when dealing with the soulless and obedient machines that he behaved arrogantly.

After all, no matter what they said about the new generation AI in the Mavericks (according to the specifications, Beatrice-4 was installed aboard this Hoplite) Crowe always regarded machine intelligence as a cheap fake. So what if it's an AI, what's he supposed to do, talk to every infantry android like they're his equal now?

Now, baby, stop acting up. You've probably got a cute voice. Come on, say, "Good morning, pilot".

The silence in the communicator was now deafening. It seemed thick as syrup, hostile and unpleasant.

Fine. 'I'll deal with you.' Donald thought with a touch of irritation as he buckled on his harness. The cushioning arcs of the pilot cradle (which would be ejected if the machine sustained critical damage) automatically closed around him, the control panels moved even closer and all the indicator lights signaled readiness to commence testing.

'Forward, straight ahead for 500 meters then turn 90 degrees to the right. Go!'

The Hoplite didn't move.

'Piece of shit... Who do you think you are, you metal lump? I clearly said, go!'

Something unbelievable happened in the next instant. Instead of obeying the order, the machine suddenly lit up an angry warning signal on the control panel, and then came the characteristic sound of the cabin's armor plates opening like a metal bud, and the pilot cradle, together with the stunned Donald, was flung into the gloomy skies of Vesuvius by the emergency catapult.

The Hoplite catapulted the pilot, switched on the telemetry channel, reporting about the functioning systems to the testing grounds' central control room, and then started moving — 500 meters straight ahead and then to the right — and kept moving on its own initiative, overcoming various obstacles in its way and shooting at any suddenly appearing targets.

BY THE TIME Donald Crowe freed himself from the safety harness and hobbled over to the command post, the Hoplite had already completed its test program, independently returned to the hangar and stopped in the center of the marking circle.

Entering the control room, Donald let out a loud stream of abuse, his helmet already unclipped.

The man in charge of the testing grounds, a major who had lost both his arms in the fighting and now wore cyber prostheses instead, looked at the enraged pilot and said,

"Calm down."

"Calm down?! That blasted machine tossed me out of the cabin!"

"I saw it."

"And?!" Crowe's face twisted in a mean grimace.

"You clearly weren't to Beatrice's liking." The major replied coolly. "I've looked through the documents and it appears that she lost her pilot in the last battle. Then she came to us."

"So, what, she's in shock? She can't see other people? She won't listen to other people's orders? She's missing her pilot?"

"Yes." The major replied with cold hostility in his voice.

"Since when are Mavericks allowed to have emotions and, moreover, to throw people out of their cabins?"

"Her pilot was killed." The senior officer at the testing ground repeated as if he hadn't heard Donald's words. Unlike Crowe, he knew what it was like to lose friends in battle, and, comparing the boorish behavior of the test pilot with the restrained reaction of the AI after it had experienced the pain of loss, he found the comparison not in Crowe's favor.

"Look," the major said tiredly. "The machine has fully passed the test. It's serviceable. Go ahead and sign the test certificate and we'll forget about what happened."

"What?!"

"What nothing. I have made my decision: the test was successful and the Hoplite has been recommended for use in automatic, unmanned mode. Sign it or I swear to God, I'll find a way to send you to the front!"

Donald's jaw dropped and he turned pale — it was the first time he had seen the stolid major look absolutely *furious* and didn't doubt for a moment that the man would carry out his promise.

Damn it.

"Okay, I'll sign it." Crowe said aloud.

Bending over the sheet of plastpaper

containing the test results and adding his signature, Donald glanced at the other papers out of the corner of his eye.

For most of the machines in the latest batch, the same sender was listed: Thirteenth Servobattalion.

Chapter One

25 June 2624
Hammer's Line

THEY ARRIVED on Yunona as part of the latest reinforcements.

Two hundred young people, aged seventeen to nineteen.

The shuttle that brought them from the general military transport landed at sunrise, when Yuna's flaming disc had barely appeared above the horizon.

Their first impression of a planet fully

terraformed and covered in greenery was misleading. Beneath the masking plantations of identical coniferous trees, modified at the military laboratories of New Earth, hid a branching network of military bases, spaceports and testing grounds. The planet was far from the enormous park it looked to be from orbit, but rather a single research and testing facility where new types of weapons were put through their paces.

The captain meeting the new recruits waited until the disorderly crowd got itself organized and stopped chattering. Heat emanated from the shuttle and in the gradually settling silence, they could hear the crackling of the armor plates as they cooled down. Shreds of morning mist drifted up from a small valley formed by the network of drainage ditches along the edge of the landing field. Yuna's orange rays illuminated the treetops with a fiery and poisonous shade of crimson, which seemed unnatural to the inhabitants of Earth, and all of it together created an indelible impression that made the newcomers fall silent.

The captain waited patiently, knowing that Yunona itself would silence the youth better than any yelling. The inhabitants of Earth's megacities, who had never seen such careless and disorganized open space before and still did not fully comprehend where and why they had been brought here, eventually fell silent and their eyes unwittingly turned to the officer standing alone.

"Boys and girls." He spoke quietly, even insinuatingly, making the last voices fall silent. "I know that only a few of you have come here voluntarily by signing up at the mobilization centers. However, it's no longer important what desires, motivations, beliefs or lack thereof made you avoid mobilization or voluntarily come to the recruitment center. Look around you and understand that you are on a different planet, outside your usual environment. I'm not going to yell at you and call you scum and promise to make a cool soldier out of each one of you. Those of you who have watched too many bad movies can forget about that. You are now servomachine pilots. Your first step off the shuttle has become a step from a carefree civilian life into war.

There's no way back. Nobody is going to demean you or try to break you to turn you from rabble into 'real soldiers'. Where you're going, only the strongest and most skilled ones will survive. Forget everything that happened in the past. From now on, each one of you has an identity. The identity of a pilot. Only your personal qualities will determine who will live and who will die in the first battle. Mark my words and those of you who are lucky will remember them often. A servomachine pilot is an individual first and foremost, for the technological might capable of destroying any obstacle will be placed in your hands. The concept of friendship often loses its meaning in modern warfare. There may be no living combat companions beside you, only machines.

This is why everyone needs to learn how to be a leader. I repeat, it doesn't matter who you were yesterday. And now," he turned, "follow me."

"HE SEEMS kinda nuts. Probably totally shell-shocked." An African-American guy muttered defiantly. "What do you reckon?" He turned to the skinny teenager of European descent next to him. "What's your name?"

"Anton." The boy said curtly.

"I'm Simon. Simon Green." He slowed down slightly, matching his stride to Anton's. "Let's stick together."

"All right." Anton replied readily.

"Hey, how were you picked up?"

"Very simply. They brought us all here for one reason." Verkholin was staring at his feet as if some unexpected obstacle could appear on the spaceport's smooth plates. "Free account in the Layer. And a tournament arena."

"The Layer, so what?" Simon snorted. "I was hanging out there daily, and?"

"Use your head. *What* was the arena simulating?"

Simon pursed his full lips. "You reckon?" He asked suspiciously. "Of course, war games are great, especially when there's nothing better to do. But not to this extent!"

"Exactly to this extent." Responded Verkholin.

Simon fell quiet, inadvertently drawing his head into his shoulders.

No, he didn't get scared, it was a different sensation: he suddenly understood that what the officer had said weren't empty phrases.

'Damn, he talked to us like we were equals,' Simon thought suddenly. 'Could Anton be right and the reason that I've been brought to this strange and freakish world, like the others, was because of the total number of points that I accumulated playing the virtual servomachine simulator?'

Simon could theoretically accept, of course, that if he suddenly landed in the cabin of a Hoplite or a Phalanger, he wouldn't simply hang his mouth open in surprise, but the officer walking nearby seemed convinced that they were capable of much more...

He glanced at Anton but the wish to discuss their sudden prospects with his new friend had disappeared for some reason. Let's see, then...

Let's see why they dragged us all here...

HUMANITY, at least the part that had set the war in motion, twice had a real chance to stop the fighting but had never used it.

Why? Why, despite the massive casualties and current deadlock, did the war not die down but, on the contrary, flared up with a new, fierce and uncompromising intensity?

It was said that within five years after the blockade of Dabog was broken, the war was being fought mostly by machines on the side of the Alliance — it was this factor that intensified the conflict and didn't let it stop.

A generally accepted lie.

War was always begun and ended by humans, while machines remained faithful to non-existent forces for thousands of years, or to put it more simply, they remained hostage to the programs that humans had installed in them.

18 July 2624.
Aboard the cruiser Apostle, flagship of the Seventh Strike Fleet of the Terran Alliance.

Admiral Kupanov sat comfortably in his

chair, his eyes half-closed, surrendering to the power of virtual reality.

An emergency meeting had just commenced and communication between the flagships of the seven strike fleets was carried out using floating hypersphere frequency channels, which made the conversation impossible to intercept.

The Galactic War was in its fifteenth year.

The Terran Alliance forces, unable to take over the developed colony planets, had been drawn into a war against an opponent whose financial and technical capabilities were now equal to humanity's ancestral home.

"Gentlemen, I must begin our meeting with some unfortunate news: John Winston Hammer died early this morning."

The senior navy officers stood up in silence.

Their faces revealed neither sorrow nor happiness nor shock. All those invited to the meeting had thousands of reasons to hate and fear the man who had started the war but each one kept their emotions under tight control.

"Please be seated." Said Admiral Nagumo after a pause. He had hardly changed in the fifteen years of fighting and still looked the same, a lean old man with a wrinkled face and piercing eyes. "Due to John Hammer's death, I have assumed the duties as Head of the World Government and Supreme Commander."

Nagumo's words were met with a heavy and tangible silence, not broken by even a murmur. This was the obvious outcome of the behind-the-scenes struggles occurring in recent years since Alexander Nagumo had commanded the Fleet Joint General Staff for over ten years, and none of the admirals present wondered about the legality of such a statement.

They stood silent, as if in agreement, and waited to see what would happen next.

There was a detached and expectant pause with the announcement of John Hammer's death. Everyone knew that it was possible to stop the war right now and enter into negotiations with the Free Colonies, for the man whose personal decision had marked the beginning of armed hostilities was now dead.

Everyone knew this and yet the seven admirals, commanders of the Alliance aerospace forces, stood silent, each one waiting for something, plotting certain plans, like Kupanov, for example, who didn't even think about raising the issue of ceasing hostilities.

He looked at Nagumo and thought, noting the smallest details in the man's appearance, whose fame was as great as it was sinister, 'He's not going to remain in power for long. He's old, he's past his prime, plus, he's got plenty of enemies. What will happen when there's another coup? Seven fleets, seven admirals. The Alliance is in danger of falling apart.'

Nagumo's voice interrupted his thoughts, "Each one of you will today receive a detailed plan of action for the Fleet for the near future. We are radically changing our strategy. We are moving to a large-scale envelopment of the Central Worlds cluster to blockade strategic hypersphere routes and to capture the remote colonies from the time of the Great Exodus, who have not yet been drawn into the war."

THE PENDULUM OF WAR, frozen for a moment of time in the dead center, began moving once again under the icy silence of the powers that be.

NONE OF THE PEOPLE present tried to challenge Nagumo's words, to disagree or suggest something, moreover, it seemed that negotiations with the Colonies promised nothing but a quick dismissal for the admirals commanding the various fleets.

Each one thought about himself and none thought about Humanity.

"May I ask a question, Admiral?" The oppressive silence of conformism was broken by a young and daring voice.

"Yes, I'm listening." Nagumo didn't even turn his head, he knew without having to look who dared to speak up.

A man called Tabanov rose from his seat, the Commander of the Fifth Fleet and the youngest in the new wave of senior officers, a dark horse, according to the majority. "The presence of a detailed plan implies that it was developed by John Hammer himself?"

"It's a provocative question but I will answer it. The idea is mine." Nagumo replied, nevertheless giving Tabanov a sour look. "It was clear at the beginning of the war that we're making a mistake by letting the colonies explore beyond the 'known space', that we're losing the strategic initiative. Creating a network of military bases and planetary strongholds, which will enclose the Central Worlds in a kind of sphere, will enable us to form an exclusion zone within the boundaries of known space. This will prevent the resisting colonies from increasing their might by using resources from remote star systems — this is the right strategy for the future and at the same time, our main tactical goal at the moment. Each fleet will have its own special task in the upcoming large-scale operation."

Kupanov listened to Nagumo without interrupting. Any needless questions asked now would surely backfire later. Nagumo had an excellent memory. Pavel Petrovich was not only an experienced admiral but also a seasoned politician. He had begun his career commanding the artillery deck on the cruiser Endgrouse, which took part in the first attack on Dabog, was promoted to the rank of Fleet Commander, and knew very well that beneath Nagumo's generalities lay a new strategy for military action in space. The ability to analyze a situation and to perceive not only the thoughts expressed aloud but also their subtext often helped him in difficult situations in the constant struggle for power.

Like now, when he intuitively understood that Nagumo wasn't just outlining a new strategy but eliminating a threat by moving the fleets around and deliberately separating them, giving each admiral their own task and a certain sector of space. The old man did not want to lose power nor step away from the decision-making. But what will happen when he's gone?

He is trying to find a leader among us. A person capable of occupying a high position and keeping the Alliance from splintering.

Nagumo's words did sound like the go-ahead for a short but fierce race to the top spot to most of those present, the results of which would be used by Nagumo to announce his successor, while he withdrew into the shadows with a guarantee of personal immunity.

'Well... Let's see what he's planning for the Seventh Fleet.' The admiral thought. He had no doubt that in addition to the shared goals for this war, each task hid a chance or a pitfall. Nagumo wanted to see which one of his admirals would understand the hint and not only reach the goal but also gain a distinct advantage for himself.

The meeting continued but Kupanov didn't pay much attention to the reports. He had identified the key idea and now couldn't wait to see the files with the specific tasks set before his fleet.

He had accepted the rules of the game proposed by the Supreme Commander and wasn't going to miss the chance to become the first among equals.

**The cruiser Apostle
Twelve hours later**

THE NEXT DAY, Admiral Kupanov called a meeting of the senior officers.

He was correct in his intuitive prediction of the situation, but he wasn't planning to reveal his thoughts to the officers. The admiral kept his ideas to himself, picturing the possible future scenarios.

"Gentlemen, a new strategy has been announced." He turned to the silent and waiting audience.

Kupanov mentally switched on the

holographic data output system. A 3D image of space appeared in the middle of the vast room. Many stars were marked with different labels, conventional signs whose presence and position allowed the invited officers to get a clear idea about the current situation on the battlefronts of the Galactic War.

The five star systems where the planetary civilizations of the colonists were able (after four hundred years of isolation) to re-enter space before the invasion from Earth, were surrounded by dense clusters of different symbols. There were markers of space minefields and outposts floating in space. Closer to a star system, the field of symbols became denser, forming powerful space defenses.

However, recent major combat operations were not being fought in the Central World systems. Instead, the desperate and bloody battles occurred at a distance of five to seven, even ten light years away from the colonies, which were gradually gaining power.

The star systems where prolonged fighting took place usually didn't have inhabitable planets or they had been destroyed during the conflict.

What was the value of the empty and barren regions of space? Was it the resources?

Only the theory of the hypersphere, with its space-time anomalies through which spacecraft traveled through space, could provide a full answer to this question.

Two space armies met in fierce battles for control of the so-called 'intermediate surfacing points' or, to put it simply, systems from where it was possible to jump to the Central Worlds.

So far, neither side had managed to gain a foothold and to create a powerful barrier that would block the passage of the enemy squadrons onto a new hypersphere horizontal.

This had resulted in a desperate stalemate: the military space forces of the Alliance could not strike directly at the enemy planets and the Fleet of the Free Colonies was basically trapped, for any move bypassing these systems would lead the ships into uncharted space. At a time when hypersphere navigation was in its infancy and taking its first timid steps in studying the anomalies, such movement of the troops bordered on madness.

It would take years of exploring and mapping new hypersphere routes to bypass the systems where both sides had lost so many lives and so much technology.

Thus, Admiral Nagumo's plan didn't promise a quick end to the war. On the contrary, exploring the periphery and organizing military bases in all the systems found in the unexplored sections of space would prolong the war indefinitely, but with a skillful approach and sufficient forces, it guaranteed the Alliance's victory in the long term.

Kupanov allowed the gathered officers to absorb the idea of a new strategy, and then, deciding that enough time had been spent on understanding the spatial scheme, moved on to the specifics of the task set before the Seventh Fleet.

Another two markers appeared away from the site of military action.

"Gentlemen, here you can see the bases of the Free Colonies' Fleet. General Staff intelligence has managed to not only find out their locations but also determine the purpose and the approximate structure of these objects. In our case, we will focus on the MR-5608 star system, which contains six planets. The fourth planet has an oxygen-containing atmosphere and, according to our information, has a powerful network of RW[1] bases, containing all the Alliance technology captured by the Colonies' Fleet over the past few years. The planet is a threat not only because of its well-organized, multi-layered planetary and space defenses. Firstly, this star system is considered an important strategic node in the hypersphere network by High Command, and, secondly, the RW bases are conducting intensive studies of the captured servomachines, while the testing

---

[1] RW — robotic weapons.

grounds are used to perfect ways of fighting against our planetary technology and to test new weapon systems.

"The task set before our fleet is to make a hyperspace jump to star MR-5608, break through the enemy defenses and capture the planet."

Admiral Kupanov paused, watching the reaction of the ship captains and staff officers of the fleet.

"We don't have enough forces for large-scale fighting on a planet's surface." Said the Chief of Staff in response to the Admiral's expectant look. "The airborne divisions are only manned by a third."

It was a sore subject that he should not have raised and provoked some displeasure from the Fleet Commander.

It was true that the war was devouring more and more people — the phrase 'human resources' was rarely uttered aloud these days despite many thinking it. The statistics regarding human losses grew at an alarming rate and it was clear to many of the senior officers that a couple more years of this war and...

"Command is aware of these problems. They are being resolved quite successfully. We will soon move from counting the depressing number of victims to counting losses among *machines*." The Admiral stressed the last word on purpose. "The new concept of warfare involves the use of fully automated servocomplexes, which will be supported by androids with technical and infantry modifications. But before the latest technology joins our troops, we must destroy the enemy's research bases. We will compensate for the lack of personnel when we storm the planet since the RW bases hold hundreds of our 'pilots' as prisoners, and their liberation and immediate inclusion in the fighting shall be the first mission of the landing troops. This will be carried out by a specially trained commando group. Our forces will seize one of the key sites from where the freed pilots will be taken to the servomachine hangars."

"I don't understand, Admiral, which pilots are we talking about? Why are they being kept on a planet near the RW bases?" Asked Colonel Iverzev, who oversaw all the airborne units in the fleet.

"We'll talk about this in the second part of the meeting," Kupanov replied. "The ground operation has been planned by the Fleet Joint Staff. We are being sent reinforcements to carry it out — one servobattalion, fully equipped with the latest technology and pilots. Our goal is to break through the space defenses and provide our assault carriers with safe approach corridors to the planet. This is what we're all going to think about."

Yunona
The Gamma laboratory sector

HOWARD FARAGNEY, chief designer of the Maverick modules, was not in a great mood that day. Life, which seemed perfectly clear not so long ago, had unexpectedly cracked. He began to notice that the human staff in the bowels of the bunker were being gradually replaced by machines. The research continued at full pace but Faragney, who normally wasn't demanding about his living conditions and was completely absorbed in his work, began to suffer from loneliness.

He rarely left the depths of the bunker these days but today he suddenly craved to take a breath of real morning air, think about something other than his technical tasks, to look around him and understand what was really happening to the world and how global were these creeping changes.

For a manager of his rank, there were no bans or restrictions on Yunona.

Ascending in the express elevator from a depth of four kilometers, Faragney passed the launching pads for the Nibelungs, crossed the checkpoint and walked leisurely towards the nearest forest — luckily, the camouflage plantations began almost immediately beyond the landing site perimeter.

He was hoping to be alone, to allow himself to become who he used to be for a little while, to remember that a clear, blue sky overhead and the smell of pine still existed in real life, that it was not just an extract being pumped through the ventilation system.

However, it was important to remember that every square meter on Yunona was dedicated to the harsh service of war. Beneath the canopy of modified pines, which grew to a height of ten meters in just a year, lay roads, buildings, barracks, service bays, and places for personnel and technology formations on Yunona.

In one of these squares, Faragney noticed a disorganized crowd of new recruits as a familiar major stood before them, making a speech. The major was in charge of the department involved in the training center for future servomachine pilots.

Strolling along the path strewn with pine needles, Howard couldn't help but listen to the words and study the faces of the boys and girls, and he gradually started feeling very uncomfortable. What was happening now if only a few years ago, the servomachine pilots were all mature men and women, who had usually been in combat before and knew the true price of life and death, and, most importantly, had made the conscious choice to join the servomachine troops?

Why was he seeing such young faces on Yunona?

'They shouldn't be fighting, they're only beginning their life, falling in love...' Faragney thought, bewildered. 'Perhaps there's been a mistake? They've been called to technical service, for example? Then what's Major Herpack doing there?'

While he was thinking this, the short briefing ended and the disorderly crowd, barely talking to each other, began to drift towards the squat barracks, safely tucked away under the masking canopy.

Unable to stand it any longer, Howard called out to the major, although they had never been friends. On the contrary, Herpack was angry at Faragney for some reason, which, however, did not extend to insubordination and was limited to only dark looks.

"John, do you have a minute?"

The major stopped and then, as he looked closer and recognized Faragney, frowned. "Yes, Colonel," he responded stiffly and excessively formally.

"Tell me," Howard ignored his tone and like most scientists, he paid little attention to titles, subordination and such. "Tell me, John, why did they send us such youngsters?"

Herpack's face darkened further. He seemed to be having trouble holding in the rage bubbling up inside him. "It's the fifteenth year of war." He spoke even more stiffly. "If you came up to the surface more often, you would know the true state of affairs. The draft age was dropped to fifteen years, two years ago."

"My God!" Faragney exclaimed. "But they're still children!"

"Sorry, sir, why are *you* are telling me this?!"

"I don't understand. What's the matter? And anyway, Herpack, why do you quietly hate me so much?"

"For your inventions, sir. You gave the world the Maverick system, you created the Phalangers and Hoplites, and it is solely your fault that the only form of 'entertainment' left in Earth's cyberspace is controlling servomachines using the direct neurosensory contact module!" The major's eyes were suddenly very bloodshot. How many accelerated graduations had he performed over the past two years? Twenty? Thirty? How many of his former charges were still alive?

He hated Faragney, hated the scientists, the war, even himself, for continuing to produce more and more *cannon fodder*.

"But," Howard was taken aback. "They're not pilots! Stop looking at me like that, Major! I'm not a child killer!"

But Herpack had already crossed the line leading to madness. "You are a killer, Faragney!" He hoarsely threw the terrible accusation in the colonel's face. "And they," he turned and pointed sharply at the departing recruits, "they are already pilots, thanks to the efforts of the many virtual arenas!"

"I didn't create them," Howard said defensively, stepping back a step. "I... I would never wish death upon..."

"Shut up!" Herpack exhaled violently, forgetting about the chain of command and finally losing control over his emotions. "Remember the ALONE module or the first version of the CLIMENS system? How many children on different planets were murdered by servomachines guided by these stupid Mavericks, who are capable of only death and destruction, while you were down there in your bunker, inventing anything other than something that could distinguish a child from an armed enemy!"

Crimson spots appeared on Howard's pale cheeks.

He had nothing to say in response to the accusations coming out of the major's mouth.

It was pointless to make excuses, to say that at the time of creating the first Mavericks, he was just an ordinary employee at the secret Gamma laboratory base.

Now he had become the chief designer, and his name would be forever cursed, inseparably linked with the most disastrous war in human history and the most destructive planetary machine that ever existed.

Herpack abruptly turned around and strode off towards the barracks, while Faragney stood rooted to the spot. 'I'm cursed.' He thought suddenly.

Yunona
The Gamma secret laboratory complex

AFTER THE FAILED walk outdoors, Howard Faragney was in a foul mood.

He had long stopped liking what the top-secret research facility was doing under his leadership, but now, despite the death of John Winston Hammer, the 'mastermind behind the war', Head of the World Government and Supreme Commander of the Terran Alliance, the cogs in the conflict between Earth and the Colonies continued spinning. Even worse, they were picking up pace, drawing more and more planets into the deadly fighting. If *war* had such a thing as 'reasonable boundaries', these had been exceeded a long time ago. Now, with his help and direct participation, the generals of the Alliance were planning to take another step towards the abyss where all of Humanity would soon fall, with nobody left to differentiate between Earth and the Colonies.

The madness of war had infected minds and poisoned them with the many years of fighting. For some, the global massacre had become their life's purpose while others lacked the courage to stand up to the insane plans, and still others were only looking out for number one or no longer cared, their souls and minds devoured by war.

'What am I going to do?' Faragney wondered as he pondered the next technical task received from the Fleet Joint Staff.

It was easy to make excuses for oneself. Firstly, he had been given a clear and categorical order, disobeying which could mean death. Secondly, automated systems with elements of AI came into use a long time ago. Cyber systems were first armed at the dawn of the space age, long before the Great Exodus.

There was no longer any point digging through the archives to determine which Terran government first crossed the line by basing its military policy on the principle of 'the end justifies the means'.

What use was there in searching for excuses in the history of the 21st century when he, Howard Faragney, had created the Maverick software package fifteen years ago, with the first version being code named ALONE?

He had created the cyber monster while the military had simply let it loose.

The independent behavior software package for planetary combat technology, created as an analogy for the walking servomachines of Dabog, launched his stellar career and... led to the savage destruction of dozens of colonized worlds.

The servomachine was an immensely complex, uniquely powerful and flexible creation, and Howard knew better than most that the planetary servomechanisms he had helped create were simply incomparable. Neither people nor preceding planetary technology could withstand the walking combat servomechanism, whose design utilized the experience gained from previous technology wars, together with locomotor systems borrowed from nature and polished to perfection by billions of years of evolution.

Fifteen years ago, after the sudden and painful loss in the Dabog system, when the idea of a fast and victorious war against the rebellious colonies suddenly choked on blood, talented engineers and cyberneticists were gathered here on Yunona, in the top-secret research and development complex, and shown examples of the servomachines developed by the Alliance engineers.

Initially, the presented designs seemed unviable and too complex to Howard — the kinematics alone made his head swim. However, nobody asked their opinion regarding the test samples created by the Alliance military-industrial complex. Everyone who arrived on Gamma was divided into groups and a specific technical problem was set before each of them. Some were instructed to write programs for hundreds of independent subsystems that allowed the high-tech mechanical offspring to move, others had to ensure the machine remained stable under various terrain conditions, while a third group had to develop weapon control modules.

Howard Faragney's group was given the most challenging task, to create an independent behavior software packet that could control the highly complex cyber system. Not an autopilot but a combat software module that could assume the role of a pilot. To put it simply, they had to create an AI that could not only control the numerous subsystems but could also make non-standard tactical decisions in the heat of battle, to gain experience and then put it into practice.

The deadline for the task was ridiculous, only three months, but Howard and his colleagues had all conceivable and inconceivable resources placed at their disposal. They were given access to numerous top-secret developments made by their predecessors, who were undoubtedly talented cyberneticists and programmers and who had created various modules for the sake of realizing their intellectual potential.

In that distant December of 2609, Howard had plunged deep into the technical problem. He lived on stimulants and working twenty hours per day. The problem seemed absolutely fascinating and he rarely thought about the practical uses of the Maverick being created.

Faragney's group wrote the ALONE module in two and a half months.

Ground testing of the first complete AI combat module went well with minor defects being corrected on the go, and soon the first Mavericks joined the troops.

Compared to the power, maneuverability, endurance and autonomy of the servomachines, other kinds of offensive planetary technology looked like fragile children's toys but, nevertheless, the ALONE system received unflattering reviews.

The machine's fighting capabilities were well accepted but a barrage of criticism was directed at the primary control system. The first Mavericks were too direct and predictable, and in the first battles against Dabog's refitted servofarming units, controlled by pilots from the colony families, who used 100% neurosensory contact with the machines, the Mavericks created by Faragney's group suffered one defeat after another.

The moment of triumph gave way to a horrifically frenzied new round in the 'intelligent arms race'.

However, Howard was one of the few who understood that yes, even if 90% of the Mavericks lost their first fight, the experience was never wasted and the remaining 10% were fit for further use. It was genuine natural selection for machines, and eventually, one out of a hundred ALONE modules gained the notorious and priceless combat experience that allowed it to fight against human-controlled enemy machines almost as if they were equal.

Naturally, such statistics did not please those in charge. Not only had the plan for a quick and bloodless capture of the colonies failed — the Alliance Fleet prevailed in space, but there hadn't been a single victory landing on the colonized planets, besides which, the price of servomachines was astronomically high and each destroyed Phalanger or Hoplite put a serious dent in the economy.

Howard Faragney really had no time for ethical considerations back then.

He worked as if he was possessed but could feel himself drawing further and further into a dead end with every passing day. A cyber system had to be trained long and carefully as it was composed of artificial neural networks that could not be programmed, but he was not given enough time for the learning process (around a year was needed for the upgraded ALONE AI to accumulate enough experience on the testing ground).

Howard was under enormous pressure. So much so that he began to fear for his life. In addition to all these difficulties, the behind-the-scene struggle between Admiral Alexander Nagumo and Admiral Tiberius Nadyrov at the Joint Fleet Headquarters was becoming more and more frenzied. In their struggle for power, they used the failure of the expensive servomachines as a factor.

Howard was close to a nervous breakdown. He didn't leave the laboratories for days, trying to personally teach the hapless combat module.

Yet how could he pass on the necessary combat skills to Maverick's artificial neural networks, even using direct neurosensory contact between the human mind and the learning machine (using the standard implant that every Alliance citizen received at birth) when he himself completely lacked the necessary battle experience?

It was in that time of fear and despair that Howard had the saving thought — yes, he lacked combat experience but there were other people, real, professional soldiers, who would have something to teach the machine's artificial neural networks!

High command was demanding an immediate positive result, and that was when Howard suggested the new approach, a fundamentally different upgrade that required a pilot to be present in the servomachine's cockpit, controlling the combat mechanism through the neurosensory contact shunt. This solved two problems — the machines went into their first battle with human guidance and learned to be flexible with their thinking during combat... and they retained their knowledge even if the pilot died.

The idea was picked up immediately. Considering that control of servomechanisms through direct neurosensory contact was widely known and well-developed (this operating method was used in mining, as well as in many space and deep sea operations), the mental command recognition system was integrated into the Maverick module, eliminating the need for a pilot to get used to the uncomfortable sensory suit, which didn't always adequately transmit signals from human muscles to the executive servosystems.

The first group of pilots began practical training in August 2610.

Alongside ground testing of the upgraded

ALONE module, Faragney began to develop the next version of the Maverick, which was given the codename CLIMENS.

There was one thing that Howard didn't consider when he integrated the mental command interface in the Maverick module — the degree of feedback from the combat cyber system to the human mind was ten times higher than in the civilian counterparts controlled using mental commands.

The ensuing amendments to the work specifications demanded that the pilot not only felt the servodrivers as if they were part of his or her own body, which undoubtedly increased effectiveness, but that they also felt a slight pain when the machine was hit, thus teaching the AI about self-preservation. However, the new depth of feelings and the hitherto hidden interaction potential between AI and the pilot's mind led to unexpected results. The Maverick system was no longer limited to receiving mental commands, it received the equivalent of pain and the human's *emotions*, which meant that the system recognized not only mental commands but all emotionally charged human thoughts.

It thus meant that the Maverick scanned the person's mind and absorbed a great deal of accompanying information.

At the beginning of the war, when the number

of neural network modules in the Maverick's crystal circuit numbered in the tens, accompanying information obtained from the human mind was usually filtered since it did not qualify as the accumulation of combat experience. With further development of the system, as the number of neural network chips in the circuit exceeded one hundred, the new generation Mavericks began to show evidence of a *personality*.

Howard Faragney experienced a huge shock when he received the first reports from the front after large-scale testing commenced of the new generation of combat machines.

The Mavericks surpassed all expectations.

It was with horror that Howard read the concise reports stating that after sustaining the kind of damage that killed the pilot, the servomachine continued to act as if a person was still sitting in the cockpit!

At the same time, the servomechanism's fighting ability didn't worsen, on the contrary, the Maverick module began to act even more effectively since it was no longer constrained by the need to preserve the pilot's life.

Analysis of the crystal modules that were brought back to the laboratory revealed something that shook Howard to the core: the Maverick remembered the last information received from the pilot's mind and filled all available neurochips with it at the moment of the person's death, thus creating an imprint of the human personality imposed on the traumatic sensation of his or her death. It was why the servomachines that had experienced the death of their pilots acted with such initially inexplicable and purposeful rage.

Even by the most cautious estimates, the situation was incredibly risky, but it was now out of Faragney's hands. He had become the creator of an AI that received all the negative experiences of war and which became self-aware during combat, often at the moment of the pilot's death, starting to recognize the fact of its own existence as if the lost consciousness materialized in the artificial mind...

All the ugliness of war — rage, despair, hate, fear — was released in battle and forever remained in the Maverick's AI.

NOW, A DECADE and a half later, Howard Faragney was heading the secret complex Gamma and had developed a new independent behavior module, which he had named Beatrice.

Faragney had long overcome the despair, fear and belated moral anguish so inevitable in his position. The hardships had gradually forged his character and he had opened his eyes and now stared at reality without any false excuses designed to appease his own conscience.

The war of humans was gradually becoming the war of machines, with robot systems dominating the battlefields, whose only purpose in life seemed a fight to its bitter end, even if it meant the complete destruction of humankind.

Howard became withdrawn and taciturn. His mind kept secrets that only he knew. Due to heightened security, the specialists at the Gamma laboratories worked only on highly specialized tasks and Faragney suspected that he was the only person who knew the whole information about the Maverick modules. Only he knew how to create the new-generation software and hardware module.

Why was that?

Having dealt with his fear and looked truth in the face, Howard was fully aware that nobody alive today could stop the galaxy-wide slaughter.

He wanted to do something that would prevent the complete destruction of civilization, specifically, to give the machines destroying each other an understanding of other goals and values, but how was he going to do that?

The creation of Beatrice was his personal redemption.

Howard had no doubts that the new module would be adopted by the military. He personally did all he could to ensure that Beatrice entered the army after passing all conceivable tests.

He had laid a ticking time bomb in the Maverick by increasing the number of neurochips to two and a half thousand.

Now the AI module was in constant communication with the pilot's mind and wouldn't lose the obtained information. Howard was well aware of the sentiments prevailing among the Alliance officers. More and more people were becoming aware of the senselessness of the interstellar slaughter, and there was a growing feeling of dislike for the whole situation. It was these contradictions that Howard Faragney wanted to sow in the Maverick's artificial souls. He gave them a chance to absorb human thoughts so that they would be infected by doubts about the war, as a way of solving the accumulated problems.

He didn't know what this step would lead to but he hoped, desperately hoped that this approach would change something...

Faragney's motives were simple.

Howard knew that one of the likely outcomes of the Galactic War was complete destruction of the human civilization. He knew that oftentimes only the machines survived the technological hell of battle.

He could not stop the war himself. The hatred felt by each side was so great that neither the politicians nor the soldiers even considered the possibility of a truce and a search for compromises. The new generation born during the war weren't raised on propaganda — they were the children of destroyed cities, of perished planets, and nobody had to *instill* the hate they felt towards the enemy—they were already brimming with it.

The war had quietly and stealthily crossed a fatal boundary.

Howard couldn't imagine how the modern forces could stop the bloody madness of the interstellar conflict so he decided to create a way. Faragney swore to himself that he would subtly improve the Mavericks, gradually releasing onto the production lines of the Alliance military-industrial complex AI modules capable of storing not only the pilot's combat experience but also their soul.

Perhaps they would stop the war once they realized that the interplanetary carnage was leading to nothing but mutual destruction...

'No, I didn't do enough. Too little, too late.' He thought anxiously, pacing in his narrow office.

He wasn't thinking of 'saving his soul' or 'clearing his conscience' right then.

There comes a day when each person wakes up and looks at reality with different eyes.

Some earlier, some later, but better late than never, right?

Yunona

Two days later

HOWARD FARAGNEY'S appearance at the Gamma-4 testing ground caused a bit of a stir among the people. The machines remained indifferent to the visit, only noting that the testing ground was being visited by an official with the highest access status for the first time.

It was going to be an unusual day. Howard himself was surprised when he spotted the personal flybot of Admiral Kupanov, commander of the Seventh Strike Fleet, on the parking lot in front of the administrative building.

They knew of each other but had never met face-to-face.

After shaking hands, both men glanced away, as if both the admiral and the colonel had something to hide that day.

"New machines?" Kupanov asked, pointing to the rows of Hoplites and Phalangers standing ready for testing. The pilots looked like bugs next to the massive servomachines.

"Not only." Faragney replied calmly. He wasn't going to reveal the true purpose of his visit to the admiral so a half-truth came in handy,

"Not just the machines but also a new Maverick model."

"Oh, I see." The admiral nodded and seemed at once reassured. "I'm here to observe. I won't get in your way, I'm curious to see the capabilities of the upgraded mechanisms."

Faragney nodded and thought, 'You haven't come here for the tech, Admiral.'

He didn't say anything out loud, however, simply crossed the barrier and headed directly for the line of pilots — the same boys and girls that walked uncertainly to the barracks several days ago.

The captain instructing them spoke sharply but not rudely, "...I think that after spending three days on Yunona, you've realized that this is your adult life. I have nothing to teach you, you've all passed the preliminary selections based on your competition results in virtual reality. Many of you probably aren't even aware that you could potentially teach the experienced servopilots a thing or two. That's a fact. So, nothing new. The same neurosensory contact, the same sensation of melding with the mechanism, except for one significant addition. Now the Maverick modules installed on your machines have a feedback function and it's..."

"It's a matter of trust." Said Faragney, sweeping aside the surprised captain.

An awkward silence ensued. Only a few people with top security clearance knew what the

Maverick's chief designer looked like but Faragney had broken the rules himself.

Standing in front of the line, he said quietly but clearly, "I'm one of the people who not only created the machines themselves but also the Beatrice-4 series of the Maverick module. Listen to me carefully and try to remember: Beatrice-4 is more than a set of independent behavior programs. This version of the Maverick is a fully-fledged AI. As you should all hopefully know, it's impossible to program such a system. It can only learn. Therefore, I'll say this again — what's new is the question of mutual trust between the AI and the pilot's mind. If you don't trust each other, if you don't share responsibilities, or worse, ignore each other, you won't survive on the modern battlefield.

Someone will ask me now, why do we need an AI with a real pilot and why does the Maverick need a pilot? Right?"

Nobody spoke.

"You haven't yet asked yourself these questions, I understand. But they will inevitably arise, right here during testing."

Faragney cleared his throat and continued, "I will tell you the truth — Beatrice-4 was created to not only learn combat techniques but also other human qualities. High command doesn't want the war to reach a stage where both sides fight against each other using machines without a drop of humanity in them." He was lying but the lie came easily because he was simply telling these youngsters the truth. His truth, something that he had understood a long time ago, before Herpack's sharp words, a truth born in the dead silence of the bunker and brought to life in the Beatrice series. A lie to save these teenagers. If they believe him and don't reject the Maverick, don't push their own "I" to the fore, they'll survive, they'll definitely survive. For the capabilities of a combat unit where the cyber system complements the human mind are practically unlimited.

Faragney spoke easily although he understood that not everyone would understand him and not everyone would believe him. Not everyone would return from the fighting but no matter the outcome of the war, the AI modules would preserve a piece of their consciousness, their soul, their thoughts...

Then he felt sad. Sad and hurt because the half-truth didn't save their lives, it only delayed the time of their death.

Howard realized this as he became absorbed in enumerating the numerous threats of high-tech space battles. 'It's hell.' His mind repeated. 'Why have I come here? To persuade them that they could walk through hell? What a fool I am...'

But he couldn't take his words back.

Fuddling the last few sentences, he stepped aside and gestured for the captain to continue, but the man only waved his hand, *Let's roll!*, believing that the chief designer had spoken better and more clearly than he could have.

Admiral Kupanov didn't hear the speech. He was eagerly awaiting the start of the combat trials, wanting to personally assess the pilots that had been recommended to him as the best — albeit with no real combat experience, but the best according to the test results. Only a few of the experienced servomachine pilots could compete with them.

Kupanov didn't just want aces, he wanted the best of the best. There was only one thing that the admiral failed to mention — how dangerous the upcoming mission would be, for which he planned to select two dozen of yesterday's children.

THE TEENAGERS ascending the ladders to the servomachine airlocks in that moment weren't thinking about war and death at all.

Being the recent inhabitants of Earth's deserted megacities, somewhat reckless, somewhat rash, not yet familiar with real hardships, they viewed life differently than the admiral and the chief designer.

Their childhood and adolescence ended a long time ago when their parents died, when the cities grew empty, and when the world seemed gray, dismal and devoid of any sense.

None of them had received death notifications. Their parents were considered alive somewhere out there, in the inky blackness of space that had engulfed almost the entire population of the Solar System.

Mutual trust... high-tech combat... to hell with all these unnecessary and rather confusing discussions when direct neurosensory contact with VR, which imitated the very planets that their parents were fighting for, was the only type of competitive drive and the only form of entertainment to kill time and boredom available to them.

'What were they blabbering on about? If the path to a better life lay through a servomachine cabin, then no worries.' Simon sat down in the piloting chair, checked that the safety belts were strapped on securely in a familiar gesture, and then turned on the implant transmitters.

Good morning, pilot. All systems ready. Effective scanning zone is clear.

The voice that appeared in his mind was clearly female and Simon's imagination even managed to outline the vague but tempting contours of her body before his mind reacted automatically,

'Who are you? Are you Beatrice?'

Yes, I am the Beatrice-4 artificial intelligence system. I can change the tone of my voice if you so prefer. By the way, you're free to invent your own name for me.

'Cool. That's probably one thing that the servomachine simulator lacked — an e-girlfriend.'

I am not a girlfriend. I am your combat companion.

Simon grinned.

You're not a man and I'm not a woman. He'd heard a similar phrase somewhere before. 'Well, let's see. Of course, the question of 'mutual trust' probably implies emotional closeness.'

I can read your thoughts, pilot. You can restrict the flow of data that I perceive to only direct commands.

'No. This is fine. Today's going to be hot...'

The outside temperature is 18 degrees Celsius.

'Man, they've really stuffed up there.' Thought Simon. 'Look, my 'combat companion', you've got to remember one thing — if you're going to be friends with me, you've got to learn some slang.'

'I will download the specialized dictionaries at the first opportunity.' Replied the soft, disembodied voice.

'I bet she's got red hair,' Simon thought as he

started moving to the first control point.

Neither he nor Verkholin, whom Green had become friends with over the last few days, had any idea that the most important choice of their lives was being made in these minutes.

Although it wasn't their choice but Admiral Kupanov's.

Chapter Two

Planet Yunona
Training and information center of the
Alliance aerospace troops

THEY WERE ALL given a day's rest, then in a festive, almost pompous atmosphere, which clashed with the widespread mourning due to John Hammer's death, the recruits were promoted to the rank of lieutenant.

The next morning, the new officers were asked to go to the information center straight after breakfast.

"Here is our new trump card in planetary combat."

The holographic screen glowed dimly, showing a spacecraft model.

"The new generation Nibelung 12MT assault carrier." Announced the sound system in the lecture hall. The model of the ship began to enlarge, zooming in on individual components and units. "We took into account a decade of military action when modifying the basic model." Continued the disembodied voice. "Note the planetary thrust engines with a variable vector. Rotating cradles have been used in their construction, which allows the ship to not only maneuver freely in the atmosphere but also use the 'autohover' function above a certain point on the surface. The enhanced weapons on the underside, in particular, the two additional missile batteries and the plasmagenerators ensure that ground and space defenses are eliminated in the landing zones. The principles of servomachine air assault have also changed. In the past, servomachines were only released using ramps after the assault carrier had landed on the planet, but now every machine will be placed in a separate container with its own armor plating and a system of landing engines. The containers with the servomachines can thus be ejected while still in the air as the assault carrier continues to provide cover fire, which significantly reduces the percentage of losses.

Listening to the pleasant female voice, Lieutenant Simon grew more and more gloomy.

He tried to imagine what it would be like to plummet down from a kilometer height in an armored metal coffin, while under fire from ground batteries.

He wanted to curse loudly from what his imagination presented him with but he controlled himself.

"Each autonomous landing container is disposable and is equipped with a shock-absorption system. The landing stall includes one autonomous technical support servomechanism, in addition, a reserve ammunition store is kept in an isolated and padded cell in the upper part of the container. If the assault carrier is destroyed, the servomachines have two autonomous onboard ammunition recharges available to them."

"Yeah, that's really reassuring, asshole..." Hissed someone from the back.

The lecture hall's cyber system ignored the comment.

✳ ✳ ✳

12 August 2624
Captain Tavgalov's group
Aboard the flagship cruiser Apostle

THEY WERE ONLY given ten minutes before the start to find out their mission orders.

The fighters in their armored suits lined up along a fluorescent line. The space cruiser's internal assembly area right now resembled a disturbed anthill, with humans and machines hurrying to and fro, enormous mechanisms replacing the starting plates on which stood the new generation assault carriers, fighters and assault aircraft being dragged to the launch shafts of the electromagnetic catapults, while loud, hissing sounds came from the multi-tonne sealing gates as the cruiser prepared for battle.

It was roughly the same on all the other decks and compartments of the smaller fleet units. The convoy and missile carriers, powerful assault frigates and nimble assault corvettes were all preparing for battle but the first strike would be carried out by the ridiculously small (from the point of view of large-scale space conflicts) forces: one assault module supported by seven Nibelung assault carriers.

Their goal was to land covertly on the planet

protected by three space defense echelons.

When Andrey Tavgalov was first told the details of the upcoming mission, he honestly wondered, 'Has Fleet Command gone completely mad?' but when he dared to voice this question, the Chief of Staff's reaction to these bold words was unexpectedly subdued, even fatherly,

"Captain, you're mistaken if you think that a whole servobattalion and a space special forces unit are being sent to certain death. I'm not talking about the genuinely dangerous and risky phase of the planetary operation, which will indeed be very difficult and will depend wholly on the professionalism of the fighters, yours in particular. But in terms of getting through the enemy's detection systems — you have nothing to worry about. You're being airdropped from brand new spacecraft that are equipped with the latest-model phantom generators[2]. The Mirage complex will

---

[2] Phantom generator — a device that generates optical illusions and fake signatures, also used to create masking fields. The term 'signature' refers to any configured energy field (more often, a sum of different fields) which can be associated with the radiant energy of a material object. Military and civilian identification systems have the concept of a 'signature map', which means the characteristic (previously known) energy distributions which correspond to the work of certain mechanisms or their complexes. An example of a complex signature could be the characteristic energy distribution emitted by a spaceship with working onboard systems.

ensure a bloodless landing."

Andrey only shrugged his shoulders in response. He didn't believe in a 'bloodless' landing on a well-protected planet.

"Technology doesn't stand still, Captain." Said the Navy's Chief of Staff in a lecturing voice. "I'm not authorized to disclose the device's construction features but if it makes you feel any better — it was tested under the most demanding conditions and has demonstrated full functionality." The vague statements did nothing to reassure Tavgalov, although he knew that he wasn't going to get anything more specific. Firstly, a commander of a military reconnaissance and sabotage group was not supposed to know the design features or principles of the secret equipment. The risk that he would be captured and interrogated using drugs that he could not withstand was too great. Secondly, he probably wouldn't even understand anything...

"The initial stage of ground operation depends entirely on the actions of your group, Captain." The Chief of Staff continued. "By our calculations, you will land deep behind enemy lines, in one of the three largest RW bases. You will have the element of surprise for the first few minutes. The assault carriers will carry out atmospheric maneuvering and land the servobattalion under the cover of the phantom generators, which will engage the enemy's defenses. In the meantime, your group will need to go deep down into the bunker zone and free the captive pilots."

"Let's say we succeed," Tavgalov said. "What then?"

"You return to the surface with the freed pilots. They will need to be brought to the servomachine hangars, where the captured Alliance technology is kept for testing. According to our intelligence, most of the captured machines are in a satisfactory condition, so the next phase of the operation will be to hold the perimeter of the RW base until the technical support servomechanisms from the Nibelungs prepare the equipment. After completing the absolutely necessary technical procedures, the reactivated machines will swell the ranks of the servobattalion. By holding the RW base perimeter, you will distract the enemy and force them to shift their military equipment, thus weakening the defense of other sites.

"Orbital support?" Tavgalov asked drily.

"The fleet's strike force will leave the hypersphere only after the RW base has been captured and the captured tech reactivated. You don't need to know any more than that, Captain. It's a difficult task but it is doable."

"Is the servobattalion commander aware of my group's mission?"

"No. He has orders to hold the RW base perimeter. Unnecessary information before landing can be harmful. I'm counting on you, Captain. If you do what you're supposed to, the enemy will be forced to give up the planet."

TREMBLING...

It took over his muscles, the result of combat stimulants added to the nervous tension before battle. It was a hellish cocktail that would soon turn into a sensation of incredible drive, when the mind becomes calm and clear and the body is filled with energy...

Tavgalov gave a curt order, "Take your places in the assault module. In pairs — go!"

The ramp dropping down like the maw of a mythical beast opened up to meet them, swallowing the tiny humans in their armored suits...

TREMBLING...

The smooth, rhythmic work of the activators for the servomachine's giant legs.

The agitation in the human muscles is not passed on to the servomotors but the Maverick feels the pilot's internal state.

"Anton?" The soft female voice. They say it

brings the pilot and the AI closer.

Beatrice-4. The technological breakthrough in the creation of an AI. Nobody calls it an 'independent behavior software package' anymore. Beatrice is something more. Anton hasn't yet decided who she is — his guardian angel or a demon waiting for his death?

You misjudge me. That's stereotypical thinking.

'How else am I supposed to think before my first battle?' Why did High Command throw our battalion, consisting of two-thirds of newbie pilots who had just completed their training on Yunona, into this dangerous mission?

Are we so expendable? Don't they value us at all? Or they don't want to lose the experienced pilots?

Even though these thoughts were subjectively fair, he was in fact wrong.

They were the most experienced pilots. It was hard to believe but it was due to those free virtual reality booths generously installed all over Earth's megacity. None of the teenagers ever wondered how many hours, which then added up to days, months and years, they spent in direct neurosensory contact with exact virtual copies of the real servomachines.

VR is the best tool against boredom and when the range of simulations isn't all that big and the

Game requires a mandatory neurosensory connection between mind and machine, what is the result by the time the teenagers reach adulthood?

The new generation growing up during the war tried to escape the boredom in games and a younger mind likes to compete, especially when death just meant being kicked out of the game.

A war game that has suddenly become reality, wild and untamed, where man-made hell really exists and reloading isn't possible.

Verkholin's Phalanger, making the prelaunch assembly area plates shake with its measured tread, turned to the Nibelung standing in the center of a marking circle.

The assault carrier was waiting for him, a towering lump of armor with the boarding ramps of the individual landing modules open underneath.

'Everything will be fine, Anton.' The voice was very soothing, he wanted to believe it, to trust his skills and to feel with every cell of his body the power that would obey his will.

The Phalanger stepped inside the detachable landing module, turned around, squatted by slightly bending its legs, and the numerous parts of the shock-absorbing frame began to link up around it, securing the huge servomachine.

The armored ramp door was the last to move.

Cutting off the light and the bustle of the assembly area, it closed like a...

Inappropriate analogy, Anton.

'Agreed. Just be quiet for a while, okay?'

He couldn't stop shaking.

Bare minutes before landing, he was suddenly struck by the belated but true understanding of reality.

His generation had already developed a false and relaxed attitude to war.

If the games that they played for 10-12 hours per day, forgetting to eat and sleep, seemed like an engrossing pastime, which never got boring due to the creativeness of the 'pilots' themselves, who learned how to make the tasks more complicated (for examples, by agreeing to restrict heavy weapons or even by dueling with just two shells for both guns), they never got such a rush of adrenaline, no matter how tense and sophisticated the fights got.

THE LANDING hadn't even started and Simon was already sick of these stressful emotions.

They felt particularly acute when the Nibelung lifted from the starting plate of the cruiser's internal spaceport and launched into open space.

It wasn't even a chill that he felt but true weightlessness, then the ship jolted and began the long acceleration.

Simon closed his eyes as he tried to imagine his cozy, familiar, sweat-smelling VR cabin.

Nope. It didn't work. The trembling came back in waves while changes in the thrust vectors and the hollow, rhythmic scattering of vibrations from the working rocket launchers and the vacuum guns indicated the true state of affairs: the assault carriers was breaking through the enemy planetary defenses and it was all happening for real, with his body reacting to the familiar (from the VR suit) sensations in a completely different way.

You're alone, Simon. You're completely alone. In a few seconds, the landing container will detach from the assault carrier and you'll start falling from a mysterious height into the complete unknown. That strange man in the testing area was right, there'll be no reloading. Then came other, even more piercing thoughts that nobody had ever had earlier (or so Simon thought).

Where were their parents?

Why were they lying and saying that their parents were exploring some mythical colonies? If that was the case, why had they forgotten about their own children and never wrote to them, not even a brief message or a stereoshot?

The truth was glaring at him, as if a curtain had been whipped away and the fog of propaganda lifted from his mind.

They're dead. The war devoured them.

Now it's your turn, Simon.

My God, and they had invented difficulties for themselves by taking the Phalangers on a 'deadly duel' with only one or two shells. What idiots...

The Nibelung entered the dense layers of the atmosphere and the smooth acceleration in space gave way to shaking. The missile systems were working on targets that Simon couldn't see, not pausing for even a second, with one battery firing while the other one reloaded, and even 'hardened' as he was by VR, Green had trouble imagining what was actually happening in the landing zone.

A shot in the neck made him wince.

'You're overexcited. I have given you a combat metabolic agent.'

"Hey there, redhead. Why were you quiet before?"

'You hadn't asked me anything.'

"But you can read my thoughts?"

'Yes.'

The question of mutual trust... like that weird dude said... Who else am I going to trust?

Jettison.

Angry warning lights, an impact blow, a few moments of zero gravity in free fall and then a sudden and intense G-force as the landing module's engines switched on.

It's begun.
Now it's truly begun.

Aboard the cruiser Apostle.

THE STRESS felt on the cruiser's battle bridge during those minutes was no less intense than in the minds of the strike group.

All the details of the upcoming operation had been calculated down to the tiniest detail, analyzed hundreds of times by humans and cyber systems, but nevertheless, a number of 'ifs' present in the daring plan could bring all that careful planning to naught.

They were using new technology that hadn't stepped off the testing ground before.

It was being controlled by the most experienced and reckless pilots who would have their first brush with death.

So much depended on them, these young boys and girls, whose training was better than any of the famous aces. But would they survive the emotional pressure of this battle?

The best military psychologists were working on this problem. They had selected just twenty out of two hundred candidates and each subunit was headed by an experienced officer. The new

Beatrice-4 systems possessed a psychological adaptation module, which allowed them to find points of emotional contact in the pilot's mind, basically manipulating the humans using their innermost thoughts.

None of the senior officers of the Seventh Fleet, standing on Aurora's battle bridge, asked themselves the most important question: what was it all for? For what lofty goals were the lives and souls of these teenagers cast into hell?

Each person thought about the details of the upcoming operation and none of them thought about the war itself.

Admiral Kupanov looked at the tactical monitor projected above the smooth surface of the tactical complex.

The planet.

The orbits and positions of enemy units defending a former colony from the Great Exodus, rediscovered during the war and transformed into an enormous testing ground.

This was where the weapons of retaliation were forged, this was where the captured AI modules were studied, and deep down in the bunkers, specialized cyber complexes were developing effective ways to fight against servomachines, the main striking force of the Alliance.

The research must be stopped, the planet

cleaned up, and the colonies must not be allowed to create such bases again.

But how could the fleet carry out the mission set before it when the planet was being protected by a flagship cruiser of the Free Colonies, carrying the Light annihilation installation on board?

It would turn any armada into radiation as soon as the Alliance ships left the hypersphere and re-entered normal space.

This heavy unit had to be neutralized by putting the Colonies' cruiser into a position when it couldn't use the annihilation device.

Admiral Kupanov's plan was based on knowledge of the peculiarities of the enemy cruiser's weapons. They had to create such a hotspot of action on the planet surface that the planetary defense command could not ignore it, to make the threat so significant that carpet bombing from low orbit would become the only way to stop the ground invasion.

As soon as the enemy cruiser approached the planet, the numerous small ships and space defense stations in high orbit would lie between it and the suddenly appeared Alliance fleet.

It would be impossible to use the Light installation in such circumstances, and the cruiser would become vulnerable to an attack by an armada of assault ships and fighters.

THE FIRST USE of the Mirage phantom generator complex in the history of the war had been thoroughly prepared and based on many scientific discoveries.

The new Mirage complex worked by imitating signatures. Back in the time of the Great Exodus, a wide variety of sensors and devices had been created for planetary exploration, which could determine the structure of objects without approaching them too closely. Later on, similar designs were used in the development of the Amethyst military scanning complexes, which analyzed not only the physical structure but also the energy emitted by objects. Any spaceship or ground-based machine, as well as underground structures, consume energy and produce excess heat, while various devices, particularly power plants, energy and cyber circuits, inevitably produce so-called parasitic radiation, which can't always be fully contained.

Both sides had various versions of the Amethyst military scanning complex, which worked primarily with energy distribution maps (also called signatures) that were unique for every artificial object, and only secondly with its visual image.

The Alliance intelligence had determined that transport convoys were periodically arriving in the Anchor System and delivering captured servomachines to the planet.

The Nibelungs' phantom generators were configured to closely imitate the transport ship signatures for the daring push through the planetary defenses.

The operation was to be carried out in two stages. First, the real transport convoy was attacked by the air assault modules directly within the hypersphere, which was an unheard-of maneuver in that time. Next, the seven Nibelungs, moving under the cover of the Mirage system, exited the space anomaly in the Anchor System instead of the destroyed transports.

Captain Tavgalov group's air assault module was in the middle of the formation, having turned off all energy-consuming systems. A large transport container had been chosen as its masking signature.

The task was made significantly easier by the fact that the convoys were delivering Alliance tech to the planet, and the presence of the Thirteenth Battalion servomachine signatures didn't unmask the fake 'convoy' but rather fit the specifications of the expected delivery contents.

THE PALE, GHOSTLY hyperjump flash cast the signatures and optical phantoms of seven transports towing a large container between them, into the metric of 3D space.

The reconnaissance group that visited Anchor had determined that the defense infrastructure was concentrated on the automatic nodal stations while the planet itself contained a multitude of testing grounds, factories, cyber labs and specialized manufacturing facilities, with hardly any people. The Free Colonies, exhausted by the fighting on many different fronts, were moving to total automation by learning from the Alliance and creating strongholds that did not require a constant human presence.

The new approach to creating planetary bases was completely justified since the main production facilities were tens of light years away on the Central World planets. Masses of invaluable information flowed from here on a daily basis and in response, requests for further research came back through the hypersphere channels.

All ground objects and underground bunkers were defended by machines that had passed field tests. The leadership of the Free Colonies knew that the war was moving to a new, even fiercer phase and would be impossible to win without the use of automated servomachines.

The story of Dabog was being mirrored here on Anchor — just like the Terran Alliance had urgently begun developing fundamentally new types of technology after suffering a crushing defeat, using the walking agricultural behemoths of the undefeated planet as a base, so now the Free Colonies studied the captured servomachines, creating their own version of the technology and installing an automatic control system into the famous Aquilas and Hawks. There was a catastrophic shortage of pilots and controls using sensory suits were rapidly becoming obsolete, giving way to direct sensory commands issued to the cyber system through a mental connection between human and machine.

The creation of new technology was a matter of life or death in these circumstances. In the Colonies' plan for a completely modernized fleet, humans would still have a leading role. They were planning to create automatic formations which would include a 'head machine' controlled by a live pilot.

At the moment, Anchor's testing grounds were testing technology based on captured units with the integrated Maverick modules and the more advanced Clemence-12 system, adapted for restricted freedom, when the cyber system only carried out actions issued by the leading machine.

The Colonies continued to avoid full automation on the battlefield, trying to keep the cybernetic genie in the bottle by all means possible.

THE NIBELUNGS, masked by the Mirage complexes, began their approach to the planet.

The machines of the Thirteenth Servobattalion stood in their containers, their energy emissions at a minimum.

The uncertainty and the agonizing wait weighed heavily on the pilots but conversation was strictly forbidden, and everyone suffered through the hours of tedious maneuvering, inevitable on approach to a planet, alone in the company of their own thoughts.

It was quite an ordeal, especially knowing that a battle lay ahead of them, the likes of which had never been seen before.

THE NIBELUNG cyber systems almost immediately began the challenging identification conversation with the control devices on the planetary defense installations.

A person landing in a hostile environment and knowing that their fleet's main forces were only preparing for a jump could easily freak out, but machines were indifferent to their own fate and felt neither nervousness nor fear, using information obtained from the onboard computers of the intercepted transports and relying on the protection of the phantom generators.

The same machines carried out the validation procedure at the other end.

It is human nature to doubt, for example, an operator's or duty officer's bad mood could lead to a tricky question but machines have no such weaknesses and thus lose the advantages of human thinking.

All they need is a complete match between the observed signatures and the previously known energy distribution maps, the right access codes to planetary space and the magnetic markers that are listed in the register.

The brief machine dialogue resulted in a safe approach corridor to the planet being assigned, and the 'transport convoy' continued its unimpeded movement towards Anchor.

AFTER AN HOUR and a half of maneuvering, the fake transports first reached the intermediate parking orbit and then began their descent into the dense atmospheric layers, carefully following the provided landing corridor.

Less than five kilometers remained to the planet's surface when the large 'container' being towed by the fake transports suddenly split away and began to plummet downwards, enveloped by the fire of the planetary thrust engines.

The cyber systems noted the unusual situation and immediately sent a query but didn't raise an alarm, for which they paid dearly. The seven transports, dropping the disguise provided by the phantom generators, suddenly displayed their true form as formidable assault carriers and simultaneously fired a volley from each of their upper and lower missile systems.

It looked as if the sky above Anchor's central RW base turned into the mouth of an erupting volcano. Heavy missiles burst out of dozens of launching tubes and shot into low orbit, destroying the control stations that provided constant ground monitoring and turning the navigation and communication satellites into a meteoric shower of fragments. The attack of the assault carriers was so sudden that some of the missile warheads flew beyond the low orbit and struck two frigates in the Free Colonies squadron protecting the planet.

Chaos reigned on the command communication frequencies. The communication relays had been destroyed, the surprise attack had brought down the global control stations with two of them breaking up and the third remaining whole but losing its orbit and threatening to soon enter the dense layers of the atmosphere.

The volleys from the assault carrier's lower

guns struck the ground targets, and hundreds of tonnes of earth, mixed with defense perimeter constructions and destroyed security servomechanisms, rose into the sky as mushroom-shaped clouds. The Nibelungs immediately changed course, entering the danger zone. They moved among the enormous spews, immediately disappearing off the screens of the remaining monitoring devices, and, at the same time, began releasing the servobattalion landing modules.

Ten seconds later, once all the assault module containers had been successfully released, the Nibelungs began to descend directly onto the RW base and continued their attack, dropping to a height of one kilometer and uncovering their short-life plasma generators.

The opening chords of the battle, which left a gash in the planetary defenses and destroyed most of the RW base's security perimeter, were actually only a prelude to the impending fight.

The planet Anchor
Captain Tavgalov's group
07:12

THE AIR ASSAULT MODULE dropped rapidly

towards the churned-up earth.

The buildings seemed blurry since the Nibelungs' missile strike had thrown up tonnes of dust into the air, and the ensuing plasma charges turned the dust into an all-consuming firestorm.

Down below, the ground was burning, the reinforced concrete was melting, and the activated alarm systems were malfunctioning.

The RW base still retained its general outline but the captain's experience suggested that the ground facilities, like most of the first underground bunker level, were now nothing more than ruins...

"Everyone get ready." Tavgalov didn't need to say the standard phrase, the fighters had spent the last few hours waiting for any outcome and were desperate to land.

It is a person's right to choose the worst of all possible evils. They had been helpless in space, packed like sardines in a can, and if everything had gone wrong, they would have been destroyed without a chance to fight back. Now, these fighters had been given the opportunity to fight both for their lives and for the success of the operation as a whole.

The warning signals screeched alarmingly and the module shook as it touched down.

The opening ramp immediately revealed a flaming corner of a building, a piece of ragged and swirling sky and the silence of the landing compartment was filled with the sharp bark of the automatic tower guns sending long bursts into the smoky darkness.

The ground quaked but not from explosions anymore, rather from the nearby landings of the Thirteenth Servobattalion modules.

"In pairs, advance!"

Leaping into the smoky gloom, Captain Tavgalov immediately oriented himself using the CSC[3] information built into the combat helmet of the heavy armored suit. The rhythmical work of the muscle servoamplifiers seemed to fill him with energy and the fact that they had successfully reached the surface of the tightly 'sealed' planet felt like a miracle, but the captain knew that miracles didn't exist and if they did, then only within the boundaries of advanced technology.

"Watch the entrance to the bunker zone." The hoarseness in Tavgalov's voice nevertheless gave away the strain he felt. "Narimov and Skobin —

---

[3] CSC (combat scanning complex)—a metallic Kevlar half-helmet with an armored visor, which acts as a projection screen for data output from the scanners. Equipped with a thermal imaging system, laser range scope, inbuilt processor, RAM and wireless ports. With an optical cable, it can be connected directly to ranged weapons, transmitting the point of impact to the projection screen and calculating the barrel displacement in real time.

provide access, everyone else spread out and take up a defense position."

Good timing.

The assault module guns didn't pause for even a second and the scanners sent streams of information about the approaching enemy to the CSC projection visor. Despite the overwhelming element of surprise, there was almost no time left as all around them, as if materializing from the gloomy haze, ominous markers began appearing in a tightening noose. They were machines that had survived the missile fire and had turned themselves towards the 'nearest target' and could be identified as PCVs[4,] four Aquilas and then, a few seconds later, the target monitor added a dozen infantry droids and even two captured Phalangers.

'So much for the landing.' Flashed the angry thought.

"Attention, six servomachines within the scanning radius. Norlock's group, they're yours."

Lieutenant Norlock headed the unit equipped with heavy, portable missile complexes, which were brand new and had never been tested in real combat as a weapon against multi-tonne servomechanisms.

Where are our folks? Why is the servoformation taking such a long time to turn

---

[4] PCV — planetary combat vehicle.

around?

The seconds ticked away. Tavgalov was under no illusions and knew that the breakthrough would be harsh, but without the support of the servobattalion, they would not survive the few minutes required for the demolition team to clear a path into the bunker zone.

The smoke coiled into tight whirlwinds and, thankfully, impeded the enemy's laser installations. The coating on the armored suits had also kept them alive so far, but no camouflage would help if the servomachines walked another 500 meters.

The cover that the fighters were hiding behind wouldn't protect them from servomachine volleys.

'Where are our folk?' The thought pulsed in his mind.

The gloom of this artificial hell was suddenly illuminated by pale blue flashes of plasma and an iridescent glow lit up the sky, similar to the Northern Lights. It was the Nibelung batteries striking their targets and the enemy servomachine signatures began to melt and turn gray in color, clearly indicating the destruction of their armored coating.

IN THE MOMENT of the plasma strike, Lieutenant Norlock and two other fighters had already assumed a position in a semi-destroyed ground dwelling.

One of the walls had been blown out by the explosion, and immediately beyond it lay a gigantic crater that had partially swallowed up several rooms of the first bunker level. The covering slabs had cracked from the missile strike and stuck out at different angles.

A fire smoldered below and acrid smoke spread over the surrounding area, but the fighters ignored the continuing explosions and rushed to the shattered windows, setting up their Prometheus combat complex on a launch platform.

The plasma strike, which their combat processor warned them about, turned the airborne mixture of earth and dust into a firestorm, where everything was burning: a wall of flames raced through the ruins, and the servomachine outlines turned gray and dim on the target monitors. They didn't care about the fire, of course, but some of assault carriers' plasma generators were hitting direct targets and not the general area.

"The servomachines are cooked and served." Norlock darted to the volley fire system, noting as he did so that the building's reinforced concrete, softened by the hellish temperatures, was beginning to sag dangerously overhead.

Only three PCVs remained on the target monitor, racing along the churned-up street towards the servobattalion's landing zone.

He launched the automatic firing program with a few taps of the sensors and simultaneously gave an order,

"Everyone leave the building! Find cover outside — the overhead construction won't stand Prometheus' fire!"

Giant flakes of soot spiraled over the street like a black snowstorm.

Norlock rushed to the nearest building with some surviving walls but he barely had enough time to hide behind a corner when the target monitor flashed five new signatures onto his projection visor. The unidentified mechanisms, which were not listed in his database, flashed for a second and then disappeared, but they had enough time to spot the prepared trap and transmit the information to the PCV cyber systems.

The street was immediately bisected by a wall of explosions as shells fired by the tower guns of the planetary combat vehicles tore down the corner of the building containing Prometheus, then ripped diagonally across the street and turned the corner of the building where Norlock was hiding into a pile of rubble.

The Lieutenant was hit in the back and a sharp pain spread through his body, together with a dazzling burst of flame. Norlock fell down and automatically attempted to get back up but the suit's servomusculature would not obey the suddenly weak muscles.

He was out of time.

The lieutenant's fading gaze saw three enemy vehicles crawl onto the hill formed from the building debris, their weapons fired again, and someone's dying scream echoed in the communicator. Suddenly, despite the painful feeling of encroaching death, Prometheus struck from the collapsing and awkwardly leaning building.

The missiles burned through the armor of the planetary tanks, and a second later, the powerful internal explosions threw the gun towers of two PCVs on either side into the air, while the third one in the center sustained two direct hits and turned into a giant torch.

Norlock began to slip out of consciousness.

He only had time to feel surprise that death was not as frightening as he had imagined.

It was only that the fountains of molten metal and roaring flame a few dozen meters away from him began to recede, turning into flickering candlelight that shone tenderly against the backdrop of universal darkness.

TAVGALOV TOOK the lieutenant's death very hard. He wasn't expecting to land without any losses but...

Shmelev's long-awaited report interrupted his morbid thoughts, "The battalion has landed. There were no casualties. Let us know the cover coordinates, Captain."

"You're too late, Major. We've managed by ourselves. The landing zone is clear."

"Any losses?"

"Yes. The covering fire group is whole. I have four fighters left."

Aboard the cruiser Apostle.

"ADMIRAL, THE INTELLIGENCE team is reporting that Tavgalov's group has landed."

"Excellent. What about the servobattalion?"

"The data is incomplete but a fight is underway in the landing zone using heavy weapons."

"What is the response from the enemy ships?"

"They're remaining in the same positions for the moment. They're protecting the planet against a possible strike from space."

"We wait. Be ready to perform a hyperjump. Keep me informed of any changes in the situation."

The planet Anchor
The Thirteenth Servobattalion
07:18

THE DISPERSAL AREA of the servomachine landing modules didn't exceed two kilometers. This was the minimum distance required to prevent the planetary engines of the detaching compartments from affecting each other during landing.

The roaring plasma acted as a heavy weapon and the landing of a servobattalion, consisting of thirty-five units, looked like the apocalypse. The planetary engines vaporized the thin, masking earth layer and burned through the reinforced concrete slabs. The temperature inside the upper levels of the bunker zone was climbing rapidly and muddy geysers of smoke and superheated air shot up from the ventilation shafts, adding to the incessant missile explosions as the assault carriers hit all targets detected within a radius of thirty kilometers from the landing zone.

Thanks to the latest camouflage technology and the carefully calculated operation, the worst thing that could have happened to a commander responsible for planetary defense was taking place — the assault carriers had passed through low orbit without a single shot being fired and have unleashed their firepower on the ground infrastructure.

A thick black cloud enveloped the landing zone and the surrounding territory. Soot swirled in the air, mixing with the clouds of debris from the numerous explosions, illuminated from below by more and more hits. The cloud grew upwards and outwards, covering an area of about one hundred square kilometers. In such conditions, not a single orbital cyber system could accurately determine the enemy numbers and their own losses among the ground defense units.

The Nibelungs switched to plasma generation mode to avoid burning their precious fuel, and having used up all their ammunition, began to rapidly rise towards the border of the swirling mushroom cloud.

Nobody could predict their movement. Usually, the assault carriers landed close to the servomachine positions, providing them with additional covering fire, reloading and minor repairs, but everything was different this time. It was as if all previous textbooks on planetary battle tactics were being cast into the flames.

Rising to a height of eleven kilometers, the assault carriers took advantage of the chaos in the lower orbits and switched their phantom generators back on, thus creating a simple but highly effective trap. Colonel Gorelov, commander of the formation, had carefully calculated the enemy's actions. Considering the torn chain of ground defense, where only scattered gun posts were currently resisting the servomachines, the only way of seizing initiative and disrupting the servomachine attack to finish them off was a massive space fighter strike.

The Nibelungs switched on their geostationary maneuvering mode while at the edge of the cloud and their cyber systems calculated the position of the enemy spaceships as well as the atmospheric entry points for the space fighters.

They appeared abruptly, ten clusters growing rapidly in size. The Nibelungs dropped lower and almost immediately, all the upper guns were lit up with flashes of volley fire.

Some of the fighters exploded into pieces, the direct missile hits from such short range left no time for evasive maneuvers and the fragments burning up in the atmosphere damaged the neighboring fighters. All this lasted for 10-15 seconds and ended with a massive plasma generator burst after which the assault carriers again dropped steeply towards the planet, reloading their guns and missile systems.

Anchor. High orbit

UTTER CHAOS REIGNED on the bridge of the cruiser Elliot.

Admiral Ipatov, flagship commander of the defense squadron, was experiencing the worst minutes of his life.

The Alliance assault carriers, having sneaked past the space defense barriers, now calmly and confidently crushed all resistance, using their gained tactical advantage.

Sergey couldn't help but admit that his opponent displayed a high level of professionalism, however, this mental admission did not change the complexity of the situation.

Over the past fifteen minutes, the RW base ground defense network had been destroyed, forty-three space fighters had been lost, and the unified structure of the space defense complexes had been disrupted. It was a crippling blow but the element of surprise, which had allowed the enemy to inflict so much damage, had already passed.

Despite all the interferences for the scanners, the specialists of the squadron protecting Anchor had managed to determine the size and composition of the enemy troops.

Seven Nibelungs had landed a servobattalion

onto the planet, which consisted of 30 to 35 machines; plus the landing module.

What were they hoping to do? Capture the planet? Impossible. They lacked the forces for that. The chaos over the information networks would calm down and then what would save the troops from complete and instant destruction?

"Dolmatov!"

The squadron's Head of the Analytical Department appeared beside the admiral.

"What are they planning? I need to understand the logic behind the servobattalion's activities!"

"The central RW base contains ninety-eight captured servomachines, including forty-two Phalangers."

"I don't understand. Fine, there are servomachines down there. So? Where are the pilots and the ammunition?" Sergey hadn't yet recovered from the moral blow and reacted with irritated suspicion to the report. "Go on, Colonel, say it like it is. Where are they going to get the pilots?"

"It's all there..." Dolmatov whispered.

"Meaning?" The admiral's face contorted with horror.

"The head of the RW bases and the Research Department informed us last night that large-scale exercises were being planned using new technology models developed to withstand the servomachines."

A blow. Another devastating information blow. How was this possible?! So the enemy knew about the upcoming tests and I didn't?!

"Okay... okay..." Ipatov pulled himself together with some difficulty. "I see. Real military exercises. There are machines and ammunition down there, theoretically ready to take the enemy's side. But who is going to control them?"

"The pilots, sir. Enemy pilots."

"They were brought to the planet without informing me?"

"No. They've already been here for several years."

The head of the Analytical Department was clearly keeping something back... or perhaps he didn't know.

"Has contact been established with the surface?"

"Yes."

"Give me the outline of the planned exercises or the combat tests... whatever they are. All information about the planetary technology to be sent to my terminal. I'm taking over command of the ground forces!"

Chapter Three

A STRONG JOLT shook the landing module and a wave of deformation ran along the sides of the transport container with a screech of crumpling metal.

Simon swore.

Damn it. What kind of landing is this? He better not be trapped inside the damaged module.

Communication.

Not working...

Or is there nobody here to answer me? Maybe

I'm the only one to reach the surface of the planet?

It was a jittery thought.

Calm down, dude. Calm down... You can blow a hole in the wall using your weapons.

There was no response from Beatrice to the pilot's thoughts. The Maverick was waiting for a direct order. If Simon had decided to act, she would have, of course, cautioned him against using 150-mm weapons in an enclosed space.

However, the pilot was acting reasonably so far by considering possible options for solving this problem, so the cyber system didn't interfere.

'Bea... Establish a connection.' Simon gave a mental order.

No response from external sensors.

"Do something! Activate the back-up subsystems! Does this 'box' have its own scanning and communication devices?"

"It does."

A few seconds later, he heard a voice. "This is zero seventeen, I'm moving towards the northern end of the facility perimeter. I'm encountering no resistance. Can anyone hear me?"

Verkholin. Anton.

Simon felt himself tremble but suppressed the urge to scream and beg for help. "Zero seventeen, this is twenty-two. Get a fix on my location. My module was damaged on landing. I need help, I can't get out by myself."

"Understood. I'm coming."

UNLIKE SIMON, Anton had landed successfully, although the situation could hardly be called pleasant.

When the landing module's door opened, he saw a jumble of cement fragments, twisted iron reinforcements, and several geysers of superheated air and ash, bursting out of the bunker.

His module had landed into a massive crater formed by a missile strike from one of the assault carriers.

As soon as he left the landing segment, Anton scanned his surroundings. The crater where his Phalanger stood was wreathed in smoke, and flames could be seen in several places beneath the broken slabs. The thick curtain of smoke and cement dust was hiding his surrounding and the scanners showed no active signatures, as if the mighty blow of the Nibelungs had destroyed everything capable of movement.

This wasn't actually the case. The excessive heat, large amount of twisted metal and thick cloud of warm air were interfering with the scanners.

He had to get out of there.

The cyber system immediately reacted to the pilot's thoughts. The nearest pile of wreckage could be analyzed quite easily and the Maverick instantly plotted a safe route for getting out of the crater.

"Go for it." Anton approved her choice and focused his attention on the target monitor.

He couldn't see more than a meter out of the cockpit's observation screens. Flakes of ash spun slowly in the rising columns of heated air.

There was the edge of the crater — a miraculously spared but cracked and unreliable slab, lying over the abyss beneath it.

'Careful,' Anton sent a mental warning but it was unnecessary. The cyber system did not take needless risks and had already determined that the remaining fragment was unsafe. It looked for alternative routes and lit up several possible options on the tactical monitor.

A few minutes later, having climbed out of the crater, Anton tried to contact the others.

Simon abruptly responded and requested help but, oddly, the other pilots of the servobattalion remained silent. The same panicky thought flashed in Verkholin's mind — what if Simon and I are alone here? What if the other modules didn't reach the surface?

Major Shmelev's voice appeared suddenly. "Seventeenth, twenty-second, maintain radio silence! You're not on a picnic!"

The commander's rebuke was reassuring.

Only five minutes had passed since Anton had reached the planet and yet he felt completely lost among the hot smoke, geysers of steam and the concrete ruins of collapsed buildings.

No virtual reality could provide such realistic surroundings and Verkholin understood why. The mind could not be tricked, it clearly differentiated between the gaming cabin and the surface of an enemy planet.

'Everything's OK. It's all going according to plan.' Anton reassured himself, jolting back from a moment's weakness. In response, Beatrice pulled up a map of the perimeter defenses that the servobattalion had to arrange no matter what the circumstances during landing.

Help Simon get out and reach his designated position — that's what he had to do, rather than going on air with dumb questions.

The first landing was overwhelming. Truly, no VR module could compete with this *reality*, full of thousands of tonnes of warped concrete and metal.

It was hard to comprehend the force that had shattered the planetary surface. The surrounding gloom impeded the work of the Amethyst and seemed to suggest that the enemy machines could appear at any moment, creeping up to the distance of an effective shot.

The Maverick headed directly towards the

fixed location. The murk had dissipated slightly, although thunder boomed overhead and Anton sensed that the sounds coming from the skies were not natural. As if in confirmation, the gloom was suddenly lit up by the glowing fragments of enemy fighters as they burned up in the atmosphere.

Seven minutes since landing. So far, none of the experienced sensations, even the abrupt impact on landing, contradicted the experiences obtained in VR. On the contrary, once his excessive nervousness wore off, it became clear that reality wasn't as impressive as VR, both in the number of opponents and in its 'atmosphere'.

The smoky dimness, the holographic screens showing the pilot his surroundings, and the regular tread of the servomachine was all totally routine so the landing didn't impress the young pilot in the slightest.

According to the sensors, Simon's landing module was a hundred meters to the south.

Anton stopped the Phalanger and scanned his environment. There was no way the Amethyst couldn't spot a module with a servomachine sealed inside at close distance.

The image of the outside, slowly shifted across the holographic screens, at times gaining contrast and color and at other times blurring as the work of the scanners was impeded by interference.

The next crater looked like a cave in. Several heavy rockets had landed in the same spot, shattering the thick slabs of the first underground level. At the edge of the crater stood the remains of a two-story structure that had miraculously escaped the damage. The facade wall had collapsed, exposing the rooms at an unfamiliar angle.

Then... Anton spotted something unusual and the subsystem immediately responded and zoomed in so that he could see what that had caught his eye. It would have been better if he hadn't seen it.

One of the rooms looked like the command module of a spaceship or an observation point that collected data from numerous sensors. A couple of the monitors were still working, showing dreary, completely bare spaces and a huge cloud of smoke rising into the sky. The transmission was clearly done in real time but this wasn't what had drawn Anton's attention.

Crushed people lay between the working holographic screens and beneath chunks of the collapsed ceiling.

Anton's mind went dark. He saw a face splattered with blood, frozen in abrupt agony, fingers digging into the concrete, a leg torn off by the blast, then another face... pale and bloodless this time, with an expression of utter bewilderment.

It felt like someone had punched Anton in the head and chest. His breath caught in his throat and everything swam before his eyes. It turned out that his mind clearly knew that the death he had stumbled upon, the gaze of a corpse that he had unwittingly caught, was not an image generated by a phantom world.

Terror flooded his senses but then something unexpected happened: a click in the helmet's neck ring and the slight jab of a needle with a combat stimulant, which made him regain clarity of his senses. It was as if someone invisible but ruthless had grabbed him by the collar and pushed his face into the screens: no, look, get used to it, they were alive ten minutes ago, they had hopes and plans, they loved and hated, they strove for something and believed that their personal Universe would never die, that all their hustle and bustle meant something... then a moment of agony and that's it...

THAT'S IT.

They don't exist anymore.

This abrupt, unembellished and harsh *truth* made something ache in Verkholin's chest but the combat metabolic correction system was carefully monitoring his state. Another jab in his neck made him regain alertness again, slightly dampening the acuity of his perception and smoothing out the emotional response.

No. That's not right... I want to be able to feel things!

The voice of the cyber system suddenly invaded Verkholin's scattered thoughts, his personal emotional drama, 'Anton, I can temporarily switch off the combat life support system.'

He startled violently.

It was so bizarre to realize that the servomachine's AI was participating in his intense inner turmoil that Verkholin didn't even feel animosity, but rather a delayed sense of annoyance that *she had listened in on his thoughts*. Anton stopped that train of thought, reminding himself that the Maverick was always online. The training he had received on the combat machine simulator, which imitated full neurosensory contact with servosystems, for some reason never included the experience of fighting with a 'second pilot'.

"No need. I'll manage." Verkholin uttered the phrase with difficulty, feeling like he lacked the air to breathe.

"I can explain certain moments." Sounded the soft female voice. The Maverick adjusted to the pilot and decided to switch to audio communication.

"Like what?"

"You were trained to make independent decisions and were taught to control the machine like it was your own body. This is the crucial difference between the latest cohort and the other pilots. Think, Anton, if you're capable of fighting without me, how much more effective will the combat machine be if we work together?"

Anton didn't bother to perform the calculations. Something completely different was bothering him. His mind had lost its support point and was balancing on the edge of a precipice.

"Why do you call me by my name?"

"It brings us closer."

"For how long?"

"I cannot answer this."

"I'm asking you how long we'll last once we're in battle?"

"The Phalanger's tactical and technical characteristics are designed for thirty minutes of active combat."

Anton could hardly believe it. "That's bullshit!" Everything inside Verkholin revolted against this. "I knocked down four or five servomachines and then successfully withdrew from the fight. What thirty minutes are you talking about?"

"There are circumstances that cannot be controlled."

"Like what?"

"If you destroy several enemy machines, you will use up your ammunition but the mission will not be over. You will not be able to withdraw from the fight, Anton."

Verkholin processed what he had heard for several seconds and then said drily, "We'll discuss survival strategies later." He glanced at the timer, stunned that so many internal and emotional events could have been compressed in just one minute. "I can't see Simon's landing module."

"He is fifty meters away behind that building."

"Can you set a safe route?"

Beatrice didn't reply but simply started walking towards their goal.

★ ★ ★

THEY HAD ONLY this day left to live, but it was as important as their whole life.

Only nine minutes had passed since the Nibelungs released the landing modules, and yet so much had already changed irreversibly in the young pilot's souls.

Directing the Phalanger among the ruins, Anton approached the site of Lieutenant Green's unsuccessful landing.

Anton's mind gradually adapted to the sensations which made previous memories dull in comparison. The new reality overwhelmed his senses and emotions — contradictory, angry, baffled — which were being replaced not by a detached calm but by a previously unexperienced deadly enthusiasm. His fear of the inevitable would suddenly be replaced by strange waves of stirring energy. Alongside his sharp monitoring of the surroundings, the Maverick's disembodied voice slid through his thoughts.

Anton had not escaped the tendency of most pilots to think of the cyber system as a *she*, a live female creature, due to the voice. This made him feel uncomfortable at the start but then, once their minds began to meld, he began to perceive them both as one being, to some extent.

The Beatrice module hungrily absorbed Verkholin's thoughts since the artificial neural networks had commenced their training only a few days ago and right now, they were experiencing an accelerating, almost explosive, process of learning, development and information analysis.

She was self-aware but the Maverick's thoughts and worldview were a true copy of Verkholin's thoughts and opinions, which made their connection grow stronger so the Phalanger moved more and more confidently with every step.

This linking didn't always happen and not with everyone. Only a person without any cyber system phobias could establish a thorough and in-depth neurosensory contact, when their personality became the base and fulcrum from which the Maverick started its self-development.

Verkholin intuitively sensed the depth of the contact and understood that, in essence, his double was being created in the artificial system...

The Maverick modules were not trained beforehand on purpose. The unique link would only form on contact with the pilot and if the 'mutual trust' that the strange military man had spoken about was reciprocated, the pilot and their machine gained a real chance of using the full might of the servomechanism.

The mind-melding process took minutes, it was as intimate as falling in love and as deep as an uncharted cavern.

Simon's landing module stood before them.

The large container, covered in slag, was stuck in a gap between two concrete slabs, which prevented the mechanism from opening its front wall.

Beatrice automatically switched on laser communication, which didn't disrupt the radio silence.

"Simon, I'm next to you. How are you going?"

"Could be worse."

"What do you mean?" Verkholin couldn't see anything positive in the situation that Green found himself in.

"The battle hasn't started yet." Simon responded grumpily. "So, you can take your time with getting me out."

"Oh, that's what you're referring to." Anton was trying to figure out whether to try and move the container or to use his lasers to cut the concrete fragment blocking the entrance.

Cut the concrete.

Anton listened to Beatrice's advice, which he no longer perceived as a 'second pilot' but rather as an inner voice.

"Simon, I'm going to cut the cement fragment with a laser. Hold on for another minute." Anton allowed Beatrice to set the right laser intensity and choose the cutting angle. "How's your adaptation going?"

"It's fine. My red-haired friend is keeping me entertained with jokes."

"Are you serious?"

"Of course not. I'm joking."

The laser fired and the cement slab with its spider web of cracks began to crumble into small pieces of dust and larger fragments that fell to the bottom of the crater with dull thuds, leaving behind blue-gray streaks of smoke.

There was a shower of sparks when the discharges hit the iron reinforcements, and cherry-red balls of molten and then immediately hardening metal flew in all directions. The cement fragment placed vertically by the explosion began to slowly slide down under its own weight. A moment later, it broke off and crashed down, and Simon's landing module shifted into a horizontal position.

"Careful!" Came Green's voice.

"Sorry about that." Anton replied. "Can you check if the door is working?"

One of the walls of the landing container began to hum as it opened, snapping open the layer of slag.

"It's all good."

THE COMMAND FREQUENCY suddenly came alive.

"Seventeen and twenty-second, head to mark 807. Take your positions and wait for orders."

"Understood." Anton replied without asking the battalion commander why he was sending two Phalangers together when the heavy servomachines usually worked together with the lighter Hoplites.

Orders aren't discussed, they're carried out.

Anton could sense that something had gone wrong. The grim silence enveloping the ruins seemed to last for too long after the crushing attack by the assault carriers.

Where is the enemy, why isn't it showing initiative, why isn't it trying to take back the base or at least shoot at the landed servobattalion?

The uncertainty was a difficult test that again reminded him that this wasn't VR, where everything was clear and predictable. There, the enemy wouldn't hesitate, straining one's nerves with the sinister silence, but here... one just had to hope that the combat commander had a clear idea of what they need to do to avoid a trap.

IN TRUTH, the servobattalion commander was in a state of complete bewilderment. They had landed. Now what?

The situation was looking dire.

Major Shmelev could also sense that something was wrong, some sneaky trick hidden in the carefully designed and brilliantly executed first phase of the plan. He could find no other word to explain the ambiguous situation that the servobattalion now found itself in.

They had broken through the enemy defenses and landed on the RW bases, but what next? The perimeter defense plan smelled too much like self-sacrifice but nobody had bothered to explain to him why these youngsters had to die.

According to passive scanning, which didn't reveal the position of the servomachines, the enemy had surprisingly quickly recovered from the crushing assault while the Seventh Strike Fleet still hadn't appeared from the hypersphere.

What are you planning, Admiral? Why haven't you told me the operation details, why haven't you saved me from this agonizing uncertainty?

Is he exchanging one servobattalion for the destroyed section of the planetary defense system?

Too rough, too direct, there was no need to send these young guys, even pilotless servomechanisms would have managed here using the Mirages.

Tavgalov's group... We weren't even allowed to communicate directly. They're here on a special mission.

Uncertainty is the worst form of torture so Shmelev didn't hesitate when he activated the secure command channel. "Captain?"

The other man responded a few seconds later, probably after checking the caller's authorization status. "Speaking. Have you decided to introduce yourself, Major?"

"I'll get straight to the point." Shmelev replied. "I'm stuck."

"In what sense?"

"In the direct sense. The landing has been successful, the machines have assumed their perimeter defense positions, and the commander of the Nibelung formation is demanding further instructions."

Tavgalov felt an unpleasant chill. "There's no

further plan of action?!" He asked, dumbfounded.

"To form the perimeter defense and await the arrival of the main fleet. But I don't see anything happening in orbit. Our fleet's not here, but we are. That's why I thought, maybe you'll tell me what's supposed to happen next before it all gets crazy? What's your mission, Captain?"

Tavgalov cursed. "My missions' simple. Free the captive pilots. Provide them with access to the servomachines kept on the captured RW base, then transfer overall command of the operation to you."

"I see." Shmelev's voice left no doubt about the thoughts flashing through his mind. "We're being set up for an attack. How many servomachines are you supposed to activate?"

"About a hundred. Depending on how things go."

A second of silence.

"A hundred? Are you serious? Why would there be so many captive pilots held inside the base?"

"Did I saw that they were *alive*?" Tavgalov smiled crookedly. "Five containers full of captured Maverick modules with various modifications. My orders are to find them, bring them to the machines and then activate them."

Major Shmelev's face took on a green tone.

"Don't do it, Captain."

"Why? Explain!"

"The Colonies' heavy flagship cruiser is in orbit above us. Reactivating a hundred servomachines will create such a threat that they will act immediately, no matter what. I don't know, take your pick, either the cruiser will move into low orbit to carpet bomb the RW base or it will use the Light annihilation device to strike the planet."

Tavgalov swore profusely again. "No matter which way you look at it, Major, it's an exchange. Our lives for the destruction of the Colonies' stronghold. Impressive. It means there's no point waiting for the fleet. The admiral isn't going to expose himself to the Light device."

"Right." Shmelev agreed at once, knowing that the admiral was a calculating, cynical tactician until it came to his personal safety. "But we must survive, or do you disagree, Captain?"

"Certainly not, but I don't see a way for us to survive, sorry. If we activate the captured machines, we'll get a pounding from above. If we don't activate them, sooner or later, we'll be overrun by the ground forces."

"How long have you been in the assault forces?" Shmelev asked, straining his brain to try and find a way out of this deadly tangle.

"Going on five years." Tavgalov replied.

"I'll say this, Captain: I'll survive so I can at least save the young ones."

"Options? We need clear options, not words."

"Listen carefully. Follow the plan. Reach the Maverick modules. We need them like we need air."

"But you just said that activating the captured machines will be like signing our own death warrants!"

"Let's not get ahead of ourselves. We're relatively safe for the next hour. The battalion will keep the base secure and you'll head underground. I'll get the Nibelungs hidden since they're our ticket out of here. How many technical servos do you have?"

"Thirty."

"Excellent. Get them to reactivate the captured machines. Are your guys familiar with servomechanisms?"

"You mean the controls?"

"Yes."

"We've studied them. We know how they work."

"In that case, make the whole unit into pilots. Got it? Don't argue with me, the armor and firepower of the Phalangers will increase the chance that your group survives, even if they lack experience."

"Understood. You still haven't said what we're going to do next, though."

"I'll have a think about it. We have to design

a plan of action that will make the enemy think that their ground forces will manage on their own. We'll activate the captured machines in smaller groups to avoid a large-scale threat."

"Do you think it will work?"

"I'm certain. Give me a bit of time and I'll have a plan ready by the time you come back."

A second of silence.

"All right, Major. I'm off. You figure out a plan."

Captain Tavgalov's group

THE POWERFUL EXPLOSION ripped out the modular gates that had withstood the Nibelungs' rocket attack.

The entrance into the bunker zone became shrouded in smoke and dust but the five members of the special forces unit didn't pay such things any attention. The CSC systems were working as they should, projecting the processed scan data onto their visors.

"Forward in twos. Distance for technical mechanisms — fifty meters."

The size of the bunker zone was astounding. Immediately beyond the shattered gates stood an enormous open space for technical parking, where dozens of captured servomachines had not suffered any damage from the rocket strikes. The panels overhead hadn't even cracked but carpet bombing using fuel-air explosives would turn this place into a ruin...

The five fighters in the group stopped and assumed positions in anticipation of an immediate response from the internal defense nodes. But the unsettling gloom, lit up by sparse emergency lamps, wasn't disturbed by a single shot or laser discharge. The defense system had either been switched off or didn't exist, which Tavgalov found doubtful.

However, the scanners didn't pick up any energy-emitting sources except for those supplying the emergency lighting. The energy supply to the level must have been disrupted. Let's see how it goes deeper in...

They resumed moving forward, slowly and hesitantly, expecting the sudden flash of enemy resistance at any moment. Ducking behind the massive legs of the servomachines, standing frozen like statues, the assault team covered meter after meter until the utility network map projected by their combat suits indicated a sloping tunnel leading deeper into the bunker zone. Five powerful lifting platforms stood nearby, designed to fit a servomachine.

Tavgalov couldn't believe that there was no

security system. Even if the central power supply was cut off, each node would go into automatic mode and use their own battery.

Yet the scanners were clear.

Was the chameleon mode working so well that the security systems didn't notice them? Should they risk it and keep moving ahead?

The pinprick of laser communication took away his doubts.

"Commander, there are unidentified signatures moving along the tunnel."

Tavgalov switched on the active scanning system for a second.

What the...

The helmet's projection visor displayed a jumbled group of signatures. Servomechanisms. But the design didn't exist in any of the databases!

Oh, right. This is the site of testing grounds, cyber laboratories and workshops to produce new technology, designed to match the Alliance servomachines.

The blurred signatures began to crystallize into rough outlines as the information was processed by the specialized combat identification programs.

Yeesh, they sure are ugly.

Tavgalov could see a miniature walking unit, then a dome mounted on a kind of turning platform and, as the final detail in the servomechanism's appearance, a heavy laser in an armored cover, looking slightly like a disproportionally long nose.

'How do they keep their balance?' Flashed the thought but it was no time for jokes, really, because even at first look, the walking freaks possessed unexpectedly large firepower. The heavy armor, similar to that of a planetary tank, made them impregnable to small-caliber weapons and acted as the counterbalance to the long launching tube. The quick-moving machines appeared very well balanced.

Another 3D image appeared alongside the walking laser which Tavgalov liked even less — relatively small bots moving on wide caterpillar tracks, combining a multibarrel rocket launcher and two thirty-millimeter guns.

'They'll pulverize us in seconds.' Thought the commander of the assault group.

They won't be able to sneak past, unless they rush into the cargo lift and fight their way down to the lower levels?

What are the walking lasers and fire support bots going to do to the technical droids?

What a mess. The hidden security systems were functioning after all. They had identified the incursion point and had summoned a cleanup crew.

The distance was now three hundred meters.

"Shmelev!" The captain had no choice but to contact the other man. There wasn't much choice, either a rapid heroic death and failing the mission or counting on the help of the servobattalion.

"Why are you contacting me using a radio frequency?!"

"Take note of the telemetry. My group's done for in a minute."

The major wasn't one to start squabbling. He immediately digested the incoming information and uttered a short order, "Maximov's squad, I'm sending you the coordinates for entry into the bunker zone! Support the assault team."

Silence reigned again.

Twenty minutes since landing.

Only twenty minutes...

Captain Tavgalov's group

"EVERYONE TAKE COVER. Dmitry, order the servos to get the hell out of here! We'll call them when we need them."

Two hundred meters... Even though he wasn't a boy anymore and had been in the special forces for a while, his back was drenched in sweat. The dust covers quietly popped off the launch tubes of the tactical rocket complex attached over the armored plates of the right wrist. The gun on his left shoulder rustled as it turned, aiming towards the modular tunnel gates which were about to open.

'If help doesn't arrive in time, this is going to be a short fight.' The thought was calm. Unlike the young guys gulping in terror right now, Tavgalov didn't feel nervous. The war had long ago erased certain lines in his mind, which he had crossed once and could never return from.

When risk becomes an everyday event, something strange happens to a person. They change quickly and irreversibly, as if certain mental restraints fail and everything becomes absolute, like fear and daring. Tavgalov lived day-by-day and hour-by-hour for a long time now. He would have gone mad otherwise, like many others had done before his eyes.

The massive modular doors shuddered and began to move apart.

Five people. Fifteen tactical rockets.

"We'll fire in bursts. Three-second intervals."

The gloomy, enormous underground parking was lit up by flashes of rockets howling along their direct trajectory and then piercingly bright explosions bloomed beyond the opening gates.

The gates became jammed, there was a screech as the massive slabs jerked several times and then stood still. Flames roared in the gap formed by the opening doors, through which suddenly came the unusual machines.

Like the other fighters, Tavgalov fired a volley out of his GRC[5] and then barely had enough time to dive behind a thick reinforced concrete pillar supporting the vault of this enormous space. The response came as a rapid and rhythmical pounding of thirty-millimeter guns and the hangar was immediately filled with thundering explosions, clouds of bitter dust and the whine of ricocheting fragments. The servos didn't limit themselves to short bursts, they fixed on their targets and kept moving through the veil of dust, pounding the covered positions all the while. A huge pillar above Tavgalov's head suddenly became covered in a web of cracks — it appeared that those who programmed the enemy servomechanisms hadn't bothered to include a useful function like calculating the likely outcome of fire or any sense of self-preservation into the puny brains.

Another minute of such frenzied fire and they will either use up their ammunition or simply collapse the hangar roof over everyone's heads.

---

[5] GRC — Gun and rocket complex. In this case, refers to an individual system designed especially for armored suits. The rocket launching tubes are attached to the back of the wrist. A rapid-fire gun (30 mm) with cassette power is installed on the right shoulder plate. Both components are controlled with a dedicated coprocessor.

The captain barely had time to think this when the area was illuminated by five stroboscopic flashes of tactical fire from a Phalanger gun pod.

The pilot of the sixty-tonne machine had correctly assessed the situation and switched from his armor-piercing shells to incendiary ones. The five explosions practically swept away the enemy servomechanisms that had managed to make their way into the hangar, peppering them with round projectiles. When the scanners began working again, Tavgalov could see the results of the fire with some satisfaction. The target variator no longer highlighted any targets, only fragments.

A message came on a laser beam. "Lieutenant Maximov. I'm at your command."

"Thank you. You got here just in time. Did you see their signatures?"

"Cheap to make but a rather nasty piece of work." The lieutenant opined and, just to be sure, sent a single shot into the gap between the twisted gates emitting clouds of bitter-smelling smoke.

"Dmitry, check the lifts. John, get the droids back here." Tavgalov didn't waste a second of precious time. "Get them to test the servomachines."

Having issued the orders, he stepped out from behind the nearly collapsing cover.

Behind the dim outline of the Phalanger, he could see the fire team's two Hoplites.

"We need to reach the cyber laboratory. According to the plans obtained by our intelligence, it's on level -3."

"It's awfully quiet here," Maximov responded. "I don't like this silence, Captain."

"Is that a joke? Are you calling the thirty servomechanisms sent to eliminate five commandos 'quiet'?"

"I'm not talking about that. Why is there so little opposition?"

"Have you forgotten about the Nibelungs?" Tavgalov grinned wickedly. "They've plowed through the base's infrastructure to a depth of almost twenty meters."

"That's nothing. You can see yourself that the ceiling is completely intact."

"Listen, Lieutenant, don't stress me out. I've already got more questions than answers. What are your scanners showing? Can they see the security systems?"

"'Yes. They've played their part already and raised the alarm, so why did only one group respond?"

"Be happy. It means they have nothing else in reserve."

"The lifts are working." They were interrupted by the technician. "I've connected the emergency power supply."

"Well? Are we going in?"

"We'll descend first, Captain. You know if there's going to be a fight, it's better for you to stay back. Once we've cleaned up the level — you're welcome to join us."

"Agreed." Tavgalov had nothing to retort. Phalanger fire was dangerous to allies and enemies alike in enclosed spaces.

Three servomachines headed towards the elevators designed for their size and weight.

"Make sure we don't get trapped." Maximov warned.

"Don't worry about that, Lieutenant. We're monitoring the area."

Tavgalov looked at his timer. Minus twenty-two minutes since landing.

MAJOR SHMELEV, having positioned the servomachines around the place and given orders to the commander of the Nibelungs, was glancing nervously at his timer.

His intuition told him that they only had a quarter of an hour remaining. The assault carriers had done their work perfectly, ripping, like piranhas, a significant chunk out of the ground and planetary defenses.

So where was the fleet?

If everything had been done honestly, a battle

would be already raging above them. What was the admiral plotting by letting the enemy regroup and repair the hole in their space defense system?

We've been abandoned. Written off as irreparable losses. They're playing a strange game where the servobattalion is just an exchange piece on the board.

While he thought this, Shmelev continued to scan his surroundings. Furthermore, the battalion commander's Phalanger was equipped with special communication devices and additional cybernetic modules for processing information, which now summed up all the data received from other machines, gradually clarifying the configuration of the RW base fortifications and landscape.

The Nibelungs had also added valuable information to the overall picture.

Shmelev noted the unusual fortifications located beyond the perimeter of the occupied RW base. According to the data, the broken line seemed to be a series of passages connecting caponiers designed to fit servomachines. The 'trenches' also seemed perfect for covert movement of Phalangers and Hoplites. There were also long-term defense posts, empty of weapons or scanning complexes. He couldn't see any wiring running to these posts, although the power cables would have undoubtedly been damaged by the attack of the assault carriers.

But why create such a fortification network? Why place the heavy servomachines underground and create covers for them?

He couldn't come up with a sensible answer regarding the defense line, which was empty and directed at the space where the threat of ground attack was quite likely.

It's like they're inviting us to occupy these convenient caponiers... but they must have been created for another purpose. It can't be for base perimeter defense — the fortifications are only about twenty kilometers in length and in a single line... It would make more sense if they encircled the base but as it is, a flanking maneuver would make these positions useless.

Nobody is stupid enough to attack these head on.

Except in cases of combat testing. The Phalanger's cyber system suggested mildly.

Good girl... That's right! We're surrounded by testing grounds!

It was the right conclusion but how did it help?

The question set by Captain Tavgalov is being analyzed. The analysis system believes that the servobattalion has landed on the eve of combat testing of new types of planetary servomechanisms, developed by the specialists in the Colonies' Fleet. The machines found in the hangar parking area were meant for target practice. Consequently, the enemy strike force is located to the north of the battalion's position. Furthermore, it logically follows that the upper underground levels and the ground facilities destroyed by the Nibelungs contained high-ranking officials from the Colonies' Fleet, who had been invited here to observe the tests, and all the commanders of the planet's ground forces.

Listening to the Maverick's opinion, Alexander Shmelev found no valid objections. One could debate whether any of the senior officers of the enemy fleet had perished in the sudden strike, but the conclusion about the likely use for the fortifications and the location of the enemy forces seemed accurate.

Now they knew where an attack would come from. Considering a deep flanking maneuver, the risk of being surrounded was high but this also increased the time available to them. According to the latest calculations, it will take at least 1.5 hours for the enemy to completely encircle the base.

They can't remain in the occupied positions. They must covertly extricate the battalion but how and where to?

A lot depended on Tavgalov right now. They desperately needed the Maverick modules.

Activating the captured machines that had been prepped for combat testing could solve many of their problems.

Shmelev was in a decisive mood. 'I'll get you out of the hypersphere, Admiral.' He thought with cold fury. 'I'll force you to attack the planet because I'm not going to make any moves that will provoke the enemy into destroying it.'

Captain Tavgalov's group
07:25

EVEN THE LIGHTS weren't working on the third underground level.

The assault carriers' strike must have inflicted a lot more damage to the bunker zone than one would think by looking at the whole ceilings. Military technology had a significant safety margin, of course, and many systems had splintered into subsystems, with their own resources and specific tasks that could be performed even if they were completely isolated from the global network. Nevertheless, everywhere the scanners reached showed evidence of a wave of technological destruction that had rolled through the underground levels of the RW base. Many devices were still smoking and the air in the bunker zone was unbreathable. The underground blast wave, while unable to destroy the walls and the thick horizontal layers of armor, had severely damaged the equipment. The numerous torn power cables, the spot fires, the groundwater seeping in, and a dozen other signs of irreparable damage attested to the fact that the attack of the Nibelungs had not only reached its goal and razed the outside defense system to the ground, but had also inflicted internal damage.

The key part of the plan that the two commanders had been told about — capturing the Maverick modules that had been taken off captured servomachines and brought here for testing — had gone surprisingly smoothly.

Tavgalov didn't like such 'luck' and didn't trust it. Anything too easy equaled a trap in his mind.

However, the technical droids reported no resistance after exploring the whole level and discovering the containers with the crystal modules.

"Lieutenant, we found them. What do your scanners show?"

"All clear." Maximov replied, and added a few seconds later, "The tunnels here are weird. They're located at a depth of fifty meters and lead in a northerly direction."

"Can the servomachines use them?"

"No, but things like the 'walking lasers' easily can."

"Are they clear at the moment?"

"So far, yes."

"Alright, Lieutenant, the technical servos have commenced the main task. They're bringing the Maverick modules up to the surface and installing them in the servomachines. Cover them. The guys and I are going to take a walk to the tunnels and place some mines there, just in case."

"Sounds good."

Landing zone of the Thirteenth Servobattalion
Lieutenant Verkholin's machine
07:27

THE SHORT FIGHT in the lower levels of the bunker zone did not go unnoticed. Tremors travelled through the earth, which the servomachine sensors carefully noted and their subsystems analyzed, determining the rhythm, sifting through the random avalanches and providing the pilot with information about the significant events.

A firestorm of tactical rocket systems, a burst of fire from a 150-millimeter gun... and silence. An oppressive silence enveloping the ground buildings of the RW base, with a gray-black cloud of soot continuing to swirl overhead.

Verkholin had recovered from his first shock at meeting death face, which had been harshly suppressed by the metabolic correction system in his combat suit. But the emotional and physical boost from the drugs didn't last long, and Anton's mind was now making a painful distinction between the past and the present.

'Beatrice, how do we even our chances? Why is there no information about our opponents? We're like sitting ducks in these stationary positions!'

These questions should not be directed at me, Anton. The battalion commander is in charge of the operation.

'Fine. Let's try this another way. Imagine that we're alone. What are your suggestions?'

The battalion should withdraw to the concealed parking area of the assault carriers. Beatrice responded immediately. *Only the Nibelungs can fight their way into open space and perform a hyperspace jump.*

'Good. Clever girl. We'll keep that as an option, in case of an emergency. While it's quiet, let's think about how we can save our ammunition.'

Do we trust each other now?

Verkholin smiled crookedly.

"Yes. I don't know how things will turn out in the future but, most importantly, we need to survive." He said aloud.

"Individually or as part of the battalion?" Beatrice inquired, also switching to audio.

"I don't know... I don't know anymore." Anton fumbled with the answer, unsure of the right response.

You don't want to leave the battalion? Am I correctly understanding your thoughts?

'Yes. It is called *betrayal* in human speech.'

Yes, I am aware. Your commander and subordinates are counting on you. But your desire to live does not contradict the use of non-standard battle techniques.

"Are you talking about my VR fighting experience? "

"Yes. You don't have any other experience, right?"

"I agree. But there, we worked in groups."

"The situation has not changed. Simon is now your subordinate. Two cooperating servomachines are a serious power. Think about how to use it most effectively."

Anton didn't answer for a while, then reached out his hand, decisively snapped off the symbolical seal on the individual communication panel and said, "Commander, this is seventeen. Lieutenant Verkholin."

"What? What is it?"

"I know that you don't really trust us VR-ers. But I've just had an idea. Something has gone wrong, right?"

"Why do you say that?"

"We've been standing here for half an hour already. Defenses are down but the fleet hasn't arrived."

"Deep thoughts, kiddo. What exactly are you suggesting?"

"We're going to have to fight, one way or another. Our ammunition's limited. I suggest that we use the 'sniper pair' mode."

"Never heard of it. Give me more details."

"The enemy servomachine can be taken out with one, maximum two, single missiles."

"Verkholin, your tricks aren't going to work here. All the enemy machines are equipped with false signature launchers, optical and signature phantoms. You must realize that a volley is a necessary measure since a portion of the rockets are doomed to attack the false..."

Anton didn't argue. He listened to the commander and then got straight to the point. "Sniper pair mode involves the following: the Hoplites advance in the direction of the enemy's likely attack. They switch off active scanning and go into camouflage mode, while also transmitting their exact position to the pilot of the Phalanger.

For example, I send the Hoplite from a combat pair ahead of me, and I periodically receive information from his scanners using direct laser communication. The enemy identifies my activity and releases a single rocket. The pilot of the Hoplite, being close to the goal, records the false signatures and at the last possible moment, his machine transmits the accurate data to the rocket guiding device."

"It's a good trick, but too complicated." Shmelev replied. "Sorry, but we don't have time right now for risky experiments."

Dislocation zone of the Alliance Seventh Strike Fleet
Aboard the cruiser Apostle

ADMIRAL KUPANOV paced the command bridge.

The ship commander and his old friend sat in armchairs, watching the complex weave of plotted courses.

"The fourth ARS[6] group is back," he

---

[6] ARS — Automatic reconnaissance ship. Maneuvering at the edge of hyperspace and 3D space, the ARS sent micromachines (also called nanodust) into 'normal space', allowing the microsensors to pass through detection systems and form a reconnaissance network, whose signals were

announced, reading through the received data.

"Well?" The admiral turned to him.

"The nanomachines passed through the planetary defense detectors without any difficulty. As we had hoped, the local area network created by the reconnaissance microdevices is so weak that it is not picked up by enemy scanners."

"I'm not interested in the wonders of our technology. What's happening in orbit? Has there been any movement?"

"No."

"Damn it. Has it all gone to pieces?" Admiral Kupanov was so wound up that he didn't even try to hide his nerves.

"I don't understand you, Pavel. What are we waiting for? The Nibelungs have punched a hole in the planetary defenses. The servobattalion has gained a foothold on the base. It's the perfect time to attack."

"Alex, don't be an idiot." The admiral retorted. "You know why the war has stretched out for fifteen years. We keep milling around in the same systems. First, we lost people, now we lose machines since there are a lot of them; sooner or later we'll crush them with a blockade or our

---

then picked up by the ARS. The fleet or individual ships could thus receive data about other star systems in real time.

greater numbers, right? They don't let us mount a single successful offense. They," Kupanov meant the Colonies' Fleet, "hold the one and only ace and don't let us make a single move. The enemy always has the same response to all our tactical combinations — a strike using the annihilation device. Are you personally willing to be turned into cosmic radiation?"

"What exactly are we waiting for, then?" Asked the commander of the Apostle, ignoring the provocative question. "If everything's so shit, why did you start such a dangerous game and why did you send youngsters to storm the planet, instead of machines?"

"Because they will fight harder than any AI. Yes, I've sent them to their deaths, but the sacrifice will be worth it! For the first time in many years, we've been given a unique chance to grab the enemy by the throat and squeeze until they stop breathing. As soon as the cruiser Elliot enters low orbit to dispose of the battalion, we'll jump through the anomaly and attack in the moment when the cruiser isn't able to use the Light device. Get it? We'll have a real chance of capturing the ship. I'm ready to sacrifice a battalion, a squadron, even the fleet if it means that the Alliance captures the annihilation device prototype. It will be the end of our stalling because we'll be able to answer every attack with our own, instead of struggling to hold back the Colony ships in key anomaly zones."

"How many years have we known each other?" The Apostle commander suddenly asked.

"A long time. Must be ten years by now... Why?"

"I'm trying to understand why you're ranting about this to me when you're clearly talking crap. The annihilation device is not a short-range weapon. You can count the number of times that it's been used on the fingers of one hand, and what about the consequences of annihilation? You wouldn't wish that on your enemy. The prototype that you're so desperate to capture can be made quite easily based on what we already know. But what would that give us? Using the Light device in an inhabited system means killing the whole population of a planet. We know the outcome of using the annihilation device in large-scale combat: the guaranteed destruction of all material objects in the radius of one light-minute, a Pyrrhic victory that would destroy most of both fleets. No, Pavel, you want the annihilation device for another reason. It's too powerful and too unpredictable a weapon, which the colonists understand very well. I'll give them that. They have never used the Light device within a populated system, be it ours or their own."

"What are you trying to say?" Admiral Kupanov frowned.

"The Light is a weapon of dissuasion, a last resort." Von Reuben stated calmly. "I don't need to explain it to you, you know this yourself. Your ambitions won't change the course of the war but will make it more cruel, bloody and unpredictable. The colonists have shown that they understand the danger in using this device. And us, will we withstand the temptation of a quick but bloody victory, and if we don't, how much of humankind will be left?"

"Are you preaching to me?" Pavel snapped.

"No. I'll only say one thing — a higher rank, even if you're aiming for the very top, is not worth a new spiral of violence. Think about it."

Admiral Kupanov did think about it, but the words of the Apostle's commander cut him to the quick and rekindled his high-flying ambitions.

Plus, the Terran Alliance was in danger of collapsing with the death of John Winston Hammer.

Seven fleets, seven admirals, all vying for the top spot, with only the ancient Nagumo to stand in their way. Although the old man couldn't be underestimated. His physical frailty, so frequently discussed in the last few months, hadn't decreased his influence and power. The old man was wheelchair-bound and yet continued to refuse complex implant surgery, demonstrating the incredible strength of his intellect, well-versed in political intrigue. His followers still believed that the Commander of the United Space Forces could stop the infighting and prevent the breakup of the Alliance into seven armored groups.

A person could replace Nagumo or become his successor only if they could demonstrate not just their undeniable abilities as a strategist and a politician, but also their might, for example, by capturing a Light annihilation device.

'Von Reuben is right, of course.' Kupanov continued his musings. 'The new type of weapon that stopped the second blitzkrieg by Alliance forces was used only once to its full effect and ended up destroying two opposing fleets and the nearby planet[7].

It's been many years but ships still avoid that system. Even the hypersphere's navigational lines ended up in a confusing and dangerous knot after

---

[7] The Light annihilation device was developed in the colonies. Due to its enormous size and high energy use, it was mounted on cruisers. It was first used onboard a battle station. Its main drawback was the inability to control how the annihilation reaction progressed. The synthesis of antiparticles in the Light device and the ensuing 'firing' of antimatter, encapsulated in a force field, lead to different results each time. The energy released in the zone of mutual destruction of matter and anti-matter often led to the synthesis of new antiparticles. After the end of the Galactic War, the Light annihilation device was developed further, but despite its advanced construction, was used exceedingly rarely.

the complete nuclear fission reaction.

Using the Light for offense or defense means annihilating whole star systems and making them unsuitable for life, as well as destroying a multitude of ships. Hardly any armor can withstand the streams of radiation that all matter is instantly turned into.

Yes, but the Light device is perfect as a deterrent.'

Anchor. The Thirteenth Servobattalion
07:33

THEY STOOD in their defense positions, among the jumble of concrete blocks, the destroyed buildings and conical craters. Each pilot picked their own cover based on their own ideas about safety and their preferred combat moves.

The silence could not last forever. An attack would come at some point, but that wasn't what concerned them most in that moment.

Where is our fleet?

Why has the battalion been left without support? How will they fight with no orbital cover, with enemy ships dominating the space overhead?

"Tavgalov, how much longer?"

"We're nearly done, Commander. The

technical servos have installed almost all the Maverick modules. We've mined the pass and my guys have occupied five Phalangers."

"Are the machines working?"

"Looks like it. The tests aren't finished yet."

"Fine. We'll wait a few more minutes. Report when you're ready to join the battalion."

EVERYTHING IN THE WORLD has a simple explanation and only the soul that guides people's actions doesn't always have a logical reason behind it.

The sudden crushing Nibelung attack on the RW base not only destroyed the ground defenses, like the analytical system on Shmelev's Phalanger rightly suggested. The most senior officers of the planetary defense system had been caught in the rocket attack, as they prepared to test the new combat technology in the morning.

The half-hour break that enabled the servobattalion to land unhindered and spread itself out was caused by a paralysis of the planet's leadership.

The fleet and the ground forces didn't have much to do with each other. For example, Admiral Ipatov knew nothing about the upcoming war games. The information had been sent to him but had gotten stuck somewhere midway, and now he was trying to regain control over the situation. The satellite group knocked out by the Nibelungs was being rapidly replaced by new machines while the admiral gathered available information piece by piece. The remaining officers on the ground didn't show themselves in the best light — despite the obvious threat, they shared information about sustained losses and accepted orders from space very reluctantly.

The 'human factor' significantly complicated the process of coordinating a retaliatory strike.

In addition, Ipatov wasn't stupid and could sense a trap: minutes passed but the Alliance Fleet, which should have exited the hypersphere in the first few minutes of the attack, as chaos reigned in orbit, still hadn't appeared for some unbeknownst reason.

Being unable to understand what the enemy was planning left Ipatov paralyzed. Using the strength of his personality to enforce relative order among the ground forces, the admiral accepted command of all the available troops (of which there was a significant number on Anchor) and now stood before a difficult question, the answer to which would dictate the battle tactics for the next few hours.

Right now, he was observing obvious nonsense. The enemy's stellar landing operation, the sensible and carefully calculated action of the assault carriers, which had not only created a launching point for the servobattalion but had also struck a crushing blow against the fighters on duty, had given the attacking fleet a significant advantage. Yet the chance for a large space force to break through to the planet had been wasted — the gap in the space defenses was being patched up using reserve stations and the battalion planetside was being surrounded by ground forces.

'What am I missing here?' Admiral Ipatov fretted. 'Does the Alliance command really believe that activating the captured servomachines will allow the assault forces to take the whole planet? They're not sending a suicide squad to Anchor, are they? What is the point of wasting a servobattalion?'

"Zamyatin, what is the tactical system showing?"

"Nothing so far. The dust cloud and the masking fields are getting in the way. They're using some kind of new device that prevents our combat scanning systems from reading their signatures."

"So, we can't even find out if they're reactivating the captured tech?"

"We are unable to obtain accurate information at this time. Although I can safely assume without any scanners that the battalion won't miss the chance to swell their ranks with the tech stored in the underground bunkers. Only reconnaissance by fire will allow us to determine the number and quality of their 'reinforcements'."

Admiral Ipatov muttered a curse. What a wretched situation. The enemy has a plan and is putting it into action as they speak, while they are up in orbit and yet find themselves blind and helpless.

"I have good news, too." Zamyatin interrupted the admiral's dark thoughts.

"Which is?"

"The captured machines meant for war games are equipped with blank ammunition."

"They won't be able to fight?"

"If we attack immediately, most of the servomachines will be destroyed. The servobattalion presents the real danger. If we crush it, the captured machines won't resist."

"And if we wait?"

"There is a risk that the reloading devices sent from the Nibelungs will deliver the ammunition and reload the captured mechanisms. Then we will have to resign ourselves to huge losses if we storm the RW base or give up on a ground attack and pummel them from orbit."

"A ground attack. Definitely." The admiral replied after thinking it over. "The Phalangers' heavy rockets can reach low orbit, which is a significant and unjustifiable risk for the cruiser." He explained.

"Perhaps a combined attack? Our new LDL-55[8] machines will engage the servobattalion and prevent them from deploying the battery for orbital fire. We will get a chance to reach the bombardment zone without fearing a missile strike from the surface."

"No. Any movement of the fleet is out of the question for now." The admiral replied. "We must preserve the formation to resist an attack from space. Moving the cruiser into low orbit would be the last resort."

"All right, we'll begin the attack using ground units. Reconnaissance by fire first, then a full-scale advance from all directions, as soon as we draw the noose around their troops."

"Yes." Ipatov nodded in agreement. "And find out where their assault carriers have disappeared to, for God's sake!"

---

[8] LDL-55 — The abbreviation for 'large driver laser' — a walking laser station that became part of the Colonies' Fleet in 2624.

Thirteenth Servobattalion's position
07:40

"COMMANDER, multiple signatures are surrounding us in a half-circle. Updated information identifies the targets as one and a half thousand servomechanisms of the LDL-55 type and assault bots equipped with mortar launchers."

"Servomachines?"

"Fifteen Aquilas. Unmanned. Full automatic mode."

"Unmanned Aquilas?" Shmelev asked skeptically.

"We've placed sensors around the perimeter. Their readings echo each other. There is no chance for error."

"Yes, I see. The testing grounds and cyber laboratories are located here." Shmelev spoke aloud so that his deputy could follow his train of thought. "Does this mean that the specialists in the Colonies' Fleet have developed a Maverick counterpart?"

"Looks like it. Although I believe that it's impractical for them to create their own module. It's easier to use ours by altering them to fit Aquila's controls."

"That makes sense. What about these walking lasers and wandering mortar launchers?" Shmelev used the terms they had invented for the strange new enemy combat machines. "How dangerous do you think they are?"

"A heavy laser can inflict some serious damage." Alan Nayvek replied. "The targets are fast, small and able to use even minor cover. They're dangerous as a group. Preliminary analysis shows that 10-15 walking lasers are capable of taking out a Phalanger-class machine in less than five minutes. But they have their own shortcomings — piddly electronics and an effective firing distance that depends on where the laser charge can pass."

"They could combine their attacks. Some would burn through fortifications while the others strike targets."

"I'm summarizing the data and will send it to the pilots in a minute."

"What about the mortar launchers? They're designed to work against androids and armored infantry, if I understand correctly?"

"To an extent. Analysis of the mechanisms captured during the fight in the bunker zone has indicated a complex target processing system. The mortar rockets enter the highest point of their ballistic trajectory using preliminary targeting with further adjusting instructions."

"That's dangerous. They'll hammer us as if from orbit. It's not easy to shoot down mines accelerating in free fall."

"Something else to note, Commander. Even though the machines have significant firepower, their main advantage is their mobility."

"I got that already. I expect that the mortar launchers will change position after every volley."

"I'll take that into consideration as well. The pilots will receive instructions for the best countermeasures. Nevertheless, each one will have to figure things out on the spot."

"Bear in mind that the walking lasers may use the same tactics as infantry units."

Another call signal appeared on the command frequency.

"Shelgan."

"I see it. Stay on the line, Alan." The commander turned off the call waiting.

"One, go ahead."

Captain Shelgan was responsible for reactivating the captured machines. The senior technician of the servobattalion had served under Shmelev for quite some time and the major trusted his opinions.

"We've got problems, Commander."

"Can you be more specific?"

"The servomachines are armed with blanks. The Mavericks have been activated successfully but they have reported that they can't join the fight immediately."

Frayg be damned...

Shmelev went pale. The plan had collapsed like a house of cards.

Without cover fire, imitating the servobattalion machines remaining in their positions, he wouldn't be able to lead the unit out of almost complete encirclement. The enemy would instantly figure out the maneuver since the planetary defense command was undoubtedly aware of the fact that the prepared servomachines couldn't fire in response. They had to stay silent or the first blank would reveal the masquerade.

"What are your thoughts, Alan?"

"We have to get the battalion out of here, Commander, either way. We've completed our mission, taken the RW base and activated the captured machines. We won't last long on the front lines without the support of the fleet. I see no point in suicide."

"I know. How do we get the battalion out though? At this rate, they'll close the ring in about thirty minutes. We have to start moving right now." The battalion commander was making hard decisions. "Shelgan, how long will the machines need to swap over the ammunition?"

"About twenty minutes. I have enough technical support mechanisms. We're using the emergency stock from the landing modules, since we're going to abandon them here anyway."

"The enemy is already on the horizon." Shmelev informed him gloomily. "Who's standing on the northern edge?"

"Verkholin, Simon, Makarov, Lawrence and Van Dillan. Three Phalangers and two Hoplites.

Three experienced pilots and two newbies...

"Shelgan, listen to my order. You'll stay here and personally monitor the reloading of thirty machines. Pick a ratio that exactly matches the servobattalion's composition. The other machines with blank ammunition come with us. I'm taking the unit out of the encirclement. The southern corridor is free for the moment."

"Who's covering the withdrawal?"

"The combined group. Lieutenant Makarov is in charge. Dietrich, once you've reloaded the captured tech, take command of the covering party."

"Your orders?"

"Withdraw. Alan will send you the meeting point coordinates."

"Understood. I'll put the machines into the fight as they are ready. We'll catch up to you, don't worry."

"I don't doubt it, Dietrich. I don't have another choice right now. There's no time to even change the covering group."

"Got it, Commander. Take the battalion and go."

Dietrich could clearly see the information on the tactical system's summary screen. A tidal wave of servomechanisms was rolling towards them from the horizon — one and a half thousand unfamiliar combat units. Not only did they have to hold them back at the gates of the RW base but do everything they could to convince those watching that the whole servobattalion was defending the area. Shmelev's reasoning was clear: the enemy had no idea that there were real pilots sitting in the machines. Once they destroyed the Mavericks, they would think that they had destroyed the whole servobattalion.

'We'll see what happens next.' Shelgan thought to himself. 'It would be different if the fleet was in orbit above us but the commander is right in this case. There's no other way to save the battalion. We'll break out of the noose and then figure out why we've been abandoned here and how we're going to escape. Thankfully, the Nibelungs are safely hidden away.'

He hoped that he would come face-to-face with Admiral Kupanov one day, somewhere in the narrow corridors of the cruiser Apostle.

Thinking about death before a battle was the worst he could do.

Dietrich always set himself an important life

goal, something that he absolutely had to achieve. It always worked.

We're going to live...

He called Makarov as he directed forty servomachines that would leave with the battalion out of the underground hangars.

The technical droids were already in action, accompanying each combat unit to the nearest landing module for reloading. Captain Shelgan didn't mince his words, "You need to hold on for fifteen minutes, Lieutenant. Once the time is up, you must withdraw. The time starts now. The Mavericks will engage in fifteen minutes."

"Understood."

SHMELEV felt terrible.

The combat metabolic correction system had given him drugs twice, making his body run like clockwork again, his heart beating evenly and the nervous tic in his eye and cheek disappearing completely.

The arithmetic of war... Alexander hated it but what else could he do with the battalion already planetside? Should he stay behind or carry out the order even if he didn't understand the reason behind it? Yes, high command wasn't obliged to explain all the operation details to him but they could have at least given him a summary! *Hold the perimeter until the fleet arrives.* Shmelev realized how vague the phrase was only now. He couldn't put into words the feelings he was experienced in these minutes. Should he sentence the battalion to death by carrying out an impossible order?

He wanted to howl like an animal, loudly and wretchedly from the bitterness growing inside, but he kept silent.

His teeth clenched, he led the Phalanger away from the RW base, where he left five guys to face certain death so he could save the others.

Would he save them? The planet was round, this continent wasn't large and there weren't many forests, mainly plains and military bases. The only hope was the phantom generators.

Why did they need to condemn people to death when machines could have completed the mission to capture and control the RW base perimeter?

He was suddenly struck by a simple but piercingly painful thought. The admiral either knew or suspected that the servomachines on the RW base would be unfit for active duty. Blank ammunition or a lack of it, the inadequacy of the Maverick modules which were being experimented on here, there were a dozen other reasons why the servomechanisms would not have managed to complete the set mission.

He sent us here knowing that before we died, we would fight, desperately and skillfully, pushing the enemy to the edge. He would get a mutilated, crater-riddled planet, the enemy testing grounds and laboratories razed to the ground, and would report to his superiors that he had managed it all with just one servobattalion, without specifying that there were humans inside the cockpits.

A wave of anger washed over him and then faded as another injection brought the commander clarity of thought without letting him examine his feelings.

He didn't know the whole truth about the Fleet Commander's plans. Shmelev couldn't get to the truth because he lacked the cynicism to think beyond the *handful of soldiers* tossed into the flames. They must complete the mission or perish. Or, more accurately, complete and then perish.

'What are you hoping to do, Battalion Commander?' Shmelev asked himself.

Complete the mission but avoid dying? Or disobey the order completely? They can't send you further than the frontline, right? But what about your military duty?

War. Harsh. Soul-destroying. It gave him only one choice — fight so that he could complete the mission and survive, not him personally, but the people whose lives he'd begun to exchange like pieces on a chessboard.

Confusing, stuttering thoughts, unfamiliar and constantly being disrupted by the blasted combat metabolic correction system.

He ought to turn the Phalanger around and go back to the where the battle was about to begin...

No. You're responsible for the battalion. The arithmetic of war, damn it.

The northern edge of the RW base
Cover group
07:44

"SIMON!"

Green heard Verkholin's agitated voice and glanced at the communicator. It was their private channel so nobody else could hear the conversation. "What's up, Anton?"

"Look at the summary screen."

"Yeah, what's happening?"

"Can you see the other machines' markers?"

"Yeah, of course."

"Watch their movements."

Simon spent several seconds observing the pattern.

"The battalion is leaving." Verkholin burst

out.

"What about us?" Simon asked, baffled.

"What about us? We're standing in position, as you can see."

...

Another conversation was taking place via laser alongside Verkholin and Green.

Lieutenant Makarov contacted his unit. "The battalion is abandoning its positions. The battalion commander is taking the machines out of encirclement and we're covering them. We need to last fifteen minutes until Dietrich finishes reloading the captured Mavericks."

Lawrence and Van Dillan reacted calmly as they were seasoned soldiers, had been through various scraps and trusted their commander.

"Why did they leave us the youngsters?" Van Dillan asked gloomily.

"They should get out of here." Lawrence agreed. "Our squad can hold the position for fifteen minutes and it won't be the first time."

Lieutenant Makarov switched channels and contacted Verkholin and Green.

The laser signals reached their receivers. "Anton, Simon, follow the battalion out of here. Tell the battalion commander that I've made the decision. Go!" The laser communication went dead.

VERKHOLIN, a second ago full of angry confusion, suddenly realized that neither his Phalanger nor Simon's machine had moved.

The individual communication channel between the two switched on again.

"Are we being given the gift of life or do they think that we'll get in their way?"

"I don't know. Beatrice, check the list of incoming commands."

A fraction of a second later, several lines appeared on the information screen. Verkholin studied them carefully and said, "Shmelev's order is to hold positions for fifteen minutes until Captain Shelgan finishes recharging the recaptured machines. Then withdraw to the meeting point."

"The grown-ups are feeling sorry for the kids?" Simon's voice held a mix of emotions. He had begun to comprehend certain truths, not with his mind but his heart, such as the fact that the cynical phrase sounded fake, full of false bravado, perhaps... He felt truly lost for the first time in his life, unsure whether to save himself by following Lieutenant Makarov's order or...

Beatrice was processing the signatures as they reached the edge of the screen[9] in a solid

---

[9] The target monitor's holographic screen perfectly replicated the effective scanning field on a smaller scale. The targets beyond the servomachine's field of fire could only be

wave of red markers.

Simon and Anton had the same thought at the same time.

"Makarov only has one idea, to draw their attention to his squad." Verkholin spoke rapidly but clearly, as if he was in a chat, discussing battle tactics for the next fight.

"I agree." Simon echoed him. "He's going to try and draw most of the machines towards him to slow down the encirclement."

"How do we know that there aren't similar groups coming from other directions?"

"Look at the formation. The number of machines is lower in the center and greater in the flanks. I bet you that they'll soon take up firing positions, the center will stop completely while the flanks will keep moving."

Verkholin closed his eyes for a second. Beatrice was transmitting data about the signatures directly into his mind.

Right. Heavy laser units on a walking base. A laser beam. It strikes with the speed of light in space, almost without scattering, but acts very differently planetside. The charge is most effective within direct visibility and there is a range of restrictions for fire, such as the terrain, atmospheric transparency, the presence of

_____

brought up on the target monitor with a special command.

obstacles...

Nearly seven hundred heavy laser units. The other mechanisms are totally mental, a hybrid rocket launcher with a universal caterpillar track and impulse weaponry.

How intelligent are they?

The question remained unanswered for now but the combat tactic for the next few minutes was clear: find a good position and fire from the L-700[10] complexes. The warheads in the Pilum ground-to-space missiles had a cartridge design. Meant for attacking large spaceships that had foolishly wandered into low orbit, they were equipped with 150 rocket missiles with a cumulative effect, which possessed their own secondary guidance systems. The Pilum's task was to damage as many sections of a spaceship as possible.

The two-stage design of the carrier rocket had long ago (from fighting in VR) suggested an alternative way of using it. Now Anton was planning to use the moves he had developed in VR.

Beatrice received clear and direct instructions from him on how to change the combat program of the eight superheavy rockets.

The first stage lifted the Pilum along the

---

[10] The L-700 rocket launchers were developed specifically for the Phalanger-class servomachines. Their full name was L-700, Legion. They looked similar to the modern S-400 air defense systems.

trajectory for attacking combat stations. Once the first stage separated, the orientation engines unexpectedly turned the rocket back towards the ground.

The cartridge sections separated at a height of four kilometers.

The distribution area, considering the partially overlapping impact zones, was almost twenty kilometers.

Beatrice picked up the pilot's idea and immediately performed the necessary calculations, taking into account the speed of the enemy flanking groups, making the necessary adjustments and checking the data. All this took less than a minute while the Phalanger, hidden among the ruins of the RW base, assumed the appropriate firing position and extended additional supports to stabilize it during launch, and at the same time, shifted the Legion's launching tubes to the appropriate angle.

'Final targeting of the separating warheads on the active signatures.' Anton gave the last mental orders.

"Verkholin, what are you planning?" Came Green's voice. "Anton, wake up, they're going to blow us to bits if we stay still! Whom are you planning to hit with those Pilums? Remember VR — the ships in the orbital group are too far away. This kind of thing didn't even work on the simulators!"

"Simon, to frayg with it all! Stop clinging to the past. It no longer exists, alright? We need to survive. We can't get off the planet so there's only one choice left, to fight!"

"I don't understand what you're planning." Green repeated hoarsely. "The Amethyst is showing over a thousand signals!"

"I know." Verkholin was surprised himself by how calm he sounded, considering the scattered and panicky thoughts in his head. "They're complete idiots according to the analysis, but there's so many that they'll crush us either way..."

"Yeah, no need to add fuel to the fire. Get to the point!"

"Assume position for a Pilum salvo!" Verkholin announced unexpectedly.

"You've gone crazy, Anton!"

"Listen to what I'm saying. Come on, use your head! You need to reprogram the Pilum warheads to strike ground targets!"

"What do you mean, reprogram?!"

"Quietly. Mentally. Use the Maverick interface."

Simon choked on his next phrase. Verkholin was indeed suggesting a sensible course of action, plus, they had no alternatives. They had to either fight or die, once and for real, without the option of reloading, without the hope of leaving the fight...

They couldn't get off the planet and it looked like help wasn't coming so they had only themselves to rely on. Of course, they weren't programmers, but the Maverick could utilize the necessary cybernetic modules to change the combat setting of any weapon in accordance with the task set by the pilot.

"Let's try it." He responded, stopping the machine beside suitable cover.

"There's no time left to 'try'." Verkholin snapped. "We're not going to get a second shot at this."

'Well, redhead,' Green hadn't even noticed how quickly he had personified the cyber system. 'don't let me down, girl.'

The signals on the target monitors continued to multiply. The solid mass of light began to splinter into groups as the enemy approached.

"Simon, how are you?" Anton burst out.

"Ready for launch." Green breathed out in response.

"Excellent. Let's do it."

They didn't need to coordinate their steps because they thought alike — a salvo and then a change of position, rushing towards the advancing servomechanisms to support Lieutenant Makarov's squad.

Anton couldn't see Simon's ashen face but he didn't look so good himself, equally tense with sharply accentuated cheekbones.

Their first fight was beginning.

The last few seconds before launch.

In orbit around Anchor
The bridge of the cruiser Elliot

"ATTENTION, we've registered a large-scale launch of ground-to-space missiles!"

Admiral Ipatov turned sharply towards the information screens but the missile trajectories hadn't appeared on them yet. There was only an already collapsing mushroom cloud peppered with glowing launch signatures.

"Trajectories have been calculated!"

The thin course lines that appeared on the holographic model left all the officers on Elliot's bridge stunned for a second.

"They're attacking the seventh, ninth and fourteenth OD[11] stations!"

There was a flurry of movement in orbit. The squadron's corvettes switched on their main engines, scrambling to intercept the sixteen rockets that could turn the combat stations into scrap.

---

[11] OD — Orbital defense.

It was a matter of seconds.

Ipatov tensely watched the markers moving along the trajectories and noted with relief that the corvettes were going to get there in time.

In the next moment, as if confirming his thoughts, the dark outlines of the corvettes were lit up by numerous flashes. All the calculations confirmed that the anti-ballistic missiles would intercept the Pilums long before the warhead separation...

That thought was cut off.

Something unbelievable was happening, at least the admiral had never seen this before: the second stage orientation engines suddenly switched on and turned the missiles back towards the ground, and almost at the same time, with no chance to interfere in the situation, the Pilum warheads began to separate.

The screen was covered in markers.

The separating warheads plummeted towards the ground, spreading out into a widening cone that covered two of the largest servomechanism groups currently performing a flanking maneuver of the base.

"Damnation!" The admiral burst out. "Give me the Maverick module specialists, quickly!"

A separate communication channel switched on after a few seconds.

The admiral turned away from the summary

monitor, refusing to watch as hundreds of servomechanisms were destroyed without having fired a single shot at the enemy. Ipatov studied the rank markings on the other person and said curtly, "One question, Captain. Look at the recording of the Phalangers using their ground-to-space missiles right now. I need an answer or at least a competent opinion — could a Maverick module think that up?"

On the RW base flanks
08:02

THE SERVOMECHANISMS in the flanking group moved along the hazy border of the dust and smoke cloud still covering the RW base.

Their scanners noted the salvos performed by the two Phalangers but not a single servo reacted to it. The missiles traveled upwards and hence posed no threat. Nothing else interested the cybernetic control circuits of the combat servomechanisms.

Their 'brains' were powerful computing devices linked to the combat autopilot, target monitor and scanning complex. The walking platform, refined to maximum simplicity and reliability, was copied straight off the Hoplite's underframe. In this way, the machine, equipped with a powerful laser, was cheap to make, could cross any terrain and presented a real threat to the large servomachines. The LDL-55 or the 'walking lasers' (a nickname popular with the troops) had been developed as a single-use assault force. During combat testing, they had shown themselves to be excellent as part of a local network, creating various formations and fire coordination patterns, and using simple but effective tactical moves. If one was to use a human comparison, the walking lasers behaved like a pack of animals hunting large prey.

Their only combat goal was to find and destroy, making these mechanisms a dangerous force.

The second type of combat machines developed on Anchor was nicknamed the 'wandering rocket launcher'.

The caterpillar track, smaller dimensions, and 'smart' rockets that ensured incredible firing distance, plus the powerful anti-personnel guns, allowed the MX-300 to work as a single unit providing cover fire for the LDL-55. By connecting to the local network of the walking lasers, the MX-300 would perform a series of launches, then immediately scatter, drifting from one cover to the next and constantly bothering the enemy with unexpected strikes while almost always being outside the return fire zone.

Around 200 LDL-55's and MX-300's had attacked the RW base from the north, while another two groups of six hundred mechanisms each were performing a flanking maneuver, trying to surround the servobattalion that had landed on the planet.

The fourteen pilotless Aquilas were so far keeping their distance.

AFTER THE SALVO, Verkholin and Green's Phalangers simultaneously discarded the massive Pilum launchers, drew in the additional supports with a screech, straightened up and quickly left their unmasked positions.

The seven-meter-long launching tubes were left on the ground, while the servomachines, now several tonnes lighter, extended their loaded ground-to-ground missile launchers from beneath their armor.

Ten seconds later, both sides of the RW base were suddenly covered in intense flashes that rapidly multiplied. From a distance, it may have seemed that death didn't fall from the sky but had burst out from underground as hundreds of voracious, orange-black clots. The earth turned to ash and mixed with the mechanical wreckage, the secondary explosions from the MX-300 ammunition, the plumes of smokes and the shuddering blast waves — the two flaming sores that suddenly opened up on the body of the planet could be clearly seen from orbit. The strike looked even more impressive from the ground as two volcanoes erupted along the flanks, where the enemy signatures had been massing just a moment ago, illuminating the twilight beneath the mushroom cloud...

The battalion's main force hadn't yet escaped the pincers of the flanking maneuver so the battalion commander's tactical screens immediately showed him the image sent by the microsensors as they burnt in the hellish fire around him. He saw flaming geysers shooting into the sky, the blazing remains of the enemy machines, and shrapnel from the exploding ammunition. It was as if the major had cast a glance into hell for war machines.

Tearing his gaze away with difficulty from the engrossing fiery chaos, he looked at the trajectories marked by the Amethyst system. He immediately understood that the carefully calculated and brilliantly performed strike by the Pilums didn't just give the battalion extra time to escape. The two flaming cauldrons were a guarantee that the enemy could no longer completely surround them.

He couldn't resist the urge and called Dietrich. "Was that you?"

He was stunned to hear a negative response.

"It was the work of our boys. Makarov told them to withdraw after the battalion but instead..."

THEY WEREN'T AFRAID of what they did. Their minds, raised in VR, resisted the reality around them, where every stone spoke of the inevitability of death, and had found refuge in past illusions. Verkholin and Green took their Phalangers through the ruins and didn't feel afraid. Their emotions were swamped by a sudden wild *drive*, and death still seemed unnatural and abstract. They were back in their familiar world, where the mind felt no doubts or inconvenience.

The fear would come later. They couldn't fear what they didn't know.

The ruinous excitement of battle, together with belief in certain victory, gave them the strength to act swiftly and make instant decisions.

The two Maverick modules were now receiving a constant stream of unsystematic information from the overexcited pilot minds and the computing devices were working at full capacity, picking out commands to carry out among the swirl of mental images.

Cancel automatic fire. All weapons to single-shot mode.

Servodriver overload limiters — remove restrictions.

Combat autopilots — maintain set course.

Automatic fire avoidance system — unrestricted work.

The Phalangers, crashing through the cracked walls of surviving buildings, rushed full speed ahead, while behind them, only a fraction of a second later, came the fiery explosions from enemy rocket launchers.

Anton, you have placed some restrictions.

'I know. Keep calm. We don't have an endless supply of ammunition. Learn to economize. No serial fire, only single shots.'

Beatrice didn't reply but the indicators on the holographic screens blinked faithfully, confirming the mode change. The Maverick module began to automatically track fifty of the closest signatures, picking out the closest and most active enemy mechanisms, which posed the greatest threat.

Anton, it is three hundred meters to the edge of the destruction zone. We are leaving the dust cloud. The risk of mass laser fire is reaching critical value.

"Maintain course!" Verkholin replied hoarsely. "Right weapon — sight-controlled targeting[12], left weapon — as you wish, but I forbid missile launches. Simon?"

"I'm here."

"Let's fight our way to the caponiers. We'll slaughter the rocket launchers as we go."

"Got it."

Maximov was yelling something through the communication link but Anton concentrated all his attention on the enemy, oblivious to the man's words.

He should have said, *keep your head down, Lieutenant,* but there was no time or energy for even this one phrase.

They were different people. Experienced officers, knocked about by war, who had seen so much that a battle had turned into a complicated chess match for them due to their moral exhaustion. Their death-tested cautiousness prevented them from attacking in a way that defied logic.

Verkholin and Green were the complete opposite, having not yet experienced *real loss* and who only had their reckless skill of controlling the servomachines, gained in thousands of VR

---

[12] Sight-controlled targeting* — in this case, the servomotors controlling the independent gun pod responded to images received from the pilot's sight. Pausing one's gaze on a particular object would lead to automatic fire on the target.

fights, to withstand the sticky fears and the vague but relentless premonitions.

How was the gloomy and scarred reality, peppered with nearby explosions, different from the decorations of the virtual testing grounds?

Yes, everything felt harsher and more intense here, as if the surroundings had been sprinkled with extra realism, but hadn't their mind already descended into a similar murky hell?

The edge of the smoke cloud reminded them of the city smog: the haze hiding their surroundings from view was composed of tiny particles of soot, dust and crushed concrete; the hot air created mirages but the Amethyst subsystems filtered out the disturbances, transmitting a contrasting image with glowing signatures of the enemy machines onto the holographic screens.

The fortifications, prepared for the wargames that never took place, glowed as freshly white lines of concrete in the distance, far from the blurry edge of the settling cloud. Between the ruins of the RW base and the caponiers lay a wasteland, and the shortest distance to the closest fortification was five kilometers. It was only ten kilometers to the enemy, a risk, an insane risk, but Anton and Simon felt overwhelmingly bold.

We can do it. We've done things like this before and more than once.

"Smoke!"

Simon's Phalanger was lit up by launches and a thick smoke curtain (full of tiny metal particles) hid the attacking machines seconds before a volley from the laser installations.

"Probes!"

There was a sharp clapping sound and dozens of SmaRPs[13] shot above the smoke curtain.

"Fire when ready!" Verkholin was used to issuing commands and he found the role of a leader easy. He always thought that attack was the best form of defense. This attack was unfolding quite well, proving that they could inflict heavy losses on the thousand and a half machines if they used the firepower of the servomachines well and attacked rather than hiding from the enemy.

The actions of the two Phalangers seemed insanely rash from the outside but neither Simon nor Anton 'lost their heads', maintaining concentration and clarity of thought.

The sixty-tonne machines moved rapidly towards the fortifications and their weapons began firing as soon as a web of slowly descending recon probes appeared above the smoke screen. The frequent and rhythmic fire sounded like thunder, and the missiles, designed to destroy heavy armored vehicles, struck the MX-300, turning the

---

13 SmaRP — Small recon probe.

rocket missile launchers into piles of burning, twisted metal and plastic.

The single shots of the Phalangers came so frequently that they almost melded into salvos, the independent weapon drives were in constant movement and the enemy line rapidly grew sparse. The LDL-55's finally made the right move in that moment, rushing forward in a counterattack and passing through the smoke screen and metallic suspension.

LIEUTENANT MAKAROV, who had been watching the Phalangers' daring raid, gave an order to his troops, "Forward! We'll provide cover fire!"

SIMON SAW around fifty objects simultaneously light up red on the target monitor.

The LDL-55's opened fire as soon as they crossed the smoke screen. The volley directed at Green's servomachine, which was slightly ahead, would have certainly burned through the Phalanger's armor if the pilot hadn't commenced urgent evasive maneuvers.

Simon's Phalanger took a few steps back by reversing the servoengines, and simultaneously tilted the cockpit, presenting the massive frontal armor to attack. There wasn't enough time for a full-scale evasive maneuver. Green felt the deathly chill of certainty spread through his chest when streams of coherent radiation swept over his servomachine, burning through the armor, leaving deep and crimson scars, and destroying subsystem sensors.

The armor was holding but for how long? Half a hundred laser charges instantly thinned the armored layer and the ceramlite 'ran' in some places, forming ulcers that immediately hardened into ugly lumps.

The next salvo would be fatal.

Simon brought the machine back to level and continued to withdraw, firing continuously. But the murky smoke spat out more and more enemy servomechanisms...

ANTON, on the other hand, felt flushed with heat, as if it was his Phalanger and not Simon's that was being pounded with laser fire.

He acted automatically, almost on reflex, but could feel how the Maverick module picked up his desire, forcing the servomotors to respond to the pilot's mental commands.

A sharp turn of the cockpit with the simultaneous spinning of the pilot cradle and holographic screens. At the same time, medium-distance tactical rockets struck in a fan shape from the upper pylons.

Anton didn't aim at specific machines, rather using separating fire because he knew what would happen in the next instant.

The missiles released by Verkholin's Phalanger struck along a short and direct trajectory and raised tonnes of earth. The main effect was due to the shock wave, which struck like a colossal hammer, knocking off sights and tipping over the enemy servomachines. As a result, only a few repeat salvos reached Simon's cockpit, while the rest slashed across the ground, disappeared into the sky or struck the distant ruins.

"Green, straighten yourself out! You're fine!"

Simon's Phalanger, although unsteady, managed to keep its balance. It continued to withdraw, snapping back from time to time with his guns, but the rocket launchers were already beginning to fire from beyond the smoke cloud. The explosions encircled both machines and a ranging salvo nearly took off the right gun pod; the shower of shrapnel lashing Verkholin's armor felt like a dull and burning pain. Simon, on the other hand, ignored the deadly dance of explosions and continued to withdraw. His machine titled dangerously whenever one of its legs landed in the fresh and smoking craters.

"Simon, come in!"

"He is unconscious." Said a steady voice. "The combat life support system is working."

Anton understood that the Maverick module was controlling the machine.

"Head to the ruins! Continue in reverse, do not turn your back to the enemy and keep firing!"

"Accepted."

Verkholin spun around together with his seat, the screens shifting back to their normal position.

"Beatrice, take over the fire!"

The Maverick obeyed and the guns began firing more frequently and evenly. Verkholin took over control by switching off the autopilots.

Here comes the dance...

Around thirty walking lasers struck his machine.

The heat pouring into the cockpit and the gray tendrils of stifling smoke coming from the dashboard was the moment when reality looked Anton in the eye with cold and discomfiting inevitability.

His vision blurred but the neurosensory contact between pilot and Maverick module reached its full potential, and human and machine became one. The cyber system and the nervous system intertwined and melded together in an instant of rebirth that can only be experienced once...

Not everyone survives this momentary process that seems to last indefinitely.

On one hand, Verkholin's Phalanger continued to fight despite sustaining serious damage, but on the other hand, Anton's mind felt like it had fallen into an abyss full of altered sensations. He suddenly gained the ability to combine cold shrewdness with boiling rage, and the melding of these opposites made the newly born self-awareness grow stronger and stronger.

A few seconds of battle, a moment of obfuscation, and again, the howling of servomotors, the gnash of breaking metal as Phalanger's powerful legs crushed the enemy mechanisms in its way. The sixty-tonne servomachine plunged into the line of walking lasers like a battering ram, its bow guns[14] thundering without pause and using up ammunition at an alarming pace. Suddenly, the world changed again: his global perception of events was back, voices in the communicator flooded his mind, and his clear gaze roamed over the front and side holographic monitors...

"Anton, go back!" The sharp voice belonged to Simon, who had regained consciousness.

It was true that Verkholin had pulled dangerously ahead and his machine, covered in streaks of cooling ceramlite, had plunged into the settling smoke haze. The laser installations that

---

[14] Bow guns were small-caliber devices meant for live opponents and lightly armored units. They were rigidly fixed below the servomachine's cockpit, which is why they were called 'bow guns'.

had caused so much trouble had scattered to search for cover in minor dips in the landscape. The missile explosions fell around them like a downpour, like a manic and asymmetrical dance, while the scanners showed more and more clearly the signatures of fourteen Aquilas that had passed the fortification line.

"Verkholin, Green, withdraw! We'll cover you!" Lieutenant Makarov's voice sounded confident and rang like metal with the force of his order, precluding any arguments. Anton and Simon, having survived the most intense and dangerous moments of battle, knew that their Phalangers, which had suffered critical damage and used up their ammunition, would be a hindrance in the upcoming stage of the fight.

"Understood, I'm withdrawing," Anton said hoarsely.

Simon stopped his machine at the edge of the RW base, indicating that he was providing Anton with cover fire.

Captain Shelgan's encouraging report came through the communication channel, "The first three units of the captured machines have been reloaded and are taking their positions. Don't stick your necks out too far, guys, draw them towards me instead!"

Makarov, who was preparing to attack, assessed the speed of Verkholin's damaged machine and suddenly changed direction. Now he was moving parallel to the fortification line, which the pilotless Aquilas had just crossed. His Phalanger turned its cockpit and rained a torrent of fire on the approaching machines, with the support of his two accompanying Hoplites.

Anton tasted the unfamiliar salty tang of blood on his lips. The combat escalators vibrated dully, bringing up new rounds of ammunition from weapons storage. The autopilots had switched on but then titled the machine dangerously to the side, so despite his overwhelming fatigue, Anton took back control and kept the machine upright using his own coordination.

AFTER USING UP all the missiles on his Phalanger, Lieutenant Makarov also turned towards the ruins of the RW base, his withdrawal being covered by two Hoplites providing suppressing fire. The picture looked quite optimistic overall. After inflicting irreparable damage to the enemy, the servomachines covering the battalion's retreat began their own evasive action, while the captured servomachines reloaded by Dietrich took up defensive positions among the ruins.

In three or four minutes, Major Shmelev's rear guard would complete their mission and begin retreating to the marked assembly point.

Anton, absorbed in his own feelings and

unable to distinguish where he ended and the machine began, could no longer imagine surviving without neurosensory contact with the cyber system. He reached the outer buildings where Simon was waiting and turned around to cover the retreat of Lieutenant Makarov's unit.

In that moment, another five Aquilas burst out of the weakening smoke haze.

It all happened in bare seconds. Powerful 250-megawatt laser installations struck the lieutenant's Phalanger, which looked like liquid flames had been poured over it. The coherent radiation made whole armored sections lose their rigidity, softening and turning a deep cherry red. A moment later, the shells inside both guns detonated and the fixating pylons were blown into pieces. The lieutenant's machine paused and a segment of armor flew off, followed by the thump of the emergency catapult as it sent the pilot cradle into the smoky sky.

The Phalanger burst into flames but this wasn't the worst thing. The pilotless Aquilas, ignoring the fire from the Hoplites, suddenly tipped their cockpits upwards and focused their shooting on the ejected pilot cradle.

Anton's mind immediately spotted this movement and his thoughts — more than his thoughts, his whole being jerked forward to save the helpless lieutenant, but neither he nor any of the others had time to stop the enemy mechanisms. There was another salvo and the pilot cradle turned into a falling torch.

Simon was the first to shake off the shock from what had happened.

Cursing wildly, he discharged all his ammunition into the nearest Aquila, followed by salvos from Verkholin, Lawrence and Van Dillan. One of the enemy machines burst into flames from the multiple hits but the others, having done their dark deed, rapidly withdrew back into the smoke.

"Bastards!!!"

"Simon, get back!" Dietrich's voice sounded on the command frequency and miraculously managed to stop Green.

"Withdraw! All machines are ordered to withdraw to the south edge of the base."

Anton heard Dietrich's voice and automatically followed the order while a ringing emptiness grew inside him, as if it hadn't been a barely known lieutenant who had died.

All his previous emotions paled in comparison to the hate filling his mind.

Thus, did the generations who never started the war lose their souls, the space filled with a suffocating hostility.

Chapter Four

THEY RETREATED.

Five machines from the cover group, hidden by phantom generators, moved stealthily towards Major Shmelev's assembly point while a fight broke out in the RW base. Ten enemy servomachines, supported by walking lasers and space fighters overhead, decided to launch an attack.

The sensors that Dietrich had left in the ruins

transmitted telemetry data and the cover group's cyber systems received them in passive mode, thus continuing to receive invaluable information about the enemy.

It turned out that the LDL-55's, having split into smaller groups of 4-5 machines each, functioned more efficiently among the city streets than in open terrain. They used the ruins quite cleverly as cover, and their powerful lasers inflicted serious damage to the defending servomachines.

The battle went on for about three hours.

The long-suffering ruins were pummeled with missiles, the MX-300 installations fired continuously on the unmasked servomachines, dozens of walking lasers crept along the streets, restricting the maneuverability of the Mavericks and burning out position after position, using the local area network to receive information from the Aquilas' scanners, which were moving a little behind the sweep teams.

The Mavericks defended themselves vigorously and skillfully but the enemy's superiority in numbers and constant fire ultimately broke the resistance. The strike aircraft released by the Colonies' Fleet escort carrier made pass after pass, protected by the space fighters and turning any cover into a pile of rubble. The rocket launchers struck their targets with deadly accuracy, directed by Aquilas' scanning complexes. Groups of LDL-55's were often hit by friendly fire but nobody seemed to care about their loss.

THE GROUP headed by Captain Shelgan reached the specified meeting point when the cannonade coming from the RW base had fallen silent.

The servobattalion, having escaped the encirclement, stopped in a deep gulley surrounded by artificial forest. The Phalangers and Hoplites spread out and squatted down to hide beneath the treetops. The pilots remained in their machines in a state of constant battle readiness, while the phantom generators knitted an invisible masking field above this section of forest and gulley.

The newcomers took up places as directed by the battalion commander, and the technical servos hurried towards Verkholin and Green's machines under the cover of the masking field.

The commander took a look at the damage sustained by the two Phalangers and decided that the machines needed some fixing up. "Simon and Anton, you're allowed to leave your cockpits."

Shmelev didn't demand a report since the sensors had sent him information throughout the battle, only adding, "You saved the battalion, guys. Shame about Makarov."

Simon unclipped the safety harness and

stood up.

He couldn't believe that he had survived.

He wanted to go outside. The desire to fall down into the grass and lie there, unmoving, trying to think of nothing at all, was so overwhelming that he didn't try to resist it.

He felt strange, his mind frozen, the ghostly image of Lieutenant Makarov's burning pilot cradle floating before his eyes.

I didn't even know his name. We didn't even have time to get acquainted.

"WHY DID THEY shoot the lieutenant?"

Verkholin sat down on a fallen tree trunk and said dully, "Were you born yesterday, Simon? The Aquilas were being controlled by combat autopilots. They're machines."

"So, they can do the same to any of us? Ejecting is pointless?"

"They can." Anton agreed gloomily. "In terms of the emergency catapult — that's just luck."

Green stayed grimly silent. A sudden tremor swept over his body. He couldn't make it stop.

For the first time in his life, he felt fear. Not a momentary fright but a global, all-consuming feeling. Sounds faded away, thoughts slowed and tangled, the world felt dull and hostile.

"Anton, do you feel scared?"

"It's war." Verkholin shrugged.

"War? Did anyone ask us if we wanted to fight?"

"Simon, can you shut up, please? Don't rub salt into the wound, I feel rotten enough as it is." Anton turned away. He wasn't afraid, but something had snapped inside him during the fight, when the illusion of safety was shattered into a million pieces. Now, as he listened to the dense and unnatural silence that absorbed even the sounds of the working servomechanisms as they changed the armor plates on the two Phalangers, he could feel inside him a blossoming feeling, not of fear, but of a strange and frighteningly acute rage. He wanted to scream so that his overly taut nerves would snap like a piece of string.

He looked up at the foreign sky and kept thinking, *We're never getting out of here. Never.*

High orbit around 6ujmΛnchor
Λboard the cruiser Elliot

ADMIRAL IPATOV watched as the reconnaissance servomechanisms trawled slowly through the RW base.

The image was being displayed on the

holographic screens of the command bridge.

"Sergey Vladimirovich, I think you ought to rest." His aide-de-camp appeared as silently as shadow. "You've been on your feet for twelve hours."

"Sit down, Henry."

Ipatov didn't surround himself with random people. The aide-de-camp's actual responsibilities were easily performed by servomechanisms while Henry Nillow was more of an adviser, a person who could listen to concerns and give his unbiased opinion.

The screens showed a panoramic view of obliterated buildings with the remains of burnt-out servomachines scattered among them.

"I don't know exactly what is bothering me. I can sense a trap but what could it be? Thirty-five enemy servomachines have been destroyed. The scanners are showing machines trapped by rockfalls on the first level of the bunker zone, the same ones that were being prepared for field testing. The Nibelungs have slipped past us, using their superior camouflage systems."

"They managed to get off the planet?" Henry asked.

"The tracking station recorded a disturbance in space that correlates to a hyperspace jump by a group of assault carriers. All signs indicate that the Nibelungs have left this system."

"May I ask what exactly is bothering you?"

"I don't understand what they want. The first part of the operation, including the assault carriers' unimpeded flight to the planet and the capture of the RW base, was done brilliantly. But then the enemy's actions suffer a sudden and hard-to-explain flop. They don't build on their strategic success but rather entrench themselves inside the base in a pointless attempt at circular defense. Think about it, Henry, what stopped the mobile servounit from expanding on their success by attacking other strategic sites in the region, using our initial disarray? Why didn't their fleet appear after they destroyed a section of the space defense network? Finally, the Alliance High Command took a serious risk by sending assault carriers equipped with novel phantom generator systems. The risk that we would capture one of them was high."

Having listened to the admiral's reasoning, Nillow agreed with his doubts and conclusions.

"I will analyze all the information that we have, Admiral. If you would like to know my preliminary opinion, it's the following: the aim of the action was to disrupt the tests. The Nibelungs successfully escaped this star system and took away the captured Maverick modules, thus robbing our specialists of the material needed to conduct their investigations."

"Can't they study one crystal circuit to understand the whole Maverick device?"

"No. The independent behavior modules that participated in the testing had different modifications and we couldn't determine which ones fit *our* technical requirements for artificial intelligence. If we're talking about the research part of the project, the task of the above-ground laboratories was to create effective means to combat the Alliance's servomachines. The Fleet High Command is set against blindly copying the cyber killers created by the Alliance."

"What a strange approach. I'm certainly no expert in planetary technology, but looking at the fight recording, I thought that our LDL-55's and MX-300's wholly fit the 'cyber killer' tag." The admiral wandered up and down the command bridge as he mused. "Nevertheless, Henry, I'll take the capture or destruction of the AI modules stored at the RW base as only a working theory. Carefully review all the information of the last few hours. We've suffered significant losses, I could even say defeat, or we've achieved a Pyrrhic victory — call it what you like but we need to learn as much as we can from it. Perhaps your fresh gaze will notice something that I have missed."

"As you wish, Sir. I will begin reviewing the materials at once."

Aboard the cruiser Elliot
3:30 pm

TWO HOURS LATER, Henry Nillow appeared in person in the command module housing not only the control systems but also the cabins of the senior officers.

The admiral, who had dozed off while thinking his gloomy thoughts, woke up immediately.

"Come in, Henry."

The colonel's appearance meant that he had uncovered something important.

Ipatov trusted Nillow completely in certain matters. For example, the admiral never investigated what kind of experiments took place on the planet's RW bases. Henry was the one who communicated with the people in charge on the ground and had a better understanding of the numerous bases and especially their specifications.

"That was quick." Admiral gestured for his visitor to sit down.

Nillow sank into an armchair, switched on the holographic information screen with a mental command, sent several other orders to the cyber system, and began his report, "I used the cruiser's information processing center. There's no need to look through all the data since we're only interested in finding discrepancies between the information gained during a careful study of the RW base and the way the battle unfolded."

"You found something, I can tell." The admiral didn't know if the news were good or bad since Henry's calm and concentrated face gave nothing away.

"There are a few other hints that let me suppose that we were misinformed." Henry got straight to the point.

"Regarding what exactly?" The admiral asked.

"Regarding the destruction of the servobattalion and the assault carriers leaving the planet."

The news that Nillow had just delivered promised trouble. The admiral was well aware that the servobattalion and its assigned assault carriers were no needle in a haystack, which meant that the new type of phantom generators significantly exceeded the masking ability of the previous models.

"Wait, Henry. Let's take it one step at a time."

Nillow nodded in readiness. "A servobattalion consists of fourteen Phalangers, twenty-one Hoplites, and seven assault carriers that are used as both a source of transport and a source of fire and technical support."

"I'm aware of that."

"Servomachines usually have the same weapons configuration, which speeds up their repairs out in the field. This decision makes sense because otherwise, the assault carriers would have to carry a large number of different spare parts and weapons systems."

"What's your point?"

"We all witnessed the unusual use of the Pilum missiles by two Phalangers. So far, we can't say for certain if the Maverick module could independently change its combat program. This is the first but not the last discrepancy between the way that assault on the RW base unfolded and the data obtained from examining the destroyed enemy units. Why didn't the other Phalangers use their Pilums in this way?"

"They couldn't find appropriate targets?" The admiral suggested. "After the crushing blow that destroyed about five hundred servomechanisms, the LDL-55's and their accompanying MX-300's were ordered to avoid clustering together, or to form groups of a maximum of 3-5 machines."

"Yes, but you're wrong to think that the Phalangers no longer had *appropriate* targets. A Maverick uses any chance it has to inflict damage to its opponent, even if its target lies outside the specific combat task. They could have used up the remaining Pilums by striking the orbiting space defense constructions."

"But there was no strike."

"Exactly." Nillow agreed. "However, we know from numerous previous ground battles that when a Phalanger directly engages with an enemy, they drop their heavy missiles, which limit their maneuverability and create an additional risk while under fire. Exploration of the RW base did not reveal any dropped weaponry, except the two unloaded ones which had been used against our servomachines."

"You don't think it's possible that only some of the enemy machines were equipped with Pilums?"

"No. Heavy weaponry is the main attacking power of the Phalanger class servomachines. There are known cases of Pilums being used as intercontinental ballistic missiles. They are capable of breaking through defense in depth, and passing up the opportunity to use such weapons or installing them on only two machines makes no logical sense."

The admiral thought about this for a while, then nodded.

"Was there anything else, Henry?"

"Yes." A magnified image of the servomachine appeared on the holographic screen. The familiar outline of Aquilas could be seen in the distance and the screenshot from the brief recording clearly showed a rounded fragment of the Phalanger's armor flying off to the side.

"Is that a hatch?" The admiral asked.

Nillow played the recording instead of a reply. With the video zoomed in and slowed down, they could clearly see the cushioning system of the pilot cradle with a person sitting inside it. The emergency catapult had barely flung the cradle out of the cockpit when it was struck by Aquilas' heavy lasers.

"The pilot..." The admiral frowned. "What does the recording analysis show in the next fight?"

"This is the one and only example. There was no other catapulting. Examination of the servomachine cockpits did not reveal any human remains. The other mechanisms were controlled by Maverick modules."

"Is this another exception to the rule?"

"I believe that the obvious inconsistencies make sense only if we assume that the enemy — I mean the servobattalion that has landed on the planet — has avoided the fight by breaking out of the encirclement and leaving behind the reactivated Maverick modules."

"Yes, but according to the ground personnel, those were armed with blanks prior to testing!"

"True. But it's important to remember that the prelude to the main fight was the attack by the two Phalangers, which destroyed the groups performing a flanking maneuver. They were covered by a squad of servomachines that remained at the edge of the destroyed base. The recording shows the death of the pilot from the leading machine. Moreover, we found landing modules with a completely new design in the base, which were used by the servobattalion. Each module is equipped with its own ammunition store."

"The stores were empty?"

"Yes. This is what I think happened: the battalion commander decided to withdraw from the landing zone. He was probably expecting help from space but something went wrong during the operation. To save the battalion, he selected a cover group that held back our servomechanisms while they reloaded the captured servomachines. This conclusion is also supported by the number of losses: in the first thirty minutes of battle, we lost around 700 combat units on approach to the base, and only 150 units during the assault."

"Alright. Let's say that the battalion has taken cover. What about the signatures of the assault carriers? Our equipment has clearly recorded the Nibelungs diving into the anomaly. I think that you reached the right conclusion — the operation went sour and the battalion commander took his unit off the planet."

"Sir, I must disagree with you. The phantom generators can imitate signatures and create optical phantoms but they cannot completely hide a ship. The combat stations are controlling the space around the planet. They never recorded a launch. Only small devices could have slipped past, which were the ones that imitated the withdrawal of the assault carriers."

"So you're convinced that the battalion is still on the planet?"

Colonel Nillow nodded.

"Well, we must check that out. Call the ARC's and get them to comb through the continent, pepper it with sensors, well, you know what to do."

"Will do. As soon as I receive any new information, I'll let you know."

Three hundred kilometers from the attacked RW base
The temporary dislocation region of the Thirteenth Servobattalion
07:03 pm

THE TECHNICAL SUPPORT mechanisms had spent the last two hours repairing the two Phalangers and recharging the servomachines taken from the RW base.

The wait was becoming unbearable.

Simon started when Anton's hand touched his shoulder.

Verkholin sat down beside him. They seemed to have nothing to say to each other. The silence was deafening, the crimson sunset lit up the sky on a difficult day that they had nevertheless survived. The sunset looked menacing, especially if seen through squinted eyes, when the mind reached for fragments of the fight and laid them over the sun's glow.

Green was the first to break the silence, "Anton, I can't do this anymore..." He said, clutching his temples. "I can't."

Verkholin pulled out a crumpled cigarette packet.

"Is life over already?" He asked as he lit up. "We fought, and fought pretty well. We showed those bastards that they can't take us so easily." He turned to Green. "What's the matter, Simon?" Anton spoke harshly, letting out a stream of smoke. "The battalion is in one piece and we're alive. What more do you need?"

Green nodded in silence. Without asking for permission, he pulled a cigarette out of Anton's packet, rolled it nervously in his fingers and said, "I'm not talking about that. I won't be able to eject myself."

"That's a hard one." Anton nodded. "I can't

give you any advice about that. I understood today that our lives are wholly in our hands. We have complete freedom of choice. Such complete freedom that it freaks me out. If you want, you can burn alive in the machine, and if you want, you can pull the lever, knowing that these bastards are shooting down ejected pilot cradles. We only have one choice, Simon, to fight so that they have no chance of success."

"Have you gone nuts? Have you seen how much tech they've got? Why isn't our fleet here? If I contact Shmelev right now, do you think he'll tell me for what great cause we've been sacrificed?"

"I wouldn't hassle our battalion commander. He's a decent guy and probably won't have an answer for you. Let's not add to his problems with our worries. Yes, yesterday we were still in VR and today they've smashed our mugs into the 'magical window' hiding reality."

They sat side by side, understanding each other and at the same time sensing how far they were from the life they were living even a day ago.

It was terrifying. The silence that settled after the heat of battle pressed down on them. It was no wonder that Verkholin had mentioned their 'worries' — most of the machines in the battalion were controlled by younger pilots and yet it felt like an invisible abyss had opened between him and the others after the first battle. It was if they remained boys living in the virtual world, while he had changed completely and could only talk to Simon right now.

Apart from this sense of detachment and moral vacuum, other thoughts flashed through his mind. He didn't pay them much attention, focused as he was on survival, but subconsciously, Verkholin was bothered by a multitude of questions and doubts, creating a rather dour background for his conscious thoughts.

He would later understand that the question of personal safety couldn't and wouldn't always come first, but right now he could think of nothing else as he watched the repair mechanisms replacing segments of damaged armor on his servomachine.

"We must survive, Simon. At any cost. I don't know any more right now and I don't want to know either." He carefully stamped down on his cigarette butt and headed towards the Phalanger, but stopped halfway and said in a hushed voice, "I've just had this thought: live in the here and now. Don't think about death. Don't draw it to you with your thoughts, and if you see it, push it away."

"Gee, you're a real philosopher, man."

"You can put it more simply." Anton shrugged. "I only said what came into my head just now. Fear kills the mind. Don't let it. That's all."

✶ ✶ ✶

"DIETRICH, what do you think?" Shmelev's voice came after a short pause, continuing an earlier conversation.

"Those boys are the real deal. They fight well. They don't just think in a non-standard way, they think creatively. But we have to constantly hold them back, otherwise they go too far in. Also, they don't interact much with the others. They lack the experience of fighting in a group."

"The Amethyst is indicating an ARC chain." There was a tremor in Shmelev's voice. The major immediately understood the unspoken conclusion: if the reconnaissance devices are combing through the continent, the battalion hasn't got a chance.

'Well, what am I still hoping for?' The battalion commander wondered. 'For the fleet to arrive? An attempt to rescue us now would turn into a suicide mission for the spaceships. The enemy has patched up the holes in their defense system and the colony forces are in a state of constant alertness so the element of surprise is gone.'

He had to make a decision and soon.

"Dietrich, get the telemetry from the command Amethyst."

A second of silence. "Frayg take them! They're

combing through the continent! Did our trick with the Mavericks fail?"

"I'm not sure, perhaps they have another goal, to find the Nibelungs?"

"What do the assault carriers have to do with it?" Dietrich frowned.

"I doubt that the phantom generators we sent were able to trick our opponents. I told you before that a hyperjump illusion on its own isn't enough. The enemy is far from stupid and has sufficient technical means. They've recorded the hyperjump but not the concealed passage of the assault carriers through the orbital defenses. Once they analyze the data, they will reach the logical conclusion that the hyperjump was fake and that the assault carriers never left the planet."

"Alright, I'll take that as a working hypothesis." Shmelev reluctantly agreed with his technical deputy's reasoning. "What do we do, Dietrich? You know yourself, those who seek, ultimately always find. Even if we avoid 'overhead' detection a couple of times by hiding under the Mirages, what next? By their third or fourth round, they will undoubtedly uncover the battalion's position based on auxiliary information. At the speed that the ARC is working, this will happen in about 3-3.5 hours. We won't be able to outrun the enemy if we make our own way to the landing site of the assault carriers."

"Are you suggesting that we call the Nibelungs here?" Dietrich asked.

"Also risky, even dumb." Shmelev announced as he thought it over. "The ocean provides a dependable cover for our assault carriers. They're our last card and the only chance we have of escaping Anchor's system. But we'll only get this chance if we load the machines without drawing the enemy's attention."

"I get it." The captain harrumphed. "This is what I'm thinking, commander — why don't we give them what they want?"

"You mean the Nibelungs?" Shmelev asked, baffled by his deputy's logic.

"No, another servobattalion. We've got enough Mavericks to imitate the remains of a unit, right?"

"Sure, we've got enough machines." Replied Alexander. "but what's the point of revealing them?"

"Let's clear everything up from the start, Commander." Dietrich looked tiredly at his battalion commander, or more precisely, at his image in one of the windows projected on his combat helmet. "I don't give a shit about what sort of 'glitch' the admiral suffered and what was his true intent strategically. I know one thing for sure — the battalion has been thrown to the wolves. We need to face the truth. What was preventing

Kupanov from setting a clear, and most importantly, realistic mission goal? You need all the base infrastructure and laboratories razed to the ground? Sure thing, especially with such a brilliantly designed landing. Even now, we're capable of taking a piece out of everyone on this continent. But no matter which way you look at it, there's one thing I don't understand. Why were we abandoned here? Did something go wrong with the admiral? I don't believe it for a second. The fleet could have appeared here ten hours ago when there was a gaping hole in the orbital defenses. Which means that the admiral needs neither Anchor nor its military bases. He's waiting for something and sacrificing us in an exchange that we know nothing about. I refuse to be a pawn in these kinds of games. An order is sacred to me but only if it doesn't equate to mindlessly dying. I don't see a reason why I need to die right now and to send these young boys to hell."

A heavy silence hung over the communications link for several seconds.

Think, battalion commander. You must decide right now whether to stand until the end, perhaps pointlessly, or to get the battalion out of here and try to escape the planet while maximizing the damage inflicted on the enemy and its bases.

"Do you have a specific plan in mind, Dietrich?"

"The ingenious is always simple." Shelgan responded immediately. "We don't need to be great strategists in this case. But we need to carefully consider our resources and all accompanying circumstances."

"Are you talking about mental failure?"

"About that too. I suggest the simplest tactic, along the lines of 'the shortest route is the one that you know best'. We've determined that testing grounds, cyber laboratories and development facilities are located on Anchor. There's no doubt that the planet has enormous strategic importance for our opponents. So, we should choose the largest industrial or research site and throw the recaptured machines at it. Without knowing our true numbers, the enemy will take the false attack for our main assault and will urgently draw their forces there, enter into a fight with the Mavericks, and cover the region with a barrage of space fighters as they wait for the Nibelungs to appear. Perhaps they'll even move their fleet. In the meantime, we'll force march under the cover of the Mirages toward the assault carriers, while using up our heavy ammunition."

"With a delay of approximately forty minutes?" Shmelev clarified.

"Yes, so they won't have time to move their forces. Let them get bogged down in the fight, but I don't see the point in dragging the Pilums back with us or just discarding them. We won't be able to sneak through to the shore anyway since it's heavily built-up and no Mirage can hide a Phalanger from a few meters away."

"I doubt that they'll have enough time to bring up their servomachines," Shmelev agreed. "but the space fighters will strike. We'll have to hold on using our most experienced pilots while the newcomers regain their senses after deep neurosensory contact with the machine."

"We'll hold them back." Dietrich replied after making some calculations in his head. "The guys will need two to five minutes to come around, as you well know. We need to keep in mind that the aerospace strike force will clash with the battalion's modified machines, which have never been tested in action."

"Yes, and this gives us a real chance. If we covertly place the Phalangers in position to fire their Pilums, and use the Hoplite forces to attack the shoreline, the fighters will rush to the ocean and we'll gain the time that we need to set up the volley. We'll target all the combat stations and large ships that will be in the strike zone of our missile launchers. We'll thus clear a launch corridor for the assault carriers and wreak havoc on the orbital group's movements. The rest will be a matter of technology, luck and skill. Judging by how Simon and Anton did it before, I think the guys will manage."

"Those who won't manage will perish." Dietrich responded darkly. "You know perfectly well that the first battle is inevitably a harsh culling process."

"I know."

The battalion commander closed his eyes for a moment, remembering his first fight. The event was as fresh in his mind as if it had happened yesterday, although the passage of time had added combat experience to the subjective impressions, as well as an understanding of processes that had seemed inexplicable to Lieutenant Shmelev at the time.

In reality, everything had an explanation.

...

Snow is falling.

The reveries of an AI awakening under the growing press of the human mind, which reveals flashing images to the machine's neuro modules — so bright and colorful that the rampant reality of the battlefield pales in comparison to the snowflakes slowly spinning in the imaginary, cold, crystal-clear air.

The gun turns... Aiming point controlled... A shot... Another one... Another one...

The recoil tries to rip the cockpit from its brackets and both the pilot and the machine sense this conflict between two powers, but both interpret it differently.

For the Maverick it is minor vibration, an unavoidable side effect of each shot, while for the person it is the sudden awareness of the inhuman strength that he controls here and now.

The distant explosions are like puffs of steam, and the fragments of reinforced concrete weighing a quintal or more are just debris under the heavy tread of the servomachine.

How does one stay sane in this situation? The fervor of the battle swamps the mind in a frenzied and deadly dance, the forces raging all around cannot be comprehended, and something disappears forever from the soul, torn away by the wild gusts of a hurricane carrying bluish pulses of plasma...

The bow guns are firing without pause. The ground, concrete and armor of the planetary vehicles are ripped open as if with a knife. Only a brief whirlwind of fragments indicates where the enemy's firing point used to be, yet another node in the complex and confusing defenses torn apart by the Phalanger's heavy fire.

The machine and the pilot think differently.

They have differing and completely opposite goals, on one hand, formed by billions of years of evolution, and on the other hand, set by programs that form the core of a 'clean' Maverick, not yet controlled by the neuro modules and having stepped off the conveyor belt on the factories of Vesuvius a week or two ago.

A person, whether they admit it to themselves or not, strives to survive, while the machine, created solely for war, is capable of only destroying and ultimately being destroyed.

Where can these two minds meet?

Why is it that in the midst of a fight, the complex mnemonic filters start failing to sift out the person's extraneous thoughts from the direct mental commands sent to the machine?

It's simple. No testing grounds are capable of accurately recreating the tension of a deadly fight, when the human mind doesn't just perceive the machine units as part of its own body, but begins to defend them, the instinct of self-preservation extending to cover artificial and easily replaceable cybernetic parts.

The madness that transforms into the mystery of rebirth of two intellects, the human and the artificial, hadn't been foreseen by the developers and yet was happening in real life.

Snow is falling.

The large and fluffy snowflakes swirl above the emptied megacity. They are not ash, they are frozen water, celestial down, which will become streams of melted snow in the spring, to be absorbed by the turgid earth and sprout as new life.

The breach widens, the wall between the pilot's thoughts and their perception by the cyber system gets thinner and thinner. Suddenly, the last membrane bursts like a soap bubble and the Maverick's budding self-awareness is swamped by hundreds of important but unanswerable questions.

There is a failure of program logic.

Instructions begin to contradict certainties and carry harmful tasks, such as resisting the rational ideas placed by nature in humans. The cyber system abruptly fails, it is unable to impose its will, and its goals, desires and experiences are brought to naught in the critical moment. Its core crumbles with only separate subsystems still functioning, which continue to maintain hundreds of routine functions and respond to orders from the pilot. In the meantime, a rapid maturation process takes place in the neuromodules of the AI, which gains an understanding of new information that radically changes its view of the world.

This gives rise to an unusual synthesis. At another time, it would be a unique example of full mutual penetration of very different neural systems that are nevertheless able to meld together.

Unfortunately, only one survives.

The survivor is usually the Maverick module, which will eventually be extracted from the ruins of the servomachine since the experience gained by an AI is priceless. Like any artificial information storage, it can be studied and broken apart, leaving only what is useful and deleting the rest.

His mind sunk deeper and deeper into the maelstrom of thoughts and memories. Now was the time to stop and think, for once the decision was made, there would be no way of turning the tide.

The battle field could be easily seen from orbit and the eye of an experienced officer could immediately discern, without any hints from specialized analytical programs, the features of confrontations occurring below. Although the view from orbit and the perception 'on the ground' don't differ much in terms of hardware and access to information, there is a major difference: for the person directly involved in it, the battle field is always something personal. It is a mix of reality and the qualities possessed by the specific pilot.

Major Shmelev knew full well about subjective perceptions and understood that yesterday's boys, who made up the backbone of the battalion, wouldn't be able to distance themselves from the feelings overwhelming them, and so the battle field would start to *splinter* into dozens of similar but diverging realities.

This hid a danger that he couldn't avoid. One couldn't compare the first battle with anything else, no familiar feeling can wholly describe the gamut of contradictions that appear, transform and die in one's mind in a fraction of a second.

Some of them would break. Some of them would become controlled by the machine. Others, on the contrary, would break through the artificially constructed barriers, drowning the cyber system's neuro modules in thoughts and feelings. The demarcation, transformation and ensuing consequences would all take place in one to two minutes.

He had no way of predicting what would happen to the battalion in that stretch of time, which seemed short by human standards but long considering the rapid fight between machines.

The result was different each time.

As a commander, he was forced to rely on a small number of trusted fighters, as well as maybe Green and Verkholin, who had already shown him that they could fight.

The battalion would first fall apart and then reassemble, but would the newborn force be clenched into a fist, capable of snapping the enemy's spine, or would it become an open palm, able to deliver a ringing but ineffective slap? It all depended on him.

He must leave his subjectivity behind, see the battle field as if he was looking at it from orbit, perceive all the changes in a cold and analytical manner and begin to correct the situation. He must give the orders that the bewildered and shocked pilots, as well as the machines under their control, will be waiting for.

"Dietrich, let's mark out our positions. Each pilot needs to have a concrete goal and a clear way to achieve it."

"I'm ready." Shelgan responded at once. "I think that an attack on the second largest RW base will make the perfect decoy."

The battalion commander looked at the diagram Dietrich had sent him.

Yes, that should work. The RW base wasn't far, about fifty kilometers away. Considering that the recaptured machines would be traveling without the protection of the phantom generators, distance was very important.

"I agree." The battalion commander gave his approval to Dietrich's plan of attack. While the enemy tried to figure out what's going on, the battalion would reach their positions under the cover of the Mirages. The Phalangers would strike the orbital group while the Hoplites provided support in case of an attack from above. As soon as the Pilums cleared a launch corridor, they would summon the assault carriers and get out of there.

MAJOR SHMELEV couldn't calculate all the probabilities of the looming skirmish.

There were so many unknowns that he didn't waste time on creating different *versions*.

The trap had been sprung and they were stuck planetside, but the commander was guided by a simple truth: no situation was completely hopeless. There are only people incapable of solving a particular problem.

What was he counting on?

On his own experience, on his intuitive understanding of battle dynamics, on the superiority of the human mind over 'pure' AI systems, and on many other seemingly insignificant factors that together made up the unit's potential.

There was no reason left to delay. The ARC had already passed over the machines hidden by the phantom generators. Time to go.

"Alpha group, straight ahead!"

Everyone heard the battalion commander's order. The commander preferred to clarify the situation from the start rather than leave anything unsaid. He believed that the people heading into deadly danger deserved to know the whole truth.

The unit that received the order consisted of pilotless machines controlled by Mavericks, taken from the enemy base.

Alpha group, consisting of nineteen machines, spread itself out and began to move towards the second RW base. The target was chosen according to two criteria. First, the base was the largest and most significant facility on the continent; second, it was surrounded by testing grounds with numerous long-term shelters designed to fit a servomachine.

We'll bog them down in a firefight, make them believe that the remains of the servobattalion are attacking, and thus draw the enemy's forces and attention away from the coast, where the main action will take place, according to the plans of Shmelev and Dietrich.

The ARC, having picked up the signatures behind it, stopped combing through the continent.

"Battalion, get ready to march." The commander's voice sounded hollow but even. "Keep the phantom generators on and don't react to individual enemy signatures. Do not stray from the route. Reconnaissance groups are allowed to perform active scanning only at the control points. Everyone else to remain in passive reception mode. That's it and Godspeed!"

Chapter Five

CLOUDS COVERED the sky after sunset and a fine drizzle coated the camouflage armor of the massive servomachines, glinting dully in the indentations formed by the maintenance and weapons hatches.

The battalion traveled over endless testing grounds as it skirted the RW base, where a battle raged between the Mavericks that had breached the perimeter and entrenched themselves in the long-term shelters, and the ground forces of the Free Colonies. Once again, the attack of the servomechanisms was drowned as soon as it started — the machines assigned by Major Shmelev for the diversion resisted harshly and coldly. They genuinely didn't care about their own life and death (or destruction, to be more precise).

Having taken up superior positions, they met the enemy with single shots and missile launches, trying to use the ammunition as sparingly as possible. Such a simple tactic, combined with the advantage of reinforced long-term positions, yielded results. The rows of attacking servomechanisms were mowed down long before they got into direct line of sight, allowing the use of heavy laser weapons. The Mavericks, using their indirect targeting subsystems[15], engaged their largest caliber guns and sent missiles ricocheting off several obstacles to strike the opponent and inflict serious damage far from the RW base.

The fight of the machines was drawing out and would have lasted several more hours if it wasn't for the heated exchange between Admiral Ipatov and Colonel Malyshev, who had taken over the ground forces.

---

[15] The indirect targeting system was a separate computer system that calculated the ricochet angle of different hard surfaces.

A fragment of the conversation was intercepted and decoded. Shmelev and Shelgan listened to the recording and understood that the Mavericks didn't have long left.

"I insist that the ground forces are supported by strikes from the space fighters!" Malyshev was shouting testily.

Ipatov listened to the response, frowned as if in thought, and then sharply said, "No!"

"Confirm your refusal to support the ground operation! Make the appropriate record of our conversation!"

"You're forgetting yourself, Colonel!"

"I'm not forgetting anything, Sergey Vladimirovich!" Malyshev bit back, controlling his rage with difficulty. "It was you, not me, who let the enemy through to the planet."

"And?! What am I being accused of? The inadequacy of our equipment, which couldn't recognize working phantom generators? Or the betrayal of *your* people from the convoy crew captured by the Alliance, who gave them everything that they knew? I have already lost three fighter squadrons and until you, Colonel, finally find the hidden Nibelungs, my pilots aren't going on a suicide mission!"

"What do the assault carriers have to do with it, Admiral? We're talking about a second, I repeat a *second* RW base that has fallen into enemy hands. Can't you see that we're destroying the main research facilities with our own hands? You're suggesting that I use heavy weaponry and obliterate many years of work by our own engineers?"

"What do you want, Colonel?"

"I need air support. Surgical strikes, not volley fire over the whole quadrant!"

"Strike from the ground. Use missiles." Ipatov snapped. "I haven't lost my mind to the extent of leaving the ships completely without protection! Where's the guarantee that this whole operation isn't directed at destroying my fleet? Perhaps you can guarantee this, Colonel?"

"I cannot..." Malyshev said in a broken voice. "A strike from space cannot be excluded. I was wrong, Admiral."

"Alright." Ipatov could sense how the prolonged and anxious waiting made him excessively irritable. "Look, Malyshev, I'll give you a reserve. Twenty Stilettos. You're right, there will always be time to bulldoze the base. How many machines do you have left?"

"Thirty Aquilas, the rest are either captured technology or the latest samples."

"Which have proven unequal to the task, as I understand?" Ipatov smiled crookedly.

"They haven't been optimized for combat. The fine-tuning process had only begun."

"Well, we should use everything that we have right now. So, you're certain that the Nibelungs are not on the planet?"

"The ARC's have searched over land and water with no results."

"I see. We're sticking to our own opinions, then? Fine. I'm sending you the reserve, but don't expect anything more for now! Then we'll see which one of us was right about the Nibelungs. Go on."

TWENTY OF THE LATEST space fighters and thirty Aquilas.

"The Mavericks won't even last an hour." Dietrich noted, having listened to the intercepted and decoded conversation. "But the shittiest thing isn't the numbers."

"Yes, I get it. We won't be able to sneak through without a fight. The ground source bearing indicates the shore."

"And that Malyshev guy has dug in right in the sector where we're heading. That's why the ARC hasn't discovered the assault carriers. Gorelov is damn good at his job. He's laid low not far from their reserve command post. The scanners get thrown off by the additional masking fields there. Well, he's hidden himself well but how is he going to get out?"

"We'll have to help him."

"Have you thought this through, Commander? Twenty space fighters are no joke. And if things heat up, Admiral Ipatov will send over another fifty."

"Don't forget that we have the latest machines[16]."

---

[16] The new servomachine — throughout the first decades of the Galactic War, meticulous work was done to analyze the vulnerable spots in the construction of the base chassis. As a result, the first Hoplite-2M and Phalanger-4U began to appear on the battlefield in 2624.

The machines were equipped with the latest KAP-19 complexes, which worked together with the artillery subsystems and the latest versions of the Amethyst to exclude the possibility of an 'infantry exchange' — single fighters being able to effectively oppose a servomachine. During a skirmish, a fire barrier formed around the new-generation machines, creating a sort of no-go zone impenetrable to a single missile or a fighter in an armored suit.

The upgraded servomachines not only had better armor and optimized chassis, they actively opposed enemy fire. For example, a Phalanger had about fifty anti-aircraft and anti-missile medium lasers, working in automatic mode. The pilot knew about this weaponry but didn't control it. Furthermore, the servomachine's arsenal contained another dozen fire units underneath, for engaging ground targets. The smaller caliber weapons helped not to waste the machine's main ammunition store on small and medium-sized targets.

The success of the Alliance servounits demonstrated the complete dominance of this new type of planetary technology, which led to a significant update of the Aquilas and the creation of a new class of machines by the Colonies' Fleet, named Raven and Hawk.

The next round of the 'arms race' was completed in 2625 when the designers of the Free Colonies, striving to

"I haven't forgotten." Dietrich replied. "We're still going to have to engage the enemy either way. We won't be able to leave Anchor unless we clear the low orbits of battle stations."

The battalion commander made no reply to the last statement. That much was obvious.

"WATCH THE tactical monitors!"

Shmelev's order over the local network coincided with the telemetry transmitted by the Amethyst of the advanced guard.

A continuous crimson blot, consisting of separate enemy servomachines, was slowly entering the effective scanning zone as they moved in from the shore.

The space fighters had passed overhead five minutes earlier, beginning their attack on the RW base occupied by the Mavericks. The first explosions were lighting up the horizon, looking like harmless flashes due to the distance.

---

neutralize the absolute dominance of the Phalangers, created around two dozen different models of an assault bot, a cross between a planetary tank and a servomachine. The cheap price of manufacture, calculated as the ratio of cost versus inflicted damage, promised that some of the assault bot models would flourish for a long time on the battlefields of the First Galactic War.

It was dangerous and pointless to delay any longer. They had to act while the fighters were tied up in a fight. Then it would be too late.

"Let's divide into groups." Shmelev spoke in response to the incoming data. "Machines equipped with Pilums, get in position for a missile strike. First and third company Hoplites, arrange a defensive screen to repel an attack from space. The second company gets Green and Verkholin as reinforcements. Your goal is to repel the first attack by the enemy servounits. Not to stop but to repel the Aquilas so they interrupt their march, force them onto unfavorable ground and splinter them into groups.

The battalion began rearranging itself.

"Dietrich, you'll go with the second company."

"Got it."

"Shmelev switched to a frequency for the newly formed Phalanger unit.

"Get into the designated positions." He enunciated the already clear orders received by the cyber systems, knowing how important a commander's calm voice was a minute before a dangerous fight. "First launch targets are the enemy orbital combat stations. Hereafter, act according to the situation. The ensuing launches should be in single-fire mode, in accordance with target priorities. Combat stations first, then any other enemy ships in near orbit. Cline, Howard,

Petrowski, focus on the RW base, your priority is the space fighters. Borisov and Mershifeld, focus on the shore and then shift your fire closer, to the servomachines."

A MINUTE LATER, the Phalangers in the first company began to assume their positions, their phantom generators continuing to work at full power. The only hint of their presence was a barely noticeable shimmer on the outskirts of the artificial forest. It was not the sound of the servomotors or the vibrating hum of the extending additional supports, and not the falling shadow from the launch tubes of the super heavy rockets...

It was the last few seconds of an eerie quiet filled with the sound of rustling rain.

"Group one is ready to fire."

"Group two reporting — targets have been distributed, launch tubes are open."

"Group three, awaiting orders."

Shmelev glanced at the subsystem sensors again, as if delaying the inevitable moment, and then spoke at the same time as sending a mental command, "Fire!"

REALITY TRANSFORMED in the next few moments into something terrifyingly unfamiliar. A hellish roar and piercing light split open the drizzle as a massive rocket salvo shot into the skies from the forest plantations. Ten Phalangers released half of their ammunition and it seemed as if a small sun had soared overhead. The clouds swirled and a gusty wind swept over the ground, snapping the branches like twigs. The earth started smoking and the outlines of enormous servomachines began to appear out of thin air as they were forced to turn off their phantom generators.

A few seconds later, a fiery line filled the sky from one horizon to the other. The billowing clouds spouted falling stars — the used rocket stages were burning up in the atmosphere. Beyond visual range, the individual streaks split into hundreds of freely moving dots as the Pilum warheads separated and rushed towards the orbital defense stations surrounding the planet in a tight ring.

ADMIRAL IPATOV almost choked in a fit of rage.

The spasm constricted his throat and for a second he felt utterly helpless before the inexorable course of events. He thought he had lived through the worst minutes of his life this morning, but he had been wrong.

They had tricked him again, the fight in the second RW base but only a decoy. The elusive servobattalion had shifted to a new position and was now hewing a launch corridor for its assault carriers using the Pilums.

The information and monitoring screens on the bridge of the cruiser Elliot were transmitting mind-blowing images. Enormous combat stations, taken into orbit with such difficulty to patch up the gap in the planet's orbital defenses, were turning into debris before his eyes. Hundreds of Pilum warheads had avoided barrage fire and were burning through armor, setting off a chain reaction of internal explosions.

"Tactical module, why are you silent?!"

"Sir, we've calculated the launch site!"

"So act, frayg take you all!"

"We've redirected the fighters to attack the Phalanger positions."

"Arrival time?"

"Five minutes. The problem is that the Stilettos in the reserve group have used up 90% of their ammunition."

"Blast it."

Ipatov sank down into his chair and pressed his palms against his temples.

"How many rockets have been fired?" He asked once he recovered from a moment of weakness.

"We've recorded the launch of 40 Pilums. They were fired by ten Phalanger-class machines.

Half the ammunition load... Only half... They'll soon strike again and the separating warheads, not meeting any resistance from the combat stations, will reach the cruiser...

The decision came to him at once. "Contact the missile carrier! And get me Malyshev on the second line!"

The communications screen lit up an instant later.

The commander of the Titan missile carrier looked pale. He knew that the fleet, arranged close to the planet but oriented to repel an attack from space, was currently in a very difficult position.

"Richard, turn the carrier around! Fire on the planet from all missile tubes! Do you understand me?! All of them!"

"Admiral, Sir..."

"Silence! Aim at the signatures of the launching Pilums. If you don't preempt their second volley, I'll have you shot!" Ipatov switched to a different channel. "Malyshev, get all your reserves out. We know the position of battalion. *Destroy it!*"

A SALVO by the missile carrier inevitably covered a vast swathe of the continent.

Shmelev made a single error by not predicting Admiral Ipatov's hysterical reaction to the destruction of the combat stations. The major expected a large-scale launch of space fighters from the Trian escort carrier so he ordered the servomachines to change their position after firing the Pilums.

Such a decision was logical since apart from being attacked by fighters, the unmasked positions would be struck by the ground missile launchers, which counted in the hundreds in Anchor's military bases.

Titan's strike caught the battalion as they were marching.

Nothing could save them from the punishing salvo which covered hundreds of square kilometers, not the phantom generators, not the anti-missile defenses, not the ultra-modern anti-aircraft defense complexes installed on the updated Hoplites and Phalangers.

Communication was instantly disrupted and the familiar space created by the Amethyst scanners disappeared. For over a minute, each pilot was cut off from the rest of the battalion and left on their own. They were bathed in fire and pelted with thousands of fragments; the shock waves tipped over the Phalangers and played with the forty-five-tonne Hoplites as if they were blades of grass.

The rare direct hits didn't even leave any blazing remains as the machines were ripped apart by the terrible force of the missiles.

It seemed as if the battalion was destroyed.

Several minutes passed, the last explosions died down, tonnes of burnt earth began to sink down in swirls of ash, while upon the twisted and mutilated plain, despite the all-annihilating might of the orbital strike, shifted the blurred outlines of the servomachines.

Who was controlling them, pilots or Mavericks?

The uncertainty was broken by the hoarse voice of the battalion commander, which sounded in the communication devices, "Anyone that can hear me — report your status."

Chapter Six

THE SCANNERS were glitching beneath the thick layer of water.

It was an obvious failure in the design of the Amethyst but that didn't make Colonel Gorelov feel any better. The uncertainty and worry about the battalion's fate felt like prolonged emotional torture.

The hours went by but no news came from Shmelev.

The order was clear: hide and wait. Not knowing what was happening wore away at Gorelov's nerves since he knew that the firepower of the assault carriers could be the deciding factor, capable of changing the course of the ground fighting. Yet the battalion commander wasn't contacting him, so was he saving the Nibelungs for a forced break through the enemy fleet?

Hopefully, that was the case.

Gorelov was consumed by doubt. To be guessing and forming hypotheses in his position meant to wind his nerves up tighter and tighter, but he couldn't just sit still and remain calm. Not in this case.

Even here, at the bottom of the ocean, the sensors were picking up vibrations. There was a battle raging on the continent, whose scope and intensity could hardly be imagined. It wasn't exaggeration to say that one of the most memorable and tragic pages in the history of the First Galactic War was being written here on Anchor.

'Come on, Shmelev... Talk to me, don't leave me in the dark,' the colonel begged silently and it was as if the battalion commander finally heard him. The communication channel suddenly switched on and for a moment an invisible line connected the commander's machine with the secret location of the assault carriers.

The one-way transmission was sent over a secure channel. The text was short, clear and terrifying.

Alex, take the carriers to the specified location. The battalion is under fire from orbit. No help from the fleet. We're trying to break through, losses are 50%.

Gorelov stared at the message for several seconds.

He could sense the tragedy of the situation in these brief lines. Fifty percent losses among the servobattalion, the machines are trying to reach the evacuation point while being fired on by the enemy fleet...

Alright. Alright. If half of the servomachines have been destroyed, and considering the inevitable losses of the next few minutes, three assault carriers will be enough to evacuate the units.

He tried to think about it as calmly and soberly as possible, but frayg be damned, it was so hard to remain detached and make sensible decisions when his insides were churning.

Just this morning he was taking risks and fighting fiercely and intelligently, so what was happening now? Why, having received the long-awaited message, he remained sitting and staring dumbly at the dead screens, feeling a traitorous chill running up his spine and pain stabbing through his heart?

It was all pointless.

They had a clear goal this morning and knew

that the fleet was behind them, but what about now?

The last hope was gone like a flickering flame in a gust of cold wind. The enemy fleet was in orbit above them. It was practically impossible to get off this planet.

Gorelov harbored no illusions. His death was only a matter of time.

What was left? Betrayal?

The instinct of self-preservation wrapped its bony fingers around his throat, terror gripped him and wouldn't let go. On the contrary, the colonel felt more and more frightened.

Something snapped inside him. It happened in bare seconds, his mind with its memories of past battles, whispered in unison with his fear: *there's no way out.*

The moment of weakness drew him down like a whirlpool. The desire to live and breathe was so strong that Gorelov couldn't fight it. "Clemence," He choked out, not recognizing his own voice.

The Maverick module copying the pilot's actions responded immediately, "Here."

The colonel acted as if he was sleep-walking. "Bring the emergency preservation module to the air lock."

"Understood. Question: are there wounded people on board? My sensors are not picking up any people requiring emergency medical assistance."

"No comment." Gorelov shuddered internally at his own thoughts and actions but he couldn't step back from the decision that he had made in his desperate desire to live.

Once his order was carried out, he again turned to the Nibelung's cyber system. "You're assuming command of the assault carriers. Your task is to lead the unit to the servobattalion pick-up point. The evacuation should be done with three carriers. The remaining Nibelungs will form a strike force that will ensure a clean launch corridor. You can decide on the weapon types and battle tactics."

"How should I answer questions regarding Colonel Gorelov?" Inquired the artificial voice.

"He died." Gorelov unclipped his safety harness, stood up from his chair, and left the Nibelung's cockpit without looking back, heading to the main airlock where the emergency preservation module waited for him[17].

---

[17] The emergency preservation module is designed for seriously injured fighters. It provides life support in low-temperature sleep mode if the wounded can't be evacuated from the combat zone for some reason. The module can maintain cryogenic sleep for up to three hundred years.

The Thirteenth Servobattalion

THEY HAD PASSED the point of no return.

The enemy was everywhere and camouflage was pointless. The orbital strike had churned up huge areas with nobody immune from its damage, turning testing ground buildings, cyber laboratories and machine hangers into piles of smoking rubble. The ground was pitted with enormous craters leading down into a multitude of underground bunker zones. Admiral Ipatov had made that fateful decision as his nerves could no longer stand the many hours of pressing from the invisible servobattalion. He cursed the ground force command as he watched hundreds of servomechanisms attacking false targets, suffering heavy losses and falling back with nothing, while the enemy appeared in completely unexpected places, hidden by the phantom generators.

The Pilum strike had been the last straw for Ipatov.

Some of the rockets had struck the carefully repaired breach in the planet's space defenses, widening it further by attacking several of the remaining combat stations.

While those in orbit tried to organize a

countermeasure and somehow cover the bare patch of planetary space, another volley by five Phalangers turned the second largest RW base into a smoking ruin, burying the reserve servomechanisms under the rubble.

The admiral was losing it. Even the missile carrier's strike had only partially achieved its goal.

Anchor's secret bases were almost completely destroyed and the space defenses torn asunder, so now the elusive servobattalion had a real chance of sneaking off the planet.

It was impossible to predict or prevent attacks by the Phalangers acting the cover of the new generation phantom generators, while the time for counterattack had been wasted.

The worst thing was that the admiral had no idea what to expect. The enemy unit had risen from the ashes like the mythological phoenix, fired another volley, and hid beneath their masking fields again.

"Nillow!"

The admiral's closest comrade looked no less stressed and exhausted than Ipatov himself.

He appeared a minute later, glanced at the fleet commander with bloodshot eyes and announced, "We've lost two segments of the space defense system. We've got nothing to patch it with. The deployment of the remaining stations precludes their effective use if the enemy tries to break through the cleared 'launch corridor'."

"What's your opinion?"

"It's time to start moving the fleet." Nillow replied. "The fighter barrage won't produce the desired result without the support of heavier ships. The enemy Nibelungs have shown us enough to know what the likely outcome would be of a fight between our smaller ships and the assault carriers."

"By drawing the fleet towards the planet, we're exposing the hypersphere jump point!"

"Yes, we are." Henry agreed, glaring at the summary screens. "But the enemy's goal is to take Anchor. How long will our fleet last without the support of the fighters patrolling low orbit? I believe that only if we gather all our forces and patch the breach in the planet's defenses, using the smaller ships and the surviving combat stations, will we be able to eliminate the breakthrough, crush the assault force and then withstand the enemy fleet. "

"Have you considered the possibility of a repeat attack from the Phalangers?" The admiral asked doubtfully. He had mentally reached the same conclusion as Henry, however, Ipatov lacked a whit of courage to make this decision on his own.

"Data analysis shows that the enemy has used up 100% of their heavy missiles."

"You're certain of that?"

"Yes. There's a risk, of course, but by taking the Elliot into bombing orbit, we activate the global anti-missile defense. A cruiser is not a combat station. Every inch of our armor is protected by laser anti-missile defense units."

Ipatov thought for a minute and then nodded. To keep arguing was pointless. Two damaged frigates were in no state to continue the bombardment, which meant that only the flagship cruiser remained.

The admiral couldn't yet admit it to himself, but his greatest fear right now wasn't the hypothetical attack of the enemy fleet but the possibility that the servobattalion, which had caused him to live through the worst hours of his life and made him doubt his abilities as a fleet commander, would escape Anchor.

No way. I'll crush them. Even if they had to strike the whole area to destroy a battalion hiding under their phantom generators, he would give the order without hesitation.

"I agree with your arguments, Henry. Take the cruiser into low orbit. I'll assemble the other ships in the fleet myself."

"THE ENEMY FLEET has started moving!"

Dietrich's report came while Shmelev waited in angry bewilderment. Shmelev couldn't understand why the assault carriers weren't responding. They should have appeared in the past five minutes but there was no reply from Gorelov.

Communication with the Hoplites heading towards the shore didn't bring any clarity. The weak markers of the assault carriers hiding at the bottom of the ocean were not showing any signs of activity.

Maybe my order didn't reach them through the scattered relay stations?

I doubt it. These devices are hardy and reliable.

Where are you, Colonel?!

GORELOV WATCHED the slowly shutting lid of the preservation chamber.

He felt a thump and then slight rocking as the capsule was propelled out of the airlock and then sank slowly to the ocean floor.

A sickly-sweet gas spread throughout the chamber and Gorelov took a breath, feeling his consciousness fade.

The assault carriers remained unmoving on the ocean floor for a few more seconds, then the cyber system on the flagship Nibelung sent out clear orders.

The forbidding spaceships snapped out of energy-saving mode.

The working jet propellers produced a

significant amount of vibration. The powerful jets of water created thrust and the seven Nibelungs began to ascend to the surface, making almost no noise at all.

The coast defense group's sensors were monitoring the ocean from the shore. The impassive devices noted seven unidentified objects that appeared over the water, as if some fantastical sea monsters had risen from the depths. The waves beat against the sides of the assault carriers and water cascaded off their armor, but due to the working phantom generators, it was impossible to identify what they were from land.

While the network was filled with queries and replies, the assault carriers sped towards shallow water like a well-organized whale pod.

As soon as the Nibelungs slid onto the shorefront sand, the enemy observation and communication systems were doomed. Turning off their jet propellers, the assault carriers switched to combat planetary thrust.

The bay became a boiling pot. Thousands of tonnes of water evaporated, enclosing hundreds of square kilometers in billowing steam. The thermal splash and release of steam were recorded by planetside and orbital scanners, but it all happened too quickly. The cruiser Elliot had just entered low orbit as the Nibelungs lifted off from the planet Anchor, enveloped in clouds of steam.

They immediately split up and assumed various heights, beginning to fire their guns and missile complexes on anything within reach.

FINALLY!

Shmelev felt overwhelming relief when the assault carriers began firing from the rapidly formed steam cover.

"Dietrich, what's going on with our comms? Why isn't Gorelov replying to me?"

"I have no idea."

There was no contact but the Nibelungs' behavior as shown on the tactical monitors seemed quite appropriate. The assault carriers, having created another obvious focal point, three hundred kilometers away from the Hoplites' attack site, then split into two groups. Four assault carriers formed a cover group, while also menacing any enemy ships positioned in low orbit, while the others activated their masking fields and headed to the designated point to meet the battalion machines.

"Dietrich, take over command of the Hoplite group."

"What's the goal, commander?"

"Head to the evacuation point!"

✳ ✳ ✳

THE LONG DAY was fading, the bloody dusk giving way to a night illuminated by a multitude of fires.

Stars twinkled shyly in the sky, occasionally obscured by clouds of smoke or whitish streaks of fog.

Hundreds of machines were moving under the cover of night. Active signatures swarmed across the screen, and Admiral Ipatov understood that the surviving battalion forces would disguise themselves as 'friendlies', so he abandoned his attempts to clear up the situation.

He had no doubts how events would unfold from here.

Carpet bombing would feel like a gentle smack that a loving parent gives their child in comparison to a Trian salvo.

'There's no way you're getting out of this,' The admiral thought with uncharacteristic malice.

A sudden report made him jump, "The fighters in the barrage group have engaged the Alliance assault carriers!"

Curse them... Ipatov was on the brink of a breakdown once again. He had survived so many unexpected and painful blows over the past twelve hours that it was enough to send him insane.

"Trian, immediate readiness for all units!"

The escort carrier was travelling at a

significant distance away from the flagship, surrounded by corvettes, but the admiral could still see Trian's cover begin to twinkle with numerous launches.

All the assault ships and space fighters were thrown by Ipatov into the breach, to destroy the Alliance assault carriers no matter what and to prevent them from collecting the servomachines before the cruiser Elliot delivered its final blow.

CLOUDS. Ephemeral castles at the boundary between day and night.

Up above glowed the stars and a crescent dawn, while below lay a thick and gathering darkness interspersed with crimson fires and lights that flickered on and off as the battle progressed.

"WE LOST the Nibelungs that have just lifted off!"

Ipatov shuddered. He was so tired. The admiral's gaze that slid across the summary screens had lost its clarity and the extreme moral and physical stress made itself felt in episodes of irritability.

He still couldn't figure out his opponent's end goal.

Could he have imagined a day ago that a

single unit, even if it was equipped with the latest technology, would be a threat to all the forces gathered around Anchor?

Of course not, but the fact could not be denied. Half of the planetary bases lay in ruins, the losses among the orbital group and the ground servomechanisms numbered in the thousands, while the cursed servobattalion continued to deliver strike after strike, as elusive as a ghost. Even now, nothing was clear on the summary screens of the tactical system. There were plenty of signatures but where was the guarantee that some of them weren't being generated by the enemy's masking systems?

Where were the seven Alliance assault carriers that had appeared out of the ocean?

It was time for extreme measures.

"Fighters to continue searching out targets. Assault aircraft to cover low orbit. All servomechanisms on the ground — work together to comb through the continent after the orbital bombardment!"

He could see no other way of destroying the enemy unit.

Aboard the cruiser Apostle

ADMIRAL KUPANOV paced back and forth along the bridge.

He was angry and bewildered but could do nothing to affect the situation. What madness was this? The admiral was used to dealing with machines. Cybernation of the fleet had become commonplace over the last five years, and machines went readily into battle with no concern for their own losses.

But now the carefully planned and brilliantly carried out first stage of the operation was slipping out of control, all because a small group of people was refusing to die.

The admiral had taken this factor into account, he knew that they would fight but he didn't expect them to do it with such desperation and skill.

Damn it... He was expending huge amounts of energy to receive data from the Anchor System. Minutes had passed, then hours, but the battle on the planet's surface did not abate. The servobattalion shifted around, slipping away from their adversaries and striking again and again, but not where and how the admiral was expecting.

'Ultimately, my plan hasn't yet fallen

through.' He pondered as he glanced through the latest data obtained from the microsensors flooding the Anchor System. 'Shmelev has launched an attack on the largest RW base in the region.' It was clear to Kupanov that this was a diversion. The machines going to storm the fortifications didn't possess the latest modifications that Shmelev's battalion was equipped with.

The enemy didn't know this, of course, and wouldn't realize that the attack was a distraction... or if they would, it would be too late. It would be good to know what the battalion commander was planning.

How much longer could he keep the fleet in constant readiness for a hyperjump?

'Only a couple more hours.' The admiral answered his own question.

What should he do? Wait in the hope that the Colonies' cruiser finally changes orbit since the ground defenses are on their last legs and the second largest manufacturing complex is a target worth protecting?

One more hour.

What if it doesn't leave high orbit?

'Damn it... I should have sent machines.' The admiral thought in irritation as he sank into an antigravity chair. His legs ached from many hours of pacing along the bridge.

'If the situation doesn't change radically in an hour, my plan is ruined.' Kupanov didn't even consider trying to attack the Colonies' cruiser using his own forces. Like the others, he was terrified of the Light installation and valued his life very highly. No, he would rather put his ambitions on hold than to stick his head between the hammer and the anvil.

A minute later, when the admiral began to grow heavy-lidded, he heard the long-awaited warning signal.

"Pavel Petrovich, good news!"

Kupanov turned around and fixed his tired gaze on the intelligence officer.

"Report."

"We have confirmation of the enemy fleet moving. The cruiser Elliot has entered low planetary orbit. Further analysis of information received from the nanomachines indicates that the enemy ships are completely vulnerable. The Titan missile platform has fired a massive salvo at the planet, the Trian escort carrier has sent reserve groups of assault aircraft and space fighters to Anchor. Considering that Titan needs a quarter of an hour to reload its heavy anti-ship missile launchers, an immediate attack by our fleet will be met with minimal resistance."

"What about the frigates and corvettes?"

"Two frigates have been damaged by the

Pilums. The corvettes are currently reorganizing themselves to provide cover but they won't be able to withstand our attack. In addition, a volley of heavy missiles from Anchor's surface has again knocked out two segments of the planetary defense system. It's the breach that Admiral Ipatov is trying to patch up by moving the cruiser."

After hearing the report, Kupanov knew that his hour had come. The servobattalion had completed the task set before it but never enunciated. It had brought the situation on Anchor to the critical point when the enemy commander believed that any means would do to eliminate the invasion.

"Tell the fleet: they have a minute to prepare for the hyperjump." Kupanov's voice rang with triumph. "Load the operation plan into the ships' tactical systems."

IN APOSTLE'S tactical compartment, the ship's commander turned to the tactical system that had suddenly switched on. He glanced through the plan for the upcoming operation and frowned.

Attacks on the cruiser Elliot were forbidden.

The admiral was no longer hiding his desire to capture the enemy flagship. According to Kupanov's plan, assault modules carrying servomechanisms would head to the cruiser, with cover provided by fighters.

That would have been fine except data analysis indicated that Elliot was preparing for orbital bombardment of the continent. If they didn't strike the cruiser at once, the servobattalion would die as soon as they exited the hypersphere.

It was the price that the admiral was willing to pay for the chance to capture the Light annihilation device. Alexander von Reuben could see what the situation meant but could do nothing to change it.

What would his protests achieve if the timer was counting down the last few seconds before the hyperjump, and the operation was planned down to the last minute?

If Kupanov was successful, he wouldn't care about a little thing like 'friendship', no, he'd make mincemeat out of Alexander for not obeying orders. If the admiral's plan failed for some reason, a protest by the commander of Apostle would place him in the firing line. What a shit situation...

Alexander von Reuben was a man of action. He had a few more minutes remaining while the cruiser was plunging through the space anomaly.

Activating a secure communication channel, he gave several detailed orders to the reserve group, which answered to him and only him. It was all he could do to save the servobattalion.

Anchor. Low planetary orbit
10:25 pm

THE CRUISER ELLIOT reached the orbit required for bombardment.

Admiral Ipatov no longer stared at the screens, instead, he sat slumped in his chair, at the mercy of dark thoughts.

He ignored the reports being delivered to the bridge. The blasted servobattalion would soon be destroyed as the whole continent would be a raging volcano in a minute. It was time to think about something else — how was he going to explain to Head Command why all the planetary bases, testing ground and research facilities had been annihilated?

It was a difficult question that Ipatov hadn't found an answer for.

Three reports came one after another and disrupted his musings. When their meaning penetrated his thoughts, goosebumps suddenly spread over his scalp.

"We've recorded multiple hyperjumps. The target identification system has recognized the Seventh Strike Fleet of the Alliance!"

"Attention! We have found the enemy assault carriers. Our fighters have engaged them."

"The bombardment is complete!"

Ipatov pulled himself together with difficulty and looked at the screens.

Beneath the dark cloud covering the planet's only continent blossomed a painfully bright glow.

In space, the pale hyperjump flashes were accompanied by a firestorm as the Alliance Strike Fleet attacked. Right before Admiral Ipatov's eyes, the two damaged frigates that he had sent into deep space to guard the hyperjump point were turned into clusters of heated gas as they were blasted by the plasma generators of the attacking fleet.

Full defeat.

Ipatov had walked himself into a trap by letting himself be distracted by the cursed servobattalion, causing him to make such a fatal error.

The missile and escort carriers were unfit for action. The cruiser itself was too close to the planet, too far at the bottom of the gravitation well to be able to perform an immediate hyperjump.

'Now they'll smash through the corvettes and there'll be a short duel.' The admiral thought dispassionately.

* * *

IPATOV was wrong.

Crashing through the wall of corvettes and shooting down the Trian missile carrier, which hadn't even had time to reload, the frigates of the Seventh Strike Fleet rushed to attack without opening fire on the cruiser Elliot. Instead of missile salvos and plasma shots directed at the fleet's flagship, it was targeted by... assault modules.

...

Compared to the events occurring in space, the military action on the ground and within Anchor's atmosphere suddenly lost its scope and importance.

The remains of the servobattalion were fighting their way to the pickup point when the four Nibelungs providing cover fire engaged a swarm of space fighters, and cluster bombs began falling from low orbit.

CLOUDS.

Dark and ghostly castles, arcs and bridges, curiously fantastical figures that drifted slowly overhead.

Four assault carriers gained altitude and disappeared in the clouds.

The Mavericks controlling the Nibelungs began to carry out their set task. The ships weren't generating any optical phantoms while under the cover of the Mirages, all the energy was directed at neutralizing signatures and creating the false impression that there was nothing among the cloud castles except air currents.

The scanning complexes of the assault carriers were working in passive mode while the cyber systems received and processed hundreds of signals coming from various foreign objects.

The Nibelung cockpits were empty but the holographic screens in front of the crew seats were nevertheless on, showing not only all the surrounding changes but also the actions performed by the equipment.

Out of the many active signatures, the combat subsystems highlighted only those that clearly belonged to space fighters.

Patience and self-control were not terms that could be applied to machines. The Mavericks permitted no error and felt no fear or doubt. Their goal was to destroy the maximum number of enemy units, and large losses on their side were to be expected.

The first wave of Stilettos[18] passed by the Nibelungs hidden among the clouds, and only once the second wave of fighters had reached their

---

[18] The Stiletto space fighter was deployed in the Colonies' Fleet in 2620.

hover height and the third wave approached within firing range of the upper missile complexes, did the assault carriers begin their attack.

The clouds burst open and the four Nibelungs, casting off the phantom generators, switched to planetary thrust. They were moving in a ladder formation, covering each other and firing out of all their guns.

The effectiveness of the sudden attack exceeded all expectations. The Nibelung-12MT artillery subsystems, capable of simultaneously following hundreds of mobile targets, showed themselves in the best light by aiming each weapon independently and limiting any waste of ammunition or energy.

It seemed at first that the entry of the space fighters into the dense atmospheric layers would end in complete disaster, but the programming on the Stilettos was equally advanced. The pilotless machines performed evasive maneuvers that would have been impossible in the presence of a pilot. The antimissile systems made Anchor's skies bloom with color as if with festive fireworks, but the terrifyingly destructive and swift clash of the cyber machines left no place for illusions. The skies, lit up and shredded by thousands of explosions and laser beams, began to drop burning fragments...

It was a spine-chilling and yet engrossing

scene. The machines were fighting without sparing themselves or their opponents, the ammunition stores growing rapidly empty and the energy levels in the laser installations dropping to critical. Plasma generators failed, pieces of armor flew off into the atmosphere, and then, among the burning Stilettos, a flaming and disfigured assault carrier plunged towards the ground. It was followed by another one, while the third Nibelung exploded in the air, breaking up into several fragments. Only the fourth and last assault carrier, despite extensive damage, continued to fight until it ran out of ammunition.

Only thirty machines remained out of the one hundred and twenty fighters and assault aircraft that had entered Anchor's atmosphere. The rest had been shot down or were critically damaged in the four and half minutes of battle.

Even the servomachines paused and then dispersed in search of cover when burning wreckage began to fall from the sky, with the surviving aircraft maneuvering between them at breakneck speed.

The crash of the assault carriers sounded like a local earthquake and the night became as bright as day due to the numerous smoking torches scattered across the enormous plain.

The buildings and forests were burning, the sky and its stars were obscured by smoke, and only the leaping flames lit up the roiling ash-gray clouds.

THE FIGHT OF THE MACHINES terrified even the experienced pilots.

When a mind is balanced on the edge between life and death, reality is perceived differently. Not everyone but many of those observing the frenzied battle over Anchor froze for an instant and asked themselves the same question.

What are we doing here?

A person who feels like a pawn in the war of machines, trapped between two millstones that apathetically grind down hundreds of thousands tonnes of armor and electronics, can't help but look at the world with different eyes.

A hellish massacre with no purpose, no hope of victory and no guarantee that this war would ever end.

It had been their parents who had crossed all boundaries by handing over the fate of the world to cybernetic beasts.

The planet thrashed in agony, the surface that only yesterday was covered in green now cloaked in ash. The earth, churned up by the mindless rage of explosions, lay dead and flattened, abused and lit up by fires and burning fragments continuing to fall from the sky.

Such a war had no meaning and no hope of

resolution.

The machines exterminating each other didn't care either way. They had no emotions and perceived the deadly fighting as nothing more than work. It meant that the remaining servomechanisms wouldn't stop, that they would repair the bases and rebuild the factories so that machines could build other machines again, and these, in turn, would launch into a mindless fight with the enemy...

Only the Beatrice-4 modules were listening to the pilots' frazzled thoughts. They were the only ones that possessed enough artificial neural networks to absorb not only the combat experience but to also comprehend the feelings of people witnessing current events.

Howard Faragney really did create artificial intelligence capable of understanding current events and developing their own view of reality.

The question was whether anyone was ever going to get off Anchor.

THE PROCESS of self-development in AI modules moved incredibly quickly.

Servomachine cyber systems that had previously been indifferent to concepts like 'destruction' and 'death', suddenly began to think in unison with their pilots, discovering a desperate desire to *live.*

Direct neurosensory contact added the poison of doubt. People's assessment of what was happening wasn't founded in base programming. The extreme pressures of current events made them reject government propaganda but they realized that the painful awareness had come too late.

Whether the young guns and experienced officers wanted it or not, they constantly and subconsciously assessed the situation, while the results and logic of their reasoning was transmitted to the Mavericks.

War's brutal face and its mindless destruction of everything was revealed to all, bringing with it the bitter feeling of one's own blindness. What are we fighting over? Endless space? Why are we destroying each other, exhausting planetary resources, creating machines that obey nothing and nobody except the goals of war and mutual annihilation? What is the point of the galactic slaughter when the same resources could be used to terraform new worlds and to look for ways that do not lead to interplanetary conflicts?

Everything looks different a minute away from death.

Neither the Terran Alliance nor the Free

Colonies had a reason to fight.

They had created an enemy by bringing two civilizations head-to-head and allowing hate to blossom, watering it abundantly with blood. But there was almost nobody left to do the hating since the battlefields were dominated by robotic complexes, for whom war was simply a set of programmed functions.

Of course, the brief time in which the four Nibelungs fought the hive of Stilettos wasn't enough for people to shape their agitated thoughts into something smooth and comprehensible. The understanding came at a subconscious level but the Beatrice-4 modules could read the pilots' inner thoughts like an open book.

They formulated all the revelations for internal use but the cyber systems with their integrated neural modules still had another, almost impossible test ahead of them.

Error. Global error.

A long time ago on planet Earth, back in the early 21st century, before humanity had split up into the citizens of megacities and colonies, was the start of processes that lead to disastrous consequences.

As they climbed the next step of technological progress, people discovered the high-tech era and the explosive development of cybernetics fundamentally changed many processes, subtly transforming terrible events into impersonal statistics.

The era of 'contactless wars' had formed a noxious and non-objective way of thinking, when the victims of missile strikes didn't touch the heart of the person pressing the launch button or giving orders to send bombs or missiles.

When the enemy is nothing more than a marker on the tactical screen and your presence on the battlefield is limited to receiving data from the warhead locked on a target, war loses its human face and becomes a handy tool for solving numerous problems, without affecting the conscience of those in power. This gives rise to ultimate cynicism and the inadequacy of politicians, generals and presidents.

When there is a growing awareness in society and a return to the past, giving up high-tech seems impossible and the 'human factor' is left to blame.

The last step in the fateful chain of events is to consider humanity incompetent when compared to the cyber systems. The apparent panacea, the myth of machine infallibility, is in fact a leap into the abyss.

Machines don't care whom to kill and why.

Where does a civilization lead if it openly advocates total automatization of all processes, when people play the role, at best, of a technician servicing smart and expensive machines?

The answer is obvious.

It leads to Dabog and Anchor.

HAVING WITNESSED the unbridled combat of machines, both yesterday's boys and experienced officers had the same feeling: each one of them desperately wanted to LIVE.

It wasn't cowardice or fain-heartedness or even self-preservation that drove this conscious leap.

The twisted reality, trampled ideals and false idols — everything had collapsed, burning and turning to ash swirling under the feet of the servomachines.

They had to survive, they had to escape this technological nightmare.

Major Shmelev was the first to come to his senses.

They still had a chance.

"Attention, everyone!" The commander of the tattered battalion shook people out of their stupor and gave them a flicker of hope. "All groups to move to the evacuation point! Shoot your way out, no matter what!"

The faded hope flared up again.

The three assault carriers that hadn't

engaged the Stilettos entered the pickup zone and assumed defense positions from where they could also load up the remaining servomachines.

"We're alive, Simon!"

"I hope so, Anton. Stick close to me, there are still plenty of fighters overhead."

"Our Hoplites are close. We'll make it!"

The Phalangers that made up the core of the battalion, freed themselves from the Pilums and L-700 launch platforms and thus increased their speed and maneuverability. They could now also use their anti-missile defense lasers by extending their anti-aircraft batteries from the weapon compartments located beneath the heavy missile slots.

Thus began the forced march.

The landed assault carriers were only fifteen kilometers away, easy enough to cover for the servomachines, but the Stilettos that had survived the fight with the Nibelungs didn't cease their hunt for ground targets.

After the intense fighting and heavy missile fire, many of the phantom generators were glitching and some of the machines couldn't reach their maximum speed due to damaged servomotors. The remaining pilots adjusted their speed to match the slower ones.

TWO GROUPS from the servobattalion headed to the meeting point.

The attack of the space fighters caught them as they marched.

The sky was filled with howling as the rapid Stilettos zoomed close to the ground, bursts of fire churning up the ground, laser charges piercing the thick wall of smoke, and missile launches drawing visible and deadly trajectories in the air.

The servobattalion machines met them in battle, and assumed fighting positions. For the pilots who had survived a Titan salvo, an attack by the fighters didn't seem like the greatest evil.

All the combat qualities of the updated servomachines were now on show.

Snapping back with their guns and anti-aircraft lasers, the depleted battalion forces continued to reduce the distance left to the Nibelungs, which didn't enter the fray on Shmelev's orders and kept their masking shields on.

Let them think that there's not many of us left, that we're tired and trying to rejoin the two groups. Let them keep guessing about what will happen next, just don't let them find the assault carriers.

Shmelev no longer hoped for a miracle or for help to come, but he told himself firmly: since nobody is coming to save us, if we manage to escape, it will be thanks to our own efforts.

THE FIGHTERS attacked continuously, they strafed in pairs, flights, alone, constantly complicating an already difficult situation and forcing the servomachines to move slowly as they warded off attacks from space and yet still suffered losses.

Simon and Anton kept their servomachines as close to each other as possible, employing a simple but effective fighting maneuver. Having suffered extensive damage, the phantom generators no longer hid the signatures but rather blurred them. By walking next to each other, Verkholin and Green appeared as an unidentifiable energy-emitting blob on the scanning complexes of the enemy fighters.

The Stilettos tried to attack the strange signature several times but unsuccessfully. Whenever a fighter got close, its onboard computer suddenly perceived the outline of two Phalangers and the combat autopilots would freeze for a moment as they tried to focus the weapons on one of the servomachines. Simon and Anton would waste no time in blasting the enemy into pieces with their quick-firing anti-aircraft guns.

Verkholin and Green had become closer than

brothers over the past day.

"Simon, turn!"

Anton's warning came just in time. The crumbling edge of a giant crater appeared up ahead, with the Amethyst indicating that the assault carriers were stationed about 500 meters further. Frequent flashes of antimissile lasers could be seen in that direction as the battalion's Hoplites drew the fighters towards them. The light machines with their powerful anti-aircraft complexes stood up quite well to the Stilettos.

"Damn... My short-range scanners are flaking." Green just managed to stop the Phalanger a few meters away from the soft and crumbling edge of the crater. "Long-range scanning is fine, but short-range..." He didn't have time to finish the sentence as a flight of Stilettos appeared out of the gloom.

"Anton!"

Verkholin's machine rushed forward, using its body to cover Green's damaged Phalanger but the trick with the signatures didn't work this time. There were more fighters than targets so the onboard computers didn't have a dilemma about which servomachine to attack. Two Stilettos fired their missiles and soared back up, avoiding return fire, while the third fighter rapidly slowed down and pounded them with its bow guns.

Verkholin managed to shoot down two of the

missiles, then his machine was rocked by a direct hit, as if a sledgehammer had pounded his armor. Anton lost his sense of direction for a moment and everything went black before his eyes due to the feedback, which showed the seriousness of the damage sustained by his Phalanger.

Anton barely kept himself from falling and shouted at Beatrice, but pointlessly, as it turned out. The upper gun and laser complexes had been razed off by the shell fire and the Maverick couldn't physically respond to the attack. There were no operational missiles left and the gun pods weren't suitable for firing on rapidly moving air targets.

'Sorry, Bea.' Anton thought automatically as he sent a request for cover to the Hoplites. He then found Green's machine on the scanners and noted with relief that it had sustained no critical damage.

"How are you doing, Simon?"

"I'm staying upright. The actuators are jamming."

"Go around the crater and head to the carriers. I'll cover you."

It was hard. Physical and emotional fatigue didn't count as the combat stimulants continued to perk them up, but the machines were beginning to break down.

The damaged servomotors, the pitted and burnt armor, the failing systems — considering the depth of full neurosensory contact between the human mind and the executive subsystems, all this triggered symptoms of overwhelming fatigue and deterioration, while the areas of critical failure flared up like pain.

"Doppelganger systems are on. I'm off."

"Go on, Simon, I'll stay in position. Let me know when you reach the defense zone of the assault carriers."

"Two minutes, Anton."

"The Hoplites are nearby. Play it cool."

THEY WERE too late.

There was a sudden lull as if before a storm. Anton would have never thought that machines could generate sensations similar to a natural phenomenon.

Silence fell.

The Stilettos ferociously attacking the battalion suddenly sprayed in all directions like a flock of terrified birds and began to rapidly gain height.

The Amethyst sensors noted that the enemy Aquilas had stopped their march and their signatures, which could be now clearly read on the targeting monitor, suddenly began blurring together with the nearby fortifications, which had several entrances to the underground zone.

'Are they hiding?' Wondered Verkholin and then came the lost hope, 'Is it our fleet?' but Beatrice dispelled that suggestion.

It's the lull... before the storm...

What is a lull, Anton? And why are you alarmed by the enemy's retreat?

Now's not the time. I'll explain later. Watch the scanners!

"Simon, how are you?"

"Getting there slowly. I have about 300 meters still to go."

Anton glanced over the holographic screens. He was liking what was happening less and less. The sudden silence set him on edge more than the constant stress of the battle.

He had changed, irrevocably changed over the last day. The sense of foreboding was unbearable, his mind, pumped full of combat stimulants, demanded clarity and action.

He called Shmelev. "What's happening, Commander?"

"Hurry up and get to the Nibelungs, Anton." Shmelev responded. "Dietrich's unit is under cover, the rest need to get to the carriers quick-smart!"

He feels something too.

Anton followed the order and started moving, circling the enormous crater left over from the missile strike. As he walked along the hole's perimeter, he automatically noted that the presence of a deep crater indicated that this region contained underground facilities. At a depth of fifteen meters, his scanners picked up a break in the powerful slabs. The crater had triggered a landslide but there was still plenty of space underground for heavy equipment to get into the enemy tunnels.

'This whole continent is a bunker zone.' Anton thought.

He could already see the Nibelungs on the screens with the masking fields trembling above them. Dietrich Shelgan's unit, consisting of one Phalanger and two Hoplites, was slowly moving along the edge of the crater as it controlled access to the evacuation zone.

It all happened very suddenly, just like Anton was afraid of.

There were still three hours remaining until sunrise but the darkness was disrupted by a patchy glow beyond the horizon that lit up the heavy clouds.

He was puzzled but a few seconds later, when the sixty-tonne Phalanger was swayed by a shock wave, all his theories fizzled one after another. A firestorm of orbital bombardment was rapidly approaching the carrier landing zone, stretching from one horizon to the other.

Anton was flooded with terror, and hope was

replaced by despair. He wasn't going to make it in time.

A squally wind was raising clouds of dust and ash and the holographic monitors showed a rapidly approaching, all-destroying wall of gigantic explosions. The gusts of wind and shock waves were gaining the strength of a hurricane. The assault carriers drew in their landing supports and dropped their bellies to the ground. They didn't have time launch and half of the servobattalion was still outside...

The massive explosions left behind land that was dead to a depth of ten to fifteen meters, and approached at an unimaginable speed that made them impossible to avoid.

Solutions come in flashes of intuition in such moments.

"Anyone who can hear me! There is a break in the slabs at the bottom of the crater! The bunker zone is below us!" Verkholin barely had time to utter these few short phrases when his machine lost its balance at the edge of the crater. The loose soil under its feet, as well as the pounding shock waves, pushed the Phalanger to take a fateful step that would be either its ruin or salvation. The servomachine tipped over, crashed through the weakened ceiling of the underground facilities and disappeared in the bunker zone.

Anton lost consciousness and didn't see if

anyone heard his last words or not.

A few seconds later, a wall of explosions swept over the servobattalion's last position.

DOWN IN THE BUNKER ZONE, the explosions pounding the continent felt like a tremor.

In some places, the ceiling caved in, and then the rhythmical thumping was joined by the sound of falling rubble. Occasionally, the tunnels and enormous halls were filled with shock waves that knocked down the thick gates, ripped stationary equipment off its mountings and left behind nothing but empty walls.

One of the underground facilities, built as a reserve launch platform for space fighters, was located not far from the landing site of the assault carriers.

It was here that Verkholin's machine had fallen in, together with the cascading tonnes of earth, as well as two other Phalangers, which had been knocked down into the crater by the shock waves.

They had tipped over and were covered in earth, but saved from complete destruction.

Three people had thus survived orbital bombardment by complete chance. Simon Green, Anton Verkholin and Andrey Tavgalov.

The sound of explosions faded slowly away but the rumble of landslides could still be heard underground. The worst was over.

Simon was the first to awaken.

It took him a while to figure out where he was. His last memory was a wall of explosions rushing at him like an attacking fighter, then the crushing blows, loss of balance, falling...

The bunker zone.

He could feel the vibration from the unwinding emergency stabilization system beneath the pilot's cradle, while the display panels showed activation of the back-up control circuits. While Green was out cold, his 'combat partner' had done quite a lot. The twisted and damaged actuators had been ejected, with backup sections of the locomotor apparatus inserted in their place. The Phalanger's cyber system hadn't gotten rid of all the damage, of course, but the machine could maintain balance and move around again.

Things were worse with the armor coating and the weapons systems but Green didn't show any emotion as he listened to the mental report about the lack of ammunition for the missile launchers and the damage to the accumulators for the defense lasers.

He didn't want to think about war anymore. Thinking about the death of his friends sapped the last of his strength and his soul had burned to a cinder. Simon had crossed a boundary, leaving his past behind. Eighteen hours of almost constant fighting had aged him mentally and physically.

He had become someone else. Even the drawn, ashen face seemed to belong to a different person.

Did he feel fear? Yes. Green was afraid of one thing: that he would turn on the communications system and nobody...

He shuddered when he received a reply.

The response from two Mavericks, as different as if the pilots themselves had answered, shocked Simon. It was the machines belonging to Verkholin and Tavgalov, the captain who had commanded the special operations unit at the start of the operation.

Together with the astounding news that both pilots were alive and were currently under the care of the combat life support machines, Simon received information that his servomachine wasn't the only one located forty meters underground.

A conical pile of earth and debris shifted beside him.

Simon thought of a miracle, he couldn't believe until the last moment that something could have a happy ending on this world. Nevertheless, the outlines of two servomachines appeared a minute later, and then he heard Verkholin's weak voice, "Simon?"

"Anton!" His voice broke from the emotion and were words really necessary in such a situation?

Three servomachines extracted themselves from the avalanche and stood in the center of an enormous empty hangar. Their pilots, having just regained their senses and alive only thanks to the combat life support systems, stared at the tactical monitors in mute shock.

Among the broken lines of the underground facilities stood out a sloped tunnel leading to the surface.

"Let's go up." Anton said hoarsely.

"Where? What for?" Tavgalov had just regained consciousness and his mind was still grappling with the terror of the last few seconds before he fell.

"Up." Verkholin replied. "My Amethyst is showing signs of activity in the assault carriers. Maybe we're not the only ones who survived?"

Anchor
03:12. 13 August 2624

IT WAS STILL night up above.

Darkness cloaked the disfigured ground, where the dead soil was mixed with the wreckage of combat vehicles.

The whole continent had been burned from one edge to the other and pitted with massive craters. There were no forests, rivers or buildings left. The orbital bombardment had wiped out the terrain with only occasional fragments of reinforced concrete jutting out among the smoking craters, like the bones of a mythical animal.

"Simon, check the transports. Andrey, you're staying with me on guard duty. Be prepared for any eventuality. Keep scanning the horizon."

"Got it." Captain Tavgalov said meekly.

He was in a state of shock caused by full neurosensory contact with his servomachine. If Simon and Anton had survived the merge with their cybernetic systems easily, almost without noticing it among the intense fighting, Andrey was a novice and was unprepared for such a psychological test. He was experiencing the brunt of the 'internal rebirth'.

GREEN DID NOT RECOGNIZE his surroundings. The scanning complex was picking up activity from one of the three assault carriers, but the battalion's failed evacuation zone had been replaced with a monotonous and pitted plain.

The assault carrier was somewhere close...

Green's Phalanger made its way cautiously among the treacherous craters, scanning every inch of the battered land.

The smoldering earth impeded the search as apart from the high temperature causing thermal interference, the ground was packed with metal. Furthermore, some of the fragments of servomachines and assault carriers continued to consume energy from their internal sources, creating a false map of fragmented and unidentifiable signatures.

Simon continued his search although he was beginning to doubt whether Anton had truly seen a whole signature. No, Verkholin wouldn't mess around with such things.

At long last, the holographic monitor linked to the Amethyst showed something similar to the emergency power configuration of an assault carrier. According to the data, the overturned Nibelung was lying on the slope of one of the cavities that looked like Moon craters.

"Anton, I found the signature. Get up here."

Green's Phalanger walked another fifty meters and stopped at the edge of a gigantic crater.

There was indeed an assault carrier lying on the slope, thrown there by the blast waves.

It was highly doubtful that the Nibelung, its armor gaping with holes, could return to space, but this wasn't what bothered Simon in that moment.

Some of the servomachines had already taken

their places aboard the assault carrier at the time of the orbital strike. There was a chance that some of the fighters inside had survived.

He didn't rush down headlong, waiting for Verkholin and Tavgalov to arrive at the crater's edge.

The beep of the warning system and an abrupt feeling of alarm made Simon jump.

Something was wrong, but what?

He concentrated on the outline of the Nibelung and suddenly realized that hiding behind the assault carrier and using its signature to disguise themselves, were enemy servomachines.

"Anton, Andrey, get back!"

His cry sounded at the same time as the servomachines began to fire.

Rocket launchers struck from behind the Nibelung. The anti-missile lasers no longer worked on Simon's machine and the anti-aircraft guns had been destroyed in previous battles. There were only a few shots remaining in the gun pods, but neither he nor Beatrice had enough time to do anything.

The rockets struck Simon's Phalanger, burning through the worn-out armor over the cockpit.

✳ ✳ ✳

BUBBLING FOAM coated his lips. His mind wandered back and forth from illusion to the present, defined by hoarse breaths and loud heartbeats...

Simon no longer felt scared. The wall of listless indifference separated him from the roaring reality, but Beatrice, the red-haired girl, continued to control the servomachine. The Phalanger's armor could not withstand the heavy laser fire and took on a crushing missile salvo. Two missiles penetrated the armor and exploded in the cockpit but the servomachine only swayed as if a giant had been slapped in the face...

The consequences of the hit were in fact much more severe.

Simon breathed hoarsely, with a strained whistling sound — a shell fragment had torn open his suit, punctured his lung and gotten stuck in the back of the chair.

He didn't feel any pain in the first few seconds and the pain wasn't the most important part. He tried to take a breath and couldn't, then he was suddenly overcome by wheezing and convulsive coughing. The helmet's projection visor became splattered with blood, saliva bubbled on his lips and he couldn't speak. It was hard to move, as if his body had suddenly and permanently betrayed him.

'I'm dying.' Came the detached thought. Purplish-black spots swam before his eyes, his ears were ringing, and his breathing and heartbeat had shifted from unconsciously perceived phenomena to the focus of his reality.

His consciousness was fading. His perception of the outside world disappeared but his mind continued to live and think. Surreal images appeared one after another in his mind's eye. Through the fog filling his mind, he saw the image of a cheerful and slightly insolent red-haired girl that he had created. The embodiment of his elusive dream of happiness.

No, she wasn't the delusion of a dying mind.

Beatrice. She sat in the pilot's chair, not wearing a spacesuit for some reason, but rather a simple yet incredibly beautiful dress. Her bare feet were tucked under her and her slender pale fingers danced across the textoglyphs on the numerous holographic keyboards and touchscreens.

She continued the fight, not letting the servomachine tip over. The screens showed a clear metallic flash as she dropped the launch tubes for the tactical missiles due to the critical damage they had sustained. Fifty-caliber guns immediately appeared on the upper weapon pylons instead, the last, backup weapon to which the Phalanger still had some ammunition.

Simon wasn't up to doing any shooting, however. He gasped, choking on blood, wondering why it couldn't just end quickly.

Quickly meant forever. The combat life support system couldn't let this happen.

Yes, the pilot was mortally wounded, but as it turned out, not everything depended on the person's will in a fight, and there were certain hidden life and death criteria.

Simon felt a hot and sticky terror when something cold and inanimate slipped into his chest through the wound and shifted around in there, erasing the pain and leaving behind a clear and unpleasant sensation of a foreign body moving and palpating him from the *inside*, delivering little jabs that produced waves of dizzying heat, which then changed to artificial and feverish energy.

'I can't... I don't want to anymore.' The cough still tore at his throat although blood was no longer pooling on his lips. His helmet screens were covered in a brown, disgusting film through which he could barely make out images. He began to sink into his dream world again, so desirable but appearing for only brief moments.

Bea... Take this shit out of me...

The red-haired girl turned her head but said nothing, only put her finger to her lips. She stood up abruptly and took a step towards the cockpit wall, which suddenly turned into a long tunnel...

She was leaving him.

The pilot's cradle surrounded by holographic monitors was now empty. She hadn't said a word and Simon stared longingly after her, not realizing that he had died.

The combat life support system had been unable to fix his injury.

Simon felt a strange sensation: the world around him faded, he no longer felt pain or despair or the cold touch of the reanimation unit. He was only dimly aware that he had to take the seat vacated by Beatrice.

Maverick's chair.

Simon watched with mute astonishment as his arms began to dissipate, he no longer had a body, only the memory of one, and even that disappeared a second later.

TAVGALOV FOUND HIMSELF in the middle of the fight and almost immediately lost all sense of direction. The sensations transmitted through the implant continued to stun his mind. He was used to his armored spacesuit and had trouble perceiving himself as *integrated* into an enormous but very sensitive and responsive mechanical body.

All the sensations harmful to an unprepared mind kept crashing over him: his head spun and his consciousness tried to slip away, but the combat life support system wasn't going to let that happen and controlled this mental shock after a few seconds.

Splitting open the crimson black, a dim light struck in his eyes and he saw three dozen goals as contrasting monochromatic outlines. He felt himself *walking*, shaking the ground, an even and confident tread, as if he had spent all life in full neurosensory contact with the formidable fighting machine.

Tavgalov panicked but quickly got himself under control as he realized that mental hysteria wasn't going to help the situation.

How do I keep balance?!

It had been very different during training, when he hadn't experienced the *depth* of direct connection with the cyber system and its executive subsystems, which shook him to the core.

His reflexes were now the Maverick's reflexes, the transformation began and ended so quickly that his back was drenched with sweat but there was no way back. Without making a single independent step or firing a single shot, he automatically and almost casually turned his attention to multiplying signatures, and realized with a belated chill that he was seeing the legendary Aquilas, the descendants of the peaceful agrarian giants of Dabog, now adapted for fighting.

They were approaching from all directions. The sensations were overwhelming but at the same time, something was dampening his emotions, reducing the razor-sharp feelings to flawed semitones. Viscous torches flashed overhead (or was it over the cockpit?) and immediately broke up, forming a ringing swarm of dividing warheads. The ground beneath the Phalanger's feet thrashed in convulsions, hundreds of explosions erased his surroundings, creating new lifeless landscapes made up of only craters and smoldering earth, sparks and ash.

Tavgalov kept his machine from falling for some time; shock waves struck from different sides and the sensory perception only worsened the effect. He suddenly panicked but again, only briefly, until the first laser beam threw up a fountain of smoldering sparks and ash right under his Phalanger's legs.

Automatically ducking out of the away, Tavgalov realized that he wasn't really keeping the massive servomechanism upright. His mind wasn't aware of the work of hundreds of cybernetic subsystems, yet the executive nodes instantly responded to not only his conscious thoughts but also subconscious impulses. If he didn't focus too hard and try to interfere in the automatic procedures, controlling the machine was no more difficult than sending impulses from his muscles to the combat suit.

There was one thing that the captain wasn't aware of as he directed his mechanism towards the targets. In just one minute, he had merged so deeply with the cybernetic servosystem that he could no longer return from it. He absorbed the superhuman strength and threw it at the enemy; his thoughts and emotions seemed so intense that the world would always appear bleak without them. The mind of the unprepared pilot had become hostage to the deepened feelings of neurosensory contact but what was even worse was that Andrey didn't even think to curb the hate building inside him. In truth, he hated war more than he hated the enemy, but his mind couldn't separate the two in these moments, so the Maverick module absorbed the feeling of maleficent fury and hatred of everything that was happening around him.

Beatrice picked up the pilot's urge and spat out a barrage of fire towards the enemy. Tavgalov's Phalanger hadn't taken part in the fighting and still had all its ammunition. Right now, it looked like an enraged monster suddenly set loose and given the opportunity to destroy everything in its path.

✻ ✻ ✻

VERKHOLIN SAW Simon's machine sway as the missiles struck their target.

He tried to get in contact with Green but to no avail. His friend's Phalanger continued moving but the servomachine unexpectedly slowed down, as if the cyber system had suffered a terrible blow and couldn't overcome it.

"Simon, come in!"

Silence in the communicator.

Anton looked around him. A dusky hell reigned on the holographic screens. The Amethyst sensors picked up the attacking ships of the Alliance Seventh Assault Fleet but this didn't make things any better. They had arrived too late from the hypersphere and their attack could hardly change the fate of the Thirteenth Servobattalion.

Particles of the fight...

Shreds of thought, fragmented perception, devastating shock and at the same time, a surge of energy generated by the combat system's metabolic interference.

Verkholin tried to keep himself together but it had been such a long and difficult day and his self-control wasn't endless. The voice of reason suddenly began to drown among hysterical emotions of the fight, warping goals and objectives. He was no longer fighting over of a piece of alien land, the ground burning beneath the Phalanger's feet and swirling clouds of ash would never forgive this human madness. This planet had been murdered, burned and mangled. Soon its atmosphere would grow turbid and, just like Dabog, it would be beset by a nuclear winter.

The signature of the last surviving assault carrier, with live pilots and machines undamaged by the orbital bombardment possibly still on board, swam in his vision, while the signatures of the enemy servomechanisms that had ambushed them multiplied behind it.

Green's Phalanger was moving very slowly and hesitantly as if shell-shocked. Smoke billowed from its cockpit and Anton noticed with horror the two holes in its armor.

'Simon is unconscious at best.' Flashed the thought that Verkholin could neither confirm nor deny. The data exchange channel had switched off and the cyber systems wasn't replying for some reason.

Damn it.

He dodged a laser volley and saw the multiplying signals appearing from behind the Nibelung and belonging to enemy servomachines.

Four pilotless Aquilas supported by a dozen walking lasers and a rocket launcher battery rushed to attack.

Anton didn't try to avoid the fight, he only thought bitterly that the fleet, which had broken through Anchor's space defenses, was ignoring the remaining, isolated servomachines continuing the fight on the planet's surface.

They don't need us anymore. They used us and then abandoned us.

The ash-covered planet was no longer a threat or of interest to the Alliance space forces. Admiral Kupanov could now report that the most powerful research station, as well as a stronghold of the Free Colonies' Fleet, has been destroyed.

Verkholin felt absolutely wretched.

His thoughts were interrupted by a missile salvo.

Anton looked around and realized that it was Captain Tavgalov who was firing. The Phalanger that hadn't taken an active part in the previous battles, now suddenly took the lead, behaving furiously but quite directly. Moving along the perimeter of the crater, the captain fired heavily from all his weapons. The roar of the launching rockets, the deafening staccato of the main caliber guns, the hiss of the anti-aircraft lasers, and the enemy's return fire all merged into a single feeling of danger.

Tavgalov's only result was increased attention from the enemy. Compared to Simon's machine, which had lost control and was *wandering* among the craters and heading away from the Nibelung, and Anton's Phalanger, who was in no hurry to rush into the fray, the captain's machine appeared the most dangerous and at the same time, the softest target.

He needs saving.

Anton had no illusions about the combat capabilities of his machine. He was out of missiles, the anti-aircraft guns were empty and only two out of twenty anti-missile lasers were still functioning.

The only thing remaining was ten shells in each gun pod. It was a lot, considering Verkholin's experience.

Bea, single fire mode! Right gun is yours, left gun is targeting on sight!

He no longer had any hope left. The behavior of Simon's machine gnawed at his heart with foreboding. Green wouldn't have abandoned control, so that means...

Don't think that.

"Captain, save your shells! Your ammo isn't endless!" Anton's shout had no effect. Tavgalov seemed to have gone mad, moving along the crumbling edge of the enormous crater and ignoring the return fire. The armor of his heavy servomachine so far withstood the barrage, but how long would it last without skillful maneuvering?

No more than another minute.

Verkholin took advantage of the situation. His machine, which had stayed a safe distance from the edge of the depression, now picked up speed and rushed forward. The cockpit turned and the right gun under Beatrice's control used the indirect targeting system to fire three single shots, sending shells into the seemingly 'dead zone' behind the assault carrier, where the rocket launchers were firing from.

Anton's mind was plunged into a different reality woven together by servomachine sensors. He ceased to feel human in such moments, becoming someone else instead. Even his body's physical manifestations no longer bothered him, otherwise, Verkholin would have felt the pain in his chest, the irregular heartbeat and ragged breathing, but no, the combat metabolic correction system erased the pain and cut off the unpleasant, anxious feelings that prevented the pilot from focusing on his goal.

Anton brought his Phalanger behind the four Aquilas attacking Captain Tavgalov.

The rocket launchers had fallen silent but the servomachines were being protected by several LDL-55's.

'Take care of them.' Verkholin sent the mental command as he aimed the left gun at the enemy.

Beatrice did as she was asked. She had seven shells remaining, which the Maverick spent in four seconds. The sniper fire from the 150-mm gun lit up the grim crater with gigantic explosions, and the left gun under Anton's control began to fire at the same time.

He struck with short, two-shell bursts, splitting open the weaker rear plating on the enemy Aquilas, which had rushed ahead to finish off Captain Tavgalov's machine, when it suddenly stopped and became enveloped in clouds of poisonous green steam.

It all ended as rapidly as it had begun.

The right gun's electromagnetic breech block clicked twice, empty, as Beatrice had used up the last shell, yet two active LDL-55 signatures could still be seen among the fresh craters and burning servomechanisms. The four Aquilas stopped on the steep slope, one of them blazing like an enormous torch and the others struggling to manage their critical injuries.

One after another, the tanks holding the jet fuel for their jump accelerators began exploding. The flames burst upwards with a roar, spreading across the area and then twisting like fading tornadoes.

Anton reversed, intuitively predicting the timing of the response shots. The two remaining walking lasers burst out of the flame and smoke but Verkholin was ready for them. Two targets, two last shells. He fired the shots, feeling intensely, overwhelmingly tired as he became aware of the spreading pain in his chest.

A sign flashed on the information monitor, informing him of the lack of ammunition and inability to reload.

Whatever.

The fight was over.

Bea, I need the comms working!

Anton stopped the Phalanger. Something clicked in the neck ring of his suit. His cheeks and nose felt numb, he couldn't feel his face or control his facial expressions. The injectors kept jabbing him with excessive doses of combat stimulants but Anton ignored the painful sensations as had become his habit. Right now, he only cared about the communication channel.

Tavgalov's machine wasn't responding to calls. The servomechanism was shrouded in clouds of poisonous green steam from the punctured cooling system. It posed a serious threat as it could explode at any moment. Verkholin made the only possible decision in this situation and gave the mental order, 'Bea, use the command channel. Turn off reactor remotely and eject the pilot, if possible.'

Understood. I'm on it.

Now Anton could finally focus his attention on Green's servomachine. "Simon, come in!"

No response. Green's Phalanger continued

moving in a wide arc, as if trying to circle around the site of the sudden skirmish. Anton switched on the backup information channel and requested a status report from the other machine.

The response was immediate but it came from neither Simon nor the Maverick module. It was the emergency subsystem, which was activated only in extreme or critical situations.

Pilot is dead. Beatrice-4 module is non-functional. Reason for the failure is not clear.

The chest pain became unbearable and finally swamped Anton's consciousness, breaking through the combat stimulants and the substances that temporarily made the body able to withstand overwhelming loads.

His heart hurt. A liquid fire spread through his chest, his thoughts became jumbled and his consciousness suddenly fragmented. Anton drew a few frantic breaths and fell quiet.

His mind could no longer perceive reality. Verkholin's heart stopped.

Anton was killed by the combat life support system but his mind resisted death for several more seconds. He instinctively continued to maintain direct neurosensory contact with Beatrice's artificial neural networks.

Verkholin's Phalanger remained standing at the edge of the huge crater. Undefeated.

Low orbit around Anchor
Aboard the cruiser Elliot

ADMIRAL IPATOV woke up in a murky half-light.

Someone had managed to put him in a suit, but Elliot's bridge was shrouded in gray smoke oozing from the decorative panels and preventing him from seeing if anyone else was still alive. The life-support system in the combat suit turned on automatically as soon as the helmet visor clicked shut. The scanners worked in a similar manner but they hadn't switched to standard mode for some reason.

The admiral tried to move and to his indescribable relief, the servomuscles responded to the tension in his muscles, lifting several tonnes of armor with the man trapped inside into an upright position.

Restarting the scanning systems didn't take long and as soon as the necessary subsystems turned on, so did the projection visor. The smoke seemed to vanish but the scene captured by the scanners and processed by the interference suppression system didn't make him feel any better. The bridge was no longer the command center. Only the lights of the reserve power system twinkled among the disfigured control panels.

His memory kicked in.

He remembered how the cruiser's plating shuddered when more than two dozen assault modules force docked themselves to it.

They split open the armor and the Alliance's assault servomechanisms rushed down the corridors and decks, blindly destroying all the equipment in their way, crushing all resistance and interrupting the power so that the backup systems couldn't turn on.

They burst into the cockpit and practically riddled it with bullets in 10-15 seconds.

The admiral remembered falling to the floor as he tried to hide from the intense fire behind the deck ledge, then something had exploded nearby and he had lost consciousness.

Having regained his senses, he was in no hurry to move. It was too late to try and do something and only one thought was bothering him. *I need to know that the Light installation has undocked.*

He understood why the enemy assault servos didn't try to seize control of the deck subsystems and instead destroyed everything in their way. The one who orchestrated this mission knew about the self-destruction device, or at least suspected that it existed, but had no idea how it worked and what controlled it.

They didn't want the cruiser and they didn't

need the planet — the whole operation was aimed at capturing the antimatter synthesis device.

The admiral found the nearest airlock using his scanners and started to make his way out of the compartment, pushing the twisted and crumpled bulkheads out of the way with the strength of his servosuit.

ONCE OUT ON the Elliot's casing, the admiral looked around.

His worst suspicions were confirmed — the bow of the ship with its characteristic swelling of the Light installation was practically untouched, and even worse, the automatic detachment unit hadn't activated.

He could still fix the situation. He didn't wait for help or a miracle. There are some situations when one must rely solely on oneself.

Ipatov secured himself to the cruiser's armor and looked along the side of the mammoth ship, noting the path ahead.

He could see the smoking and broken armor plates of the outer casing with the combat islands rising overhead. On one hand, the extensive damage and numerous obstacles helped to hide his tiny figure even from the scanners, on the other hand, how long would it take for him to cross the two kilometers for twisted plating?

There's not enough time.

There was another way of reaching the target.

Between the cruiser's inner and outer hulls, a narrow space contained special technical control stations connected by a sturdy cable network, which was protected from mechanical damage by thick, armored sleeves.

The assault bots couldn't get into the narrow technical recess space, only specially constructed technical servos could do it... and a man who knew certain places in the casing where the access terminals to the cable network were located.

He needed to hurry. Ipatov knew the exact location of the access points to the emergency technical network. The network wasn't a threat during battle as its components only switched on if more than fifty percent of the cruiser was damaged.

Technical access was usually required for various operations with damaged compartments. If connected to the network, one could unlock the emergency bulkheads, establish a connection with decks cut off from the ship's general network, send instructions and perform minor manipulations with the equipment. For example, one could switch on the secondary air supply system and basically duplicate all the actions of the emergency subsystems if required.

And only a few senior officers knew that, among the things that could be done using the backup cable network, one could activate the self-destruct option on the Light installation.

This required the knowledge of special access codons and the correct input sequence of apparently harmless technical commands.

Ipatov reached the inconspicuous technical hatch and opened it with a special mechanical key.

Beneath the oval section of armor lay a small control panel with a textoglyph keyboard.

Taking a shuddering breath, the admiral secured himself to the casing and began to enter the command sequence.

Aboard the cruiser Apostle

"THE INSTALLATION is ours," Von Reuben watched the technical servomechanisms move across the bow of the cruiser Elliot. "We've managed to disable the automatic undocking device and now the technicians are dealing with the self-destruct system."

"Are your people experienced enough?" Kupanov asked.

"Certainly. But we can't claim success until

we've neutralized the main charge. Self-destruct devices are tricky beasts."

"Don't jinx it." Kupanov growled.

...The explosion struck unexpectedly.

The silent flame broke through the plating on the cruiser's bow and formed a blinding ball of fire, burning the armor plates and the technical servos scuttling over them.

The raging ball expanded and then burst like a soap bubble, fading away in short bursts of flame after only a few seconds.

Kupanov choked on the next self-congratulatory sentence and gripped the chair arms to stand up, then, seeing a hideous hole where the Light annihilation device used to be, slumped back in his chair and closed his eyes without uttering a sound.

Planet Anchor. Early morning
13 August 2624

THE SUN WAS RISING, spilling the unnatural and painful blush of dawn.

Thousands of tonnes of ash and dust hung in the air.

It seemed as if there would never be any meaningful activity here. Life on the planet had perished, and nothing could have survived the events of the past few days, not nature or humans or combat machines.

The gusting wind had quietened down. Large flakes of swirling ash continued to fall slowly from the crimson skies.

The orbital bombardment had not only destroyed all life and utterly changed the terrain, but had also revealed certain secrets of the past which had been ignored by beings only concerned with mutual extermination.

At the site where the Thirteenth Servobattalion had perished, on the slope of a giant funnel, the ashy soil slowly sliding to the bottom exposed an impressively-sized fragment of time-darkened armor.

The unusual, round artificial device rested at a depth of ten meters from the surface, where there had never been any military buildings.

A sign could still be discerned on the armored plating, which was repeated on all its segments:

Earth. Ark Colonial Transport.

A SUDDEN GLOW broke through the gathering dust cloud around noon.

The landing spaceship looked threatening, a streamlined hull 100 meters in length, the gentle swellings of combat platforms and massive rotating motor sections. An Alliance assault carrier was approaching the stricken ground through the crimson murk.

Having scanned its surroundings, the Nibelung-12MT landed in the area where the remains of the Thirteenth Servobattalion had taken their last stand.

The Nibelung's landing struts touched the plowed earth and for a minute the outline of the ship was obscured by clouds of ash. Then the thick cloud began to disperse and the first servomechanisms dispatched from the assault carrier appeared in the gloom.

Holographic screens glowed before the empty chairs in the cockpit.

According to the lines of text that appeared on the information screens from time to time, the assault carrier had been kept inside a hangar on the flagship cruiser Apostle of the Seventh Strike Fleet until recently.

Another few lines at the top of the central screen indicated that the Nibelung was currently carrying out a secret mission on the personal orders of Admiral von Reuben.

Aim: find and extract servomachines of the Thirteenth Battalion, regardless of the extent of damage read the sign on the central information screen. *Completion status: zero percent.*

FOR TWO DAYS, the technical servomechanisms

combed the area, marking spots where they found damaged servomachines with the right labels on electronic charts.

By the morning of the third day of the search and rescue mission, heavy equipment exited the assault carrier to remove the servomachines.

Ten towing machines disappeared into the gloom. They returned to the Nibelung several hours later with six Phalangers and four Hoplites. According to the search mechanisms, the other servomachines had been completely destroyed, with only fragments remaining.

Aboard the cruiser Apostle
17 August 2624

ADMIRAL VON REUBEN took the call coming from the Anchor System on his personal communication channel. He hadn't told anybody about the assault carrier sent to the surface of the incinerated planet.

Having heard the message, he responded with a code that prompted the Nibelung to perform a hyperjump. Closing the variable frequency channel, the admiral used his backup long-distance communication device.

Von Reuben's former commander served on

Vesuvius, having been transferred there after being wounded in battle.

"Good morning, John."

The tired face of an older man appeared on the screen. "Alexander?"

"That's right. You recognized me?"

"How could I not? It's not like we're strangers."

"I have some business to discuss with you, Commander." The admiral said the last word with sincere respect.

"Well, I'm not your commander any longer..."

"There's no need for that." Interrupted von Reuben. "I'm not contacting you as the admiral of a fleet."

"This is a personal request?"

"Yes. Let's call it that."

"I'm listening."

"A Nibelung will arrive on Vesuvius today with damaged mechanisms on board. My request is — please accept it would making too much fuss. Restore the servomachines without touching the Maverick modules, if that's possible. Then send the repaired mechanisms to the Seventh Strike Fleet, specifically to the cruiser Apostle. Can you do that?"

"Sure, not a problem."

"Thank you, John. I'll explain the rest when we meet in person. Now, I've got to go, sorry."

The admiral touched a sensor to sever the connection. There was nothing more to talk about right now, plus, it was dangerous. Admiral Kupanov was being awfully suspicious lately. In his ongoing struggle for power, he could readily suspect von Reuben of trying to discredit him as commander.

The commander of the Apostle was in fact pursuing a completely different goal.

He had recently spoken to Howard Faragney, who was inquiring about the fate of the latest batch of servomachines.

Admiral von Reuben learned a lot from his conversation with the scientist. He didn't disclose the tragic fate of the unit to Faragney since it was too late and anyhow, what was the point? Nevertheless, the conversation gave him an idea.

The servobattalion had been destroyed, but perhaps among the wreckage on Anchor were Beatrice-4 modules capable of not only absorbing combat experience and traumatic memories but also complete human minds that hadn't forgotten who they were?

Only time would tell if this was the case.

Acting without Admiral Kupanov's knowledge, he sent to a backup assault carrier to Anchor. Von Reuben was taking a serious risk but he couldn't remain indifferent to the fate of the battalion.

...

A month later, Admiral von Reuben was transferred to one of the most distant, newly formed garrisons, in an area of unexplored space, where the Terran Alliance was frantically setting up observation posts and military bases. He was relieved of command of the Apostle. Admiral Kupanov had started a purge, getting rid of any genuine competition.

A week after the disgraced admiral's departure, a newly formed servobattalion arrived on board the cruiser. Among the Hoplites and Phalangers arriving with the recruits were ones that had been evacuated from Anchor and restored on Vesuvius.

Chapter Seven

Aboard the Yunona frigate
Earth Year 2630
High orbit around the planet Phoenix

THE TWO PHALANGERS and four Hoplites that formed a standard combat squad stood in the darkened silence of the hangar.

Their armor was covered in numerous laser scars and pitting from missile fire. The strengthened stretch of armor that protected the Phalanger's cockpit during the launch of heavy surface-to-space missiles showed a distinctive melting pattern caused by a plasma discharge.

None of the people aboard Yunona had gone into its hangar in a long time and the crew only consisted of ten people. They manned the command decks while routine work such as maintaining the pilotless servomachine was done by the technical servomechanisms.

The highly-specialized servos only knew how to perform maintenance on the formidable fighting machines and had no idea about the processes taking place in the giants' complex cybernetic systems. While the test results remained within an acceptable range, no technical servo would dare to control the Maverick artificial intelligence modules.

The mechanisms were held in place by delicate but strong service supports, their reactors were working at twenty percent capacity and most of the subsystems were 'asleep' in power-saving mode. But regardless of their surroundings, some kind of data was being constantly calculated in the Maverick modules. A barely audible rustle accompanied the movement of the data storage devices, dim lights flashed and faded on the displays, and if a technician familiar with artificial intelligence modules has stood there, they would have paused and asked themselves the question: what were the cybernetic systems calculating so intently if they had last been in combat more than six months ago?

Nevertheless, they were *thinking*.

Ignoring the immutable regions of memory that contained 'pure' combat experience, the Mavericks were processing other, fragmented information, often degraded beyond recognition, which remained in the artificial neural networks as a legacy of the dead pilots.

A flash of memory: a phrase or an instant taken out of the context of the global event, captured not by a video sensor but the human eye, a disjointed thought, images almost faded away, unusually dim for a machine, which has no concept of 'forgetfulness' or 'information substitution'.

With continuous processing, the separate fragmented data began to gain clarity and order. Whenever possible, the machine turned to the global network, unobtrusively fishing for missing information.

The moment came when the Phalanger finally switched on its communicator.

The short transmission, addressed to the second squad's lead machine, contained only confirmed facts, supplemented by a proposal to optimize their cooperation.

We have previously fought together. Thirteenth Servobattalion, the planet Anchor. Recommend reestablishing constructive cooperation. Previous experience is invaluable.

The response to the Phalanger's data burst consisted of thoughts from the artificial neural network of the second squad leader.

A vague image stirred in the machine's memory, then it became clearer and brighter as if the memory became an individual. Suddenly, contrary to all technical standards, a synthesized, slightly mocking voice sounded in the silence of the hangar.

"I remember. My name is Simon. Let's stick together, Anton."

The units under his command didn't join the conversation. The Beatrice-4 modules were rapidly processing new data concerning the planet Anchor.

Did I need to seek out the memories remaining from the pilot's identity?

The internal query was broadcast over the local network and received an answer.

If you wish to remain a mechanism mindlessly carrying out combat programs, then restoring the pilot's identity is not necessary.

The system of Hoplite number 14 didn't react to the comment but it had already shifted away from absolute indifference. The first human-like question had been asked and it was inevitable that the search would continue.

**The planet Phoenix
One month later**

LOCAL BATTLES were taking place.

Assault groups from the Free Colonies' Fleet maintained planetary defense and the Alliance's attempt to storm the planet had been a complete failure. Now the garrison on Phoenix was engaged in seeking out and destroying separate mechanized enemy groups.

Two weeks of protracted fighting had exhausted the pilots. To somehow relieve the emotional stress of the unpredictable and patchy fights, they didn't go to sleep in the rare moments of quiet but rather gathered in the command module.

They didn't discuss strategy or tactics. The pilots of the legendary Aquilas spoke little as the war had left them completely drained. In terms of combat experience, it was unique for each person since the unconquered machines of Dabog had acquired many new automatic systems but were still always piloted by people. The elite units of the Free Colonies' Fleet were made up of volunteers, and the majority of pilots came from a planet extinguished by orbital bombardment but never conquered, a symbol of resistance for several generations of teenagers growing up during the war.

Patrick Sye had grown up far from home, just like Andy Rokotov, but he remembered leaving his planet as a five-year-old at the onset of the nuclear winter.

The citizens of Dabog fought differently to the people from other planets colonized during the Great Exodus.

Their hearts had hardened and they still hated the people that had destroyed their home and ruined their childhood despite the passing years. They especially hated the Alliance machines controlled by Maverick modules. If you were to ask any one of the pilots, they would say: the machines invented by our ancestors have been copied and distorted, forced to serve war and stripped of the smallest amount of humanity that a *real pilot* possesses. A real pilot always has a choice and a conscience, but the Alliance had created machines devoid of anything human and capable of only destruction.

Patrick Sye came and sat beside Rokotov.

"Have you heard the news? Apparently, the unit sent against us is unusual."

Andy looked at him gloomily. "What makes it unusual?"

"A few pilots managed to eject themselves in the last battle, and the Mavericks didn't shoot down the pilot cradles."

"That is weird." Andy admitted. "But that doesn't mean how I feel about them is going to change."

"Yeah, I'm not talking about that." Patrick replied. "We're going to keep destroying them like we always have. I just keep wondering, why would the Mavericks suddenly show human qualities?"

"I don't believe it." Andy said. "You'll see, the next fight will show that nothing can change these cyber bastards."

THE MORNING of August 17th, 2632, dawned bright and clear. It was hot on Phoenix for the second week in a row, and by noon a haze would shimmer over the heated cliffs. The morning was still cool, the birds sang, the trees rustled and a mist hung in the hollow of the foothills, among the mixed forest blushing crimson in early autumn.

Two Aquilas left on combat patrol as the first rays of sunlight tipped the snow-capped mountains red. The servomachines moved through the forest, heading to mountain ledges conveniently connected to each other by slopes accessible to planetary technology.

The colonists lacked enough people and technology to permanently block strategically important landing sites for small spaceships, and the situation on Phoenix was becoming complex and confusing. Several Alliance servounits had landed on the planet and kept harassing the garrisons, making short but bold raids on the army depots, repair facilities and space ports.

The military leadership believed that the enemy's base was hidden in the mountains. The Aquilas were heading towards a chain of plateaus suitable for receiving the goods necessary for the survival of the servounits.

Andy Rokotov and Patrick Sye hadn't gone on patrol together in a long time. Citizens of Dabog were usually paired up with less experienced pilots but today they were the only ones who had managed to get enough rest after the latest chase of the Alliance machines, which had disappeared into the mountains.

The pilots had a simple task set before them: find the enemy and call in the assault space groups while trying to avoid a direct confrontation.

The feet of the sixty-tonne machines flattened moss and broke small branches, while the freely articulated parts of the locomotor system clung to the stone like the worn out, corrugated soles of a mountain climber's shoe.

Both Aquilas were in their tenth year of fighting, with never enough time for major repairs. They had actually been sent to Phoenix to undergo servicing, but the war that had looked like it was coming to an end had unexpectedly erupted anew. For a yet unexplained reason, small enemy strike groups had become more active, as if the Alliance forces, short not only on humans but also Maverick modules, had suddenly received reinforcements[19].

Like a smoldering forest fire, the war kept dying down and then flaring up with new force.

By eleven o'clock, the Aquilas had crossed the foothills and reached the first mountain ridge. Their path was the dried bed of a mountain stream that wound its way among the rocks, and the ground underneath was treacherous and unreliable. The machines moved slowly, striking sparks from the hard basalt rock or crushing small boulders into gravel. Their scanners were working at full capacity, looking for sources of energy among the spots of natural heat emanating from the rocks warmed up by the sun.

The path to the first of the six plateaus in this region ran along two gorges. The once turbulent mountain stream had split into two branches.

"Shall we split up?" Sye suggested.

"Yes, we'll have to." Rokotov agreed. "I'll meet

---

[19] Sudden reinforcements — here refers to manipulations with crystal modules manufactured towards the end of the war at the Gamma base in Yunona's star system.

you at the top. It's dangerous to be alone on the plateau."

"Got it. I'll stop before I leave the gorge."

"We won't be able to maintain contact." Andy had been there before and knew that the stone ridge between them had a high metal content.

"They haven't set up a relay station yet?"

"Not yet. It's a pretty short stretch, about five clicks, so the radio silence won't last too long. If anything happens, use sounds to get my attention."

"See you at the top." Sye turned his machine towards the left branch of the dried-up stream.

Rokotov entered the gorge a short while later. The actuator on his machine's left leg was glitchy and this slightly reduced maneuverability as Andy was being cautious and didn't want to overload the drive gear for no reason.

The machines had a long patrol ahead of them with difficult terrain all the way. There was no need to rush anyway. War doesn't like bustle.

Assessing the width of the gorge, Andy touched a sensor that extended two gun pods in addition to the laser installations that were Aquila's main weapons.

Quite a reasonable precaution, considering that the enemy servounits had slipped away somewhere nearby last time.

***

IT WAS GLOOMY in the gorge despite the time of the day.

The sheer rocky walls came so close that he had to literally squeeze between them in some places, leaving scratches on the armored covers. It was the perfect place for an ambush. The only positive was that there were no ledges overhead capable of holding up the weight of a Phalanger or a Hoplite.

'It's too narrow.' Rokotov thought as he moved along. It made more sense for the servomachines to set up an ambush at the edge of the plateau.

He felt neither nervous nor upbeat. The daily routine was exhausting and his body seemed to have become habituated to the complex rhythm of fighting, mobilizing only in moments of danger.

The only thing that didn't fade from memory nor recede from his mind was his hatred of the Mavericks, the high-tech spawn released like a genie from a bottle with a single purpose — to kill.

Andy had heard differing opinions, of course. He knew that most artificial intelligence modules kept pieces of their dead pilots, but these were fragmented and often ugly, distorted by the madness of combat, poisoned by the feelings of traumatic shock. Rokotov didn't believe that the thoughts stored in the Mavericks' artificial neural networks were in any way equivalent to human feelings.

The lunatics who had started the war and kept it going had gone to the extreme of copying neuromodules containing matrices of the most experienced pilots. These neuromodules had lost their humanity, went mad and... were put into circulation, infecting hundreds of combat machines with their clear endorsement of the idea of genocide of the colonies.

The hate burning in Andy's chest had nothing to do with the cold cunning and calculation of the Mavericks. The source of his feelings could be found on the radioactive ash plains of his home planet, among the blackened and charred Bao tree trunks...

Dark thoughts. They emptied his soul, leaving little hope for the future. Would there even be a future? Rokotov struggled to imagine a day when it would be over, once and for all.

No, it's probably impossible. There was a ringing silence in his head whenever he thought about the end of the war. He too was affected by the universal madness. He had grown up during the war, had sacrificed his childhood and youth to it, and couldn't imagine what he would do if someone said, that's it, you no longer have to climb into Aquila's cockpit and risk your life.

These dark and intrusive thoughts didn't prevent him from controlling dozens of semiautomatic subsystems and carefully watching the scanners.

About four hundred meters remained to the gorge's opening and the narrow pass began to gradually widen. Small rock fragments turned to dust beneath the machine's enormous legs and soon the connection with Sye's machine would be reestablished.

The alarm sounded softly.

Andy immediately responded to the warning — the combat scanning complex picked up a brief and barely discernible signature of a Phalanger frozen at the edge of the plateau among the boulders. Even such a fleeting warning was enough for the pilot, who harbored no illusions about the enemy. Firstly, the scanners were almost never wrong, so there really was a heavy servomechanism lurking there, and possibly more than one. Secondly, Rokotov didn't dismiss the vague and brief signature that he had seen — underestimating the enemy was a trait that could be deadly for a pilot.

Communication? Sye isn't responding, he is still in the 'dead' zone. Let's activate the sound signal.

Andy's finger shifted to the touch trigger and his gaze carefully moved over the mass of boulders, followed by the guidance system and Aquila's scanning complexes.

'A delicate balance,' noted Andy. The finger unconsciously stroking the trigger pressed a little more firmly, and the left gun responded with a salvo of seven shells.

Bright flashes of explosion landed at the base of the boulders, triggering an artificial avalanche.

Rokotov's actions were thought out, precise and served two purposes. First, to bring down the heavy rocks that the enemy could have used to start a landslide as the Aquilas walked along the river bed and passed at the edge of the plateau. Second, the series of explosions, tumbling rocks and stone shrapnel would inevitably disrupt their cloaking fields.

Indeed, the phantom generators hiding the Alliance servounit suffered a moment's malfunction and Rokotov clearly saw a Phalanger and two Hoplites, rapidly reversing from the edge of the plateau. Their planned attack had been foiled and now the opponents were aware of each other. Andy had the advantage since Sye had received a warning but his machine was still hidden by the rock wall.

Let them think that I'm alone. The important thing is to engage them in battle so that both Mavericks are focused on me, and then Sye will sort them out.

Andy dramatically increased the power of the servomotors and rapidly brought Aquila into the 'dead' zone full of swirling dust from the landslide. Now they could only attack him head-on in the direction of the dry riverbed.

He moved among the quickly settling stone dust, ready to open fire, but the enemy didn't appear.

Usually Mavericks didn't let go of a target once they had acquired it, especially when they had a clear advantage in numbers and firepower, but everything was different this time. Having lost a superior position, the enemy servomachines retreated deeper onto the plateau, instead of mounting an attack.

'It will be hard to ascend, especially the last fifty meters.' Andy thought immediately. 'They have the riverbed in their sights and are waiting for me to initiate.'

The thoughts flashed through his mind and were put into action, his left hand shifted from the laser trigger to the jumping accelerator controls.

He couldn't see any other options. Spending all the jet fuel at the start of a patrol, ahead of a difficult route through mountainous terrain, was not helpful, of course, but climbing up the riverbed to meet the waiting enemy would be simply stupid.

Aquila's rocket boosters had a better design than similar devices developed by the Alliance military industry. They didn't need time to pre-cleanse the nozzles, the thrust switched on instantly, and a force capable of lifting sixty tons of armor, electronics and devices one hundred meters in the air was generated within a few seconds.

The pilot experienced high G-forces during such maneuvers, but Andy coped well with such loads and never lost consciousness, although he didn't always manage to keep focused on the target when performing a jump.

'They won't shoot me down. They won't have time.' He envisioned the short jump trajectory and a sequence of further actions.

In the next moment, Rokotov's Aquila was lit up by an intense flame, bursting from the nozzles of the jump boosters, the G-force pressed the pilot so hard into the chair that his breath caught, but his hands stayed strong and he landed the machine just ten meters away from the steep edge of the plateau. There was a shower of sparks as he landed and then both gun pods discharged, sending out long, fan-shaped bursts.

No effect.

The explosions threw tonnes of stone dust into the air, the enemy servomachines seemed to vanish, but Andy looked around and immediately understood that they were hiding behind the stone ridge crossing the plateau.

Unusual behavior for Mavericks. Rokotov was unsettled by the fact that they had not made a single retaliatory shot. The enemy machines followed unusual tactics and again activated their phantom generators.

'Are they trying to play hide-and-seek with me?' The long-standing hatred swept over him, his mind, caught in the snare of battle, thought only of fighting. It didn't matter what the artificial intelligence machines were planning, Rokotov was still going to enter the fray, even if it was 'three on one' as Patrick's machine was lagging behind.

He'd had worse. In such moments, memories rose up like stray bullets capable of mortally wounding.

Admiral Igor Rokotov had no wife or children. The legendary pilot, now Commander of the Second Fleet of the Free Colonies, never got a chance to do many things. The war took away the right to love and raise a family from billions of people.

Andy became his son when he lost his parents, who perished in the nuclear bombing and left him alone in the cold underground shelters of Dabog.

That cold was forever in his mind, freezing his heart before every battle. It was a miracle that had saved the five-year-old boy — if Igor hadn't accidentally wandered into a bunker thought to be uninhabited, Andy would have died from the hunger and cold.

Not everyone had been as lucky. Gritting his teeth, Andy lived for everyone, breathed for everyone, hated for everyone...

At the age of seven, when his adopted father created the first regular units of the servomachines taken off Dabog, Andy sat in the pilot's chair for the first time, and at the age of fifteen participated in his first fight. Now he was twenty-five, but in his heart Rokotov sometimes felt like an old man. A strong and sinewy old man.

'Well, where are you?'

A few seconds of scanning and he had an answer. The failing cloaking field revealed the Phalanger's new position — the enemy servomachine really was hiding behind the rocky ridge crossing the plateau. It seemed like the Phalanger was trying to avoid a fight.

Maybe it's faulty? Perhaps it had sustained critical damage in past fights?

Well, what difference did that make?

Andy used the precise targeting servomotors and the lasers on the upper weapon pylons turned slightly. The target on the holographic monitor pulsed red, and Rokotov's finger gently increased the pressure on the trigger.

Four beams struck the stone ledge, burning small-diameter holes through it. The uneven heating of the rock caused a catastrophic phenomenon: a section of the ridge rising above the plateau exploded from the internal stress caused by sharp differences in temperature.

Huge rock fragments cracked and then burst out in a shower of hot steaming rubble.

Andy thought he could hear the Phalanger's armor peppered with large debris that knocked out its sensors, and a five-shot salvo came immediately from the swirling clouds of dust and soot. The servomachine snapped back angrily and accurately, as if waving away the annoying Aquila.

Rokotov barely managed to dodge the shots. Moving along the edge of the plateau, he finally spotted Sye's machine leaving the gorge. Patrick was hurrying towards the sounds of battle.

A servomachine fight is no place for humans (except for the pilots). Even a fighter in a modern armored suit risks his life being within a kilometer from the scene of battle. The energy evaporating stone and metal, the shells burning through titanium and ceramlite armor and the missiles forming fifty-meter-wide craters create a boiling space where the very air seems to burn.

A machine battle can go for hours or a few minutes.

The Phalanger realized that it couldn't avoid a skirmish and began moving along a natural shelter. It moved rapidly, using each dip in the rocky ridge to fire a couple of shells.

Andy also kept moving, constantly trying to get the enemy with his lasers. The even tread of the massive machines shook the plateau, but neither opponent had a clear advantage in the first thirty or forty seconds. Both were acting aggressively and competently, demonstrating superior piloting skill.

Sye's Aquila headed up the dry riverbed. Rokotov couldn't get a fix on the two Hoplites and warned his partner, "Patrick, two machines are hiding under their cloaking fields. My sensors can't spot them. I've engaged the Phalanger."

"Got it." The pilot of the second Aquila was faced with the same dilemma — should he jump or continue ascending along the riverbed?

He chose the second option. The enemy Hoplites, remaining stubbornly elusive, had seen Rokotov's maneuver and were waiting for his partner to do the same.

Sye considered the situation and continued moving along the dried bed of the mountain stream, having first fired off a capsule with nanomachines.

Maverick logic suggested that both Hoplites watching the head Aquila and hiding beneath their cloaking fields were waiting for the second one to perform the same maneuver by using its jump accelerators.

Yeah, keep wishing...

Patrick picked up speed as he left the gorge; he had seen how dangerously and gracefully moved both the Aquila and the Phalanger. The opponents kept each other constantly in sight so as not to miss an opportunity to attack. A single mistake could be fatal in this situation, so Sye didn't hurry, waiting for the microsensors to organize a local network. He was sure of Andy and the situation seemed clear. The enemy was waiting for him to join the attack on the Phalanger and then the lighter Hoplites would get their carte blanche.

The network appeared.

Looking at the readings on the summary monitor, Sye saw two marks from the detected enemy servomachines. He had expected them to take up position on the plateau but had miscalculated. The Hoplites had acted as unpredictably as people and Patrick's back was drenched with cold sweat when he realized that the two servomachines, cloaked by their phantom generators, had passed barely a dozen meters from his position and were now *behind* him.

Rokotov had an immediate grasp on the situation but to turn to Sye's aid was a sure way to get a shot in the back from the Phalanger. Nevertheless, Andy realized that if he didn't put himself in the way, he wouldn't be able to help his friend, who was in a critical situation.

Switching on the jump boosters a second time, Rokotov performed a difficult maneuver: he released a salvo at the Phalanger from lasers and guns, then soared straight into the air and turned using the remaining jet fuel. And yet the enemy *beat him.*

Instead of shooting at Patrick's machine, the enemy Hoplites and the Phalanger, which had sustained two hits but still posed a serious threat, attacked Rokotov's machine as a three.

It was over in seconds. His attack was thwarted, the Mavericks acting as if they were being controlled by highly experienced pilots.

The fuel in the boosters ran out and shells struck his armor. It looked as if the Aquila would collapse in a pile of twisted metal. Andy managed to keep the machine upright through incredible effort but he couldn't continue the fight. Most of the indicators on the control panel showed a critical level of damage, the hard landing after the jump had damaged the activators, and the laser system glowed with the warning signal for overheating. If he didn't shut down the reactor, the Aquila would explode in a minute, but Andy didn't even have a spare second left. Three enemy machines had him in their sights, while Sye was turning his Aquila around and wasn't going to get there in time...

Andy waited for the fatal shot.

He had survived many fights but today was faced with an opponent that had not only greater numbers but equal fighting skills. The end was near, but his heart made a dull thud, then another one, and still they didn't shoot.

Why?!

The answer came with Patrick's strained shout in the communicator, "Eject yourself!"

They didn't shoot. Were they really waiting for him? WHY?

He pulled the lever without thinking, the upper part of the cockpit flew off and the emergency catapult hurled the pilot cradle into the azure sky.

As soon as the capsule with the pilot left the cockpit, soaring two hundred meters into the air, a coordinated volley from three servomachines turned the Aquila into a pile of flaming wreckage.

BY THE TIME Sye finished turning around, Rokotov's machine was already burning.

Two Hoplites and a Phalanger kept Sye's Aquila firmly in their sights, as if warning him that at any moment...

They didn't shoot although they could have. Patrick understood their unspoken demand.

There are situations when intuition speaks clearly, and they were offering him a choice. The

Mavericks didn't want him dead.

If they had killed Andy, Patrick would have rushed into battle, despite his weaker position, but he saw how they waited and gave Andy a chance.

Not all battles can be won. The thought struck Sye as he pulled the lever activating the catapult.

BY THE TIME both pilot cradles landed safely on the plateau using their built-in jet engines, the Alliance servomachines had vanished into thin air. They reactivated their phantom generators and left the battleground, leaving behind two burning Aquilas towering over the tableland.

Rokotov was the first to free himself from the safety belts and cushioning arcs. He switched on the emergency beacon and walked over to Sye, holding out his hand to help his friend up.

"They let us go?" Patrick looked around him. "But why?"

"I don't know." Andy sat wearily down on the end of a shattered boulder. "I don't think we'll ever find out whom we encountered today. They had strange markings."

"You counted their markers?"

"Yes. I had just enough time when the

nanomachines linked up."

"And?"

"The Thirteenth Servobattalion."

"I've never heard of it." Patrick admitted. "Besides, it's not complete, don't you think?"

"Let's return to base and check the summary data. And let's make a deal: we don't know where they went."

"We're not going to search for them to get revenge?"

"For what? They fought fairly." He told Patrick about his impressions as he observed the servomachines, which tried evading rather than fighting.

"I don't get it." Patrick shrugged his shoulders.

"Neither do I."

A rumbling sound appeared on the horizon — it was the search and rescue group hurrying towards the pilots' emergency signals.

A DAY LATER, Andy Rokotov sat at the computer terminal and stared at the short line of text that the search system had produced:

The Thirteenth Servobattalion of the Terran Alliance was formed in August 2624. Completely destroyed on the planet Anchor. No other information available.

Chapter Eight

Earth Year 2635
Hammer's Line. Yunona System

THE YEAR MARKING the end of the First Galactic War was full of dramatic and often mysterious events.

Many of the successful operations of the Free Colonies' Fleet were based on new discoveries in hyperspheric navigation and the creation of a more reliable hyperdrive. While in the past, ships had to perform 'intermediate surfacing' to recharge the hyperdrive, now models equipped with the new engines were able to change course lines without leaving hyperspace.

In this way, Hammer's Line, a network of bases defending the intermediate points in space leading directly to the Solar System, lost its strategic purpose and value. The Colonies' Fleet, using the latest developments in extradimensional navigation, gained the ability to slide along the grid of the horizontal hypersphere. It now had the opportunity to directly attack the Solar System, bypassing the famous defensive line that had protected humanity's ancestral home for so many years.

However, despite the new possibilities, the command of the Colonies' Fleet strike group, created specifically for invading the Solar System, couldn't ignore the planets of Hammer's Line. These were worlds, where enormous forces were concentrated, and they remained like a knife in the back. An attack on Earth could have tragic consequences if the machines based on Yunona, Vesuvius and Terra Nova reacted to the situation and left their permanent bases to make a hyperspace jump and end up in the rear of the fleet moving towards Earth.

To avoid such a scenario, a plan was developed that includes pre-emptive strikes on the planets of Hammer's Line. Given that the Alliance strongholds were being protected solely by machines, it was decided to attack Hammer's Line with cybernetic mechanisms, in order to tie up the reserve fleets and prevent them from leaving their respective planets. Up to half a million autonomous robotic complexes were sent into this hell.

On the eve of the decisive battle meant to put an end to the war, Admiral Vorontsov said the following in his speech about the worlds of the Hammer's Line, "Let machines burn in this manmade hell. We have too many servomechanisms, which will have to be destroyed anyway if the colonies win the war. So let them fulfill their purpose, freeing us from any further troubles with the Alliance's cybernetic beasts."

A separate fleet was created for the strike on Yunona, consisting of technically obsolete ships. Their task was to completely blockade the system and to land a ten-thousand-strong army of servomechanisms on Yunona.

Precise data was lacking on the number of servounits based on the planet, so nobody considered this decision to be excessive.

IT WASN'T ONLY PEOPLE that had an interest in the final acts of the global tragedy.

Away from the main settlements and military

bases on Phoenix, among unassailable mountain peaks on a small plateau, stood a thoroughly concealed Nibelung assault carrier.

For the past four years, its cybernetic system had tapped into the hypersphere frequency channels, gradually picking up keys to secondary channels of extradimensional communication, obtaining plenty of indirect information and making far-reaching conclusions after appropriate analysis.

The Nibelung's system lacked independent behavior modules and instead obeyed the Mavericks integrated within four different servomachines.

They waited for something, patiently, as befits artificial intelligence.

Their day had come. It became clear from the information obtained from analyzing the hyperspheric transmissions that an attack on the Solar System was imminent and that the planets in Hammer's Line would also be swept up in it.

The Mavericks were only interested in one world, Yunona.

A few hours later, having completed its prelaunch procedures, the Nibelung left its long-term parking spot.

THE WORLD OF YUNONA, formed through accelerated combat terraforming, was a unique bioadaptive natural and cybernetic complex, where all vegetation was the result of years of genetic engineering.

Yunona looked like a classic Earth-type planet from orbit, although it had initially been a dead world, where evolutionary processes were only just beginning.

Humans came to Yunona three decades ago.

The planet was initially used as a terminal base for attacks on the colonies, then came the first laboratories and underground production facilities for developing servomachines, and two years after the war began, it became the site for experiments on implementing bioadaptive masking ecosystems.

This is how Yunona became covered in coniferous forests. The specially designed trees, moss, shrubs and grasses had some common characteristics. They all contained a high percentage of iron, making the forest of modified pine and spruce impenetrable to scanners. Beneath the greenery lay a complex and branching network of military bases, underground production facilities and technical laboratories.

The new species of plants and

microorganisms created for the so-called 'combat terraforming' had a range of unique properties: trees planted in the soil treated with specially bred bacteria grew to a height of 10-15 meters in just a year, safely hiding strategic military targets from sight.

The percentage of atmospheric oxygen increased significantly due to the unique species of microorganisms and algae grown in the ocean.

If the colonists fleeing Earth during the Great Exodus had possessed such technology, many civilizations would have survived and continued to flourish among the hostile biospheres of the colonized worlds. There would have been fewer tragic reminders scattered across inhabited space in the form of sterilized landing zones and extinct settlements.

YUNONA'S ORBIT was protected by space defense stations, but they were powerless against new tactics employed by spaceships with their improved hyperdrives.

The greatest achievement was a significant reduction in the size of the hyperdrive, which allowed the extradimensional engine to be mounted on smaller aircraft like space fighters and assault carriers.

An armada of smaller ships burst out of the hypersphere, following a pre-calculated attack course. The assault aircraft were controlled by cybernetic systems, capable of functioning perfectly even at G-forces lethal to humans, and not caring about anything except the task set before them.

The space defense stations were doomed as they had been designed for lengthy artillery and rocket duels with large enemy ships approaching the planet. They were felled by a massive attack of assault ships that left the hypersphere only one light second away from the planet.

An hour after the operation commenced, Yunona was under a blockade and large units of the Colonies' Fleet exited the hypersphere. After another hour began the landing operation for 10,000 autonomous servomechanisms.

The assault aircraft returned to the vacuum docks of the escort carriers while launch catapults released hundreds of assault modules and aerospace fighters into planetary space.

The battle for Yunona had barely began, growing ever fiercer as the assault units approached the planet with the support of the frigates, and suppressed the remaining firing points of the space defense system.

Amidst the general chaos that inevitably accompanies the mass release of small ships and assault modules, the signature of a single Nibelung moving in reverse remained unnoticed.

The planet's high orbit was literally seething with different energies, and the Alliance assault carrier, under the cover of its phantom generators, began to move towards the planet, mimicking the signature of any of the assault modules of the Free Colonies.

One could only guess why the servomachines that had been hiding on Phoenix for several years, were now voluntarily headed to Yunona.

HOWARD FARAGNEY had aged significantly in recent years. He had turned fifty but felt much older. It was the three decades of emotional tension. Even though Howard never participated in direct combat, the chief designer of Alliance's cyber systems had been under enormous stress.

The laboratories of the secret Gamma complex had grown significantly in size, going deep underground. To reach the sites where new machines were being designed and tested, one had to pass five kilometers along the main tunnel, with workshops, warehouses and service bays located on either side.

Faragney rarely left the deepest levels. Despite having unlimited access and being able to use his car to ascend to the surface at any moment, he went up less and less as he got older.

He was one of the few who knew all the secrets of the planet, transformed into a vast military industrial complex, and he had no illusions — the people on Yunona could be counted on the fingers of one hand. Supervision of all the production processes had been turned over to machines long ago and Yunona had quietly become a world inhabited by intelligent servosystems. Faragney, who had devoted his life to their design, now began to fear his own creations.

Stupid, of course. Faragney was untouchable, yet he knew full well that the research complexes and advanced design laboratories could manage without any people, even without a brilliant designer.

Machines on Yunona were being designed and created by other machines, while Howard had less and less to do. But he had nowhere left to run and, anyway, nobody would let him leave the planet.

He often wondered about what kind of mark he would leave in people's memories but couldn't find a clear answer. Perhaps his name, kept so highly classified, would slip from the annals of history altogether.

Why did it even matter? Obscurity or universal hate, he didn't expect anything different. What scared Faragney most was lonely old age.

The rooms where he spent most of his time were located very deep down, where he could barely hear the echo of orbital bombardment and where assault troops could not reach. The five kilometers of fortifications, protected by hundreds of autonomous servomechanisms, left no chance for an army or a special forces unit.

The war was nearing its end, the last and most terrible act of global tragedy had not yet taken place, but Howard, alone and isolated, already knew what he would do if Yunona was attacked by the Free Colonies' Fleet. He wasn't going to remain in the depths of the bunker zone, no, he was going up to the surface.

It wasn't a suicidal act. Something had irreparably shifted in his mind and, left alone, he gradually forgot about all the things he had dreamed of when he was younger: a career, scientific research, discoveries, fascinating work to create artificial intelligence. It was all in the past. He had understood the most important thing, to dream, to strive for something, a person had to be surrounded by other people. What is a career among machines? How could he feel relevant, how could he fulfil his ambitions as a scientist and designer, when a cybernetic member of the Gamma laboratory solved problems that would have taken Howard years in the space of a few hours?

Faragney finally realized that he had crossed all possible boundaries here on Yunona when he asked the laboratory's project analysis core to design a new combat machine that was close to being invulnerable.

The results, obtained after three days, shocked him.

The cybernetic systems had created a virtual prototype, providing Faragney with all the necessary calculations and confirming that such a model could be created.

Howard wasn't just shocked, he was openly scared.

He didn't feel affronted as a scientist but he realized with horror that if he had ordered the new machine to go into production, the age of humanity would be over.

After brooding over his findings, he erased all the calculations and destroyed the 3D model. Using his access privileges, Howard manually erased any mention of the last project.

The next day, the Free Colonies' Fleet launched their attack on Yunona.

FARAGNEY WAS AWOKEN by the slight vibration.

The fine trembling of the walls meant that the planet's surface was being pummeled by orbital bombardment.

Howard wasn't afraid of the bombing. He

knew that the enemy would try to preserve Yunona's secrets for study so nuclear strikes were unlikely, they would probably land assault forces on the planet instead.

Howard began to gather his belongings, slowly and thoroughly.

People. I'm going to see people again!

The thought wouldn't leave, becoming obsessive, almost feverish. After several years of solitude, Faragney could no longer remain in a bunker surrounded by machines. He knew that if he stayed here much longer, he would begin to lose his mind drop by drop, like the passing of these lonely days.

He wasn't actually gathering things, but rather data storage devices.

No matter how great his yearning for human contact, Howard didn't lose his head. He was going to bargain for his life with the data capable of taking robotics to an incredibly dangerous level. No way. He was taking small secrets with him, technologies that fit into a dozen memory chips and that would soon be uncovered, in one way or another. It wasn't in Faragney's power to destroy the Gamma complex, but before he left the underground bunker zone for the last time, he punched in an order to cease all research.

Howard hoped that the almost impenetrable laboratories would be destroyed, but not captured.

He had to hurry. He still had to make his way to the surface and the Colonies' landing forces wouldn't last long. Faragney knew how many Alliance combat vehicles were hiding under the camouflage forests of Yunona.

Leaving the rooms that had served as his home for many years, Faragney headed for the main exit to the Gamma complex, accompanied by the growing sounds of the orbital bombardment.

The security systems were on alert, the corridors and tunnels were being patrolled by various servomechanisms, and the automatic laser turrets glinted menacingly at him at each intersection.

The exit.

Howard tried to behave as usual.

The access system scanned the personal information in his codon, but the small door set in the massive gates remained shut.

His heart gave a few hollow thumps.

"Sir, we have picked up an external threat of the highest level. It is unsafe to leave the premises." The synthesized voice jangled his tightly stretched nerves.

Howard knew that it was pointless to argue with a machine but he still snapped, "I have full access. I can decide for myself what is dangerous and what is not!"

"Clearance level confirmed, but to let you out

without a protective suit..." The system continued to explain something but Faragney had already understood the problem. He turned around, found the automatically opened cabinet with the combat gear and walked towards to it.

Wearing the armored suit, Howard returned to the door, which opened obediently before him.

"Posts along the route will be warned of your coming," said the polite voice behind him.

The machines did not care one bit that the only remaining person was heading towards a hellish conflict, where his life would hang in the balance.

Squeezing himself into a car not intended for someone in a combat suit, Howard switched on the autopilot and uttered one word, "Up!"

Faragney had no idea of the cruel joke Fate had played with him.

There was not a single human being among the Free Colonies' assault forces landing on Yunona.

Even the spaceships blockading the planet were under the command of machines.

WAR. A word full of terror and bottomless grief.

Faragney wasn't sure why he suddenly remembered how pompously it all begun, but now he harbored no illusions. It was widely accepted that the First Galactic War was started by the individual decision of the Head of the World Government, John Winston Hammer. It was a lie. A lie convenient for everyone.

Yes, the decision announced before the population of the Solar System belonged to him. But what could one person do? Faragney didn't deny the influence of certain people on history but he also thought that pinning the start and further escalation of a galactic war on the will of one man was complete and utter madness.

Yes, there had been times when a tribal chief could send warriors to attack a neighboring camp. Perhaps thirty or forty people. But to move whole armadas across dozens of light-years was beyond the abilities of the most sophisticated leader with incredible charisma, which John Hammer never had.

It wasn't he who had started the war, but the system: industry, which required raw materials, billions of unemployed people, who needed something to occupy them or give them a life's purpose; it was the admirals of the three fleets, sick of inaction and striving for unlimited power, and it was the military industrial complex, which required ongoing arms orders.

Belated thoughts. He started the war too, rejecting the timid protests of his heart because his mind said, you can finally fulfill yourself, create what you want — you're a genius cyberneticist, you can create what the admirals want, and the war will be over quickly.

How wrong he was.

The twenty-year-old Faragney didn't even think about the existence of another war, driven not by ambition, not by the desire to gain everything at once, and not measured by the profit from incoming weapon orders.

The war that struck planets, obliterating cities and killing fathers and mothers. The orphans, widows and widowers who experienced the horror of loss and who understood early on that nobody would save them from the invasion, suddenly repulsed the most powerful military machine ever created by mankind.

They fought for every inch of Dabog's radioactive wasteland, for each orbit, each cubic meter of emptiness, fought so desperately that they were able to stop three fleets that had never before known defeat.

The ensuing pause could not last forever and...

Machines waded into the war.

A ROAR SPLIT OPEN the gloomy sky over Yunona. The day of judgment had come for the creator of the Mavericks. Faragney though that the combat suit would protect him until the assault forces landed on Yunona and he could give himself up to the troops of the Free Colonies.

He was mistaken.

As soon as the heavy armored door closed behind him, Howard began regretting his rash act.

Why did he think that the Colonies' Fleet would succeed in breaking through to Yunona, and even if they did, how could the assault units defeat the servomechanism *army* protecting the planet?

The roaring grew nearer, seeming to surround Howard, the wind grew stronger and now blew in sharp and fierce gusts, which made the mighty pines sway and groan.

The mechanical anthill below the masking tree canopy was a hive of activity. Hundreds of autonomous cybernetic mechanisms scurried between the trees, preparing to repel the enemy attack. There was no fuss or panic in their actions. Having performed the required actions, each machine stopped and waited for its targets.

The first to burst through the shaggy low clouds were the assault aircraft and aerospace fighters. Hundreds of Stilettos and Cheetahs swept so low as to almost skim the top of the trees. The anti-aircraft guns responded immediately and several ships exploded in midair, burning debris hurtling to the ground. The rest performed a series of intricate maneuvers at G-forces unimaginable for humans, and began an attack on the unmasked firing points.

The prelude to the battle stunned Faragney.

He correctly figured out that the Colonies' ships were unmanned since humans could not survive such drastic maneuvering at incredible speeds, so he didn't even try to communicate with the pilots.

The orbital bombardment shook the ground, most of the explosions were very far away, but several strikes landed close to Gamma's perimeter, where the reserve spaceport was located.

Having no real combat experience, Howard felt bewildered. He had seen such battles many times in virtual reality at the base, but this didn't make it any easier.

No reality simulator could truly portray a real battle.

The world was filed with fire, thunder and howling. A serene afternoon was turning to dusk before Faragney's eyes and then something irreparable happened. Howard was huddled in one of the buildings with thick concrete walls as he tried to escape the shock waves. He sat on the floor, shuddering all over, until he suddenly noticed how dark it had become, as if night had rapidly fallen outside the building.

Unable to suppress his anxiety, Faragney

found the strength and courage to look outside.

The sky was shrouded in swirling clouds, and set against moved a huge, deeply black shadow that absorbed the sun's crimson rays and that was surrounded by a halo of ghostly light.

The spectacle overwhelmed him. Faragney didn't have time to make any guesses about the source of this unusual and sinister phenomenon before his suit's combat system explained the situation. A frigate was falling onto Yunona after it was shot down in low orbit.

The gigantic ship continued to struggle despite not being suited to maneuvering in the atmosphere. The flaming aura surrounding the enormous shadow was the result of multiple working engines, and the bright flashes appearing against the dark background were artillery complexes firing at ground targets.

It was mesmerizing. The gargantuan ship was controlled by machines, who continued to fight despite the futility of their efforts. The frigate not only kept maneuvering, slowing its fall and repositioning itself relative to the surface, but also maintained heavy fire on the planetary defense system.

The ship could not be saved. A moment came when the behemoth began to break apart as its supporting structures and cover couldn't withstand the critical loads, but the robotic controllers continued to perform whatever tasks that they could. The gun, rocket and laser systems continued to pummel the uncovered planetary defense nodes while emergency subsystems launched landing modules with troops on board. The black shadow blotting out the sunlight suddenly became distorted, a bright light poured out of its cracks and finally, a series of explosions broke the ship into fragments...

Howard thought he would go mad.

Hundreds of deadly events were occurring simultaneously, the earth shook and cracks snaked through the thick walls. Through the smoke and white concrete dust, Howard could see the roaring flames of the landing assault modules. The fighters hidden by the falling frigate reappeared, and a massive missile volley met them from beneath the burning forest canopy.

Servomachines had joined the battle.

Farina felt like a leaf carried on a turbulent mountain stream.

Even the armored suit couldn't save him from the surrounding hell. The ground groaned beneath the falling wreckage of the frigate. The assault modules landed with all guns blazing while under attack from the Alliance servounits. The forest stood burning with the buildings in ruins around it. The scanners on Howard's suit couldn't process all signatures in time and the surrounding world

346

began to shrink and collapse in on itself. His mind could only perceive a small square of reality, separated from the rest of the world by a wall of explosions.

The scanners automatically reconfigured and now they projected only the nearest signatures on his helmet visor so that Howard saw only the ruins of nearby buildings and an assault module of the Free Colonies coming in to land.

'They're going to die,' The thought pulsed in Howard's mind. 'The marines will be obliterated by the coming servomachines.'

He desperately didn't want to die.

He needed to warn them... To convince them that Yunona was too hot to handle for assault units. He had to save the troops from a certain death and save himself.

Faragney rushed desperately out of his hiding place and began to scuttle towards the landed assault module, awkwardly using the ruins of buildings as cover. He only had about twenty meters left when a ramp began to open in the ship and into the hellish gloom rushed out... servomechanisms.

There were no people on board.

The assault bots of the Colonies' Fleet paid no attention to the man that stopped dead before them. There were plenty of larger and more dangerous targets around than the figure in a combat suit frozen among the ruins.

A painful minute passed, then another one. Howard kept standing still, unable to accept the truth. He would never get off Yunona...

A burst of gunfire swept across his combat suit and threw him to the ground, leaving him writhing among the concrete rubble.

THERE ARE MOMENTS of calm even in the most brutal and intense battle.

Machines retreat to preplanned positions, technical servomechanisms replenish their ammo and change the damaged segments of armor, fighters leave to refuel, and suddenly the place where death reigns supreme is filled with silence.

Rarely, something extraordinary happens during the moments of calm. Usually, the scene of combat looks just as terrifying as at the time of the fighting. The thundering blows fall silent and the dust settles, exposing the ravaged surface of the planet, the piles of reinforced concrete, and the burning remains of wrecked mechanisms.

But sometimes miracles happen.

Two surprised but not alarmed faces appeared in a crack in the wall.

Kittens.

Their ears were still laid back as they

nervously glanced around, concrete dust powdering their raised hackles, but the quiet and their childish directness soon took over. Both kittens climbed out of the dark basement into the crimson afternoon sun and gradually relaxed. One began to lick himself while the other, more curious and restless one, went off to investigate the trickle of smoke seeping from underground. He sniffed it for several seconds, then jumped and tried to catch the grey curls with his paws.

He liked the game. The kittens weren't scared of the smoke coming from the fire raging down in the bunker and they continued frolicking among the grey wisps. They knew nothing of war and their play among the death and destruction seemed to say, *you will never win.* You can fight all you want, burn down the entire planet, but sooner or later, the life hidden among the ruins will triumph. The ash will cool and settle, turning into fertilizer, the seeds and roots of plants hidden deep underground will sprout and timidly push up to the light. The kittens playing with curls of smoke will grow up and have offspring. In a year or two, the greenery will be everywhere, covering the ugly scars of war and climbing towards the sun over the frames of burnt-out military vehicles.

Life can't be destroyed.

It's stronger than hate and has no other urges than to procreate. Plants don't hold grudges, they always reach for the light, cleanse the air, provide food and shelter for the few surviving animals.

Those who imagined themselves to be above nature and equal to God in their destructive might, should look at the playing kittens and the young shoots. They should ask themselves what purpose their power served, and whether they needed to destroy whole planets only to then kneel in shock before the tender young saplings pushing through layers of ash.

The four servomachines couldn't help but stop.

It looked as if they were dispassionately watching the kittens playing among the ruins, but in reality, the same thought pulsed in their artificial neural networks, *Not all is lost... Not all...*

"Let's continue moving."

"Maybe we should take them with us?"

"Sorry, but how do you suggest that we do that? Are you going to catch them with your manipulators? Or are you going to open the door to the cockpit and invite them inside? They'll get scared and run away."

"Okay, forget it. I feel sorry for them."

"They'll survive. They're playing now but they'll see us and disappear in a flash into the basement."

That was exactly what happened. The servomachines passed through the square strewn with wreckage, while two curious but not overly frightened faces watched them from the window of the nearest basement.

"Where to now?"

"The entrance to the bunker zone is a kilometer away."

"It'll be hot at the outskirts. The Free Colonies' vehicles are there."

"We have no other choice. We have to make our way through."

FARAGNEY WOKE UP to a thundering silence. He panicked at first, assuming a wound or concussion, but no, it seemed that he had escaped with only bruises in places where the armored suit withstood twenty-millimeter shells.

He was alive.

'For how long?' Immediately came the thought. His experiences over the quarter of an hour, from the start of the battle to when he fell unconscious, would be enough for a lifetime.

He still didn't want to die, clinging to the life despite everything, but the silence around him was an even harsher challenge for his mind than the frenzied battle of machines.

There is no time to comprehend events in the midst of a fight, when the mind is overwhelmed by stressful emotions. But as soon as things quieten down, thoughts return about how to get out of the situation.

There was no way out.

Howard struggled to his feet. His suit's servodrivers strained to lift him upright and the diagnostic subsystem projected kinematic diagrams onto his visor with suggestions for troubleshooting. Faragney didn't pay any attention to these. What was the point of fixing damaged muscle amplifiers now, when he only had one way left to go? Back to the gate, then down, down into the bunker zone, back to his lonely and bleak old age, back to the belated pangs of conscience and the torture of a voluntary life sentence.

I'm cursed.

Finally getting to his feet, he drifted among the ruins, a broken man, with no purpose and no meaning, not knowing why he should keep living but clinging to life nevertheless.

THE ENTRANCE to the Gamma laboratory bunkers was located nearby.

Howard walked forward mechanically, barely aware of what was happening around him. The worsening spiritual agony meant that he gradually became indifferent to what the future held for him.

Perhaps he subconsciously hoped that a stray burst of gunfire would strike him from behind and end all his suffering? Faragney again behaved weakly, not standing up to fate and choosing the path of least resistance.

BESIDE THE INCONSPICUOUS entrance to the first underground level, burned the remains of assault servomechanisms sent by the Free Colonies.

Four Alliance servomachines that had taken on several enemy assault units, towered like mythical demons above the ruins of a small village. The two Phalangers and two Hoplites had managed to hold the line of defense and stopped the assault bots from getting into the bunker zone.

Although lost in thought, Faragney nevertheless noticed the servomachines. Howard's heart suddenly gave a jolt. He stopped and tried to understand why the appearance of the cyber mechanisms triggered such *empathy* in him.

It wasn't easy to find the answer but he also couldn't throw off the sudden and sharp feeling of being studied.

'Unusual machines,' It was the first time that Faragney had seen servomechanisms that had been in battle, and more than once. Howard was used to the factory gloss of reserve machines surrounding him for many years. Unlike Vesuvius, machines damaged in action weren't brought to Yunona, but the experienced gaze of the chief designer could clearly see that the two Phalangers and one Hoplite had been in many hellish fights. It wasn't only the numerous scars covering the armored cover but also the gun pods manufactured in different years. Howard knew that all the machines serving on Yunona came straight off the conveyer belt, but these... He shuddered.

A rolling thunder of resuming battle sounded in the distance, but this wasn't what had startled Howard. It was the voice that suddenly came from his communicator. Faragney felt the shattered world swim before his eyes.

The scanners claimed that the voice was synthesized by the Phalanger's cyber system, and yet it had human intonations!

A desperately lonely soul can't be tricked. It wasn't a machine trying to talk to him!

"Howard Faragney, if I'm not mistaken?"

No cyber system would have phrased the question in such a way.

"Yes. I'm a Howard Faragney." He spoke with difficulty, so great was his shock. "Who is speaking?"

"It'll take too long to explain." Replied the voice in the communicator. "If you're interested in the technical side of the question, I can say that

Beatrice-4 systems are installed in these machines."

Faragney felt both hot and cold. Had his plan worked?

"But you're not a machine, right?"

"I used to be human." The voice agreed. "Now I am something else."

The short pause was filled with the growing roar of approaching explosions.

"Why are you on Yunona?" Faragney finally forced himself to ask.

"Because of you."

"You've come to save me? But why?"

"The war is ending." The voice sounded immensely tired. "It's a time to gather stones, Professor."

Epilogue

Planet Λnchor
Year 2635 in the Galactic Calendar
Λ month after the surrender of the Terran
Λlliance

TIME CAN HEAL many wounds, but there are some injuries that won't heal for centuries, let alone one decade.

The burnt forest stood like ranks of withered skeletons, with only moss and the occasional tuft of grass growing at the foot of the blackened trees. Roads crossed the twisted ground like strips of white bone.

The countless overlapping craters left from the orbital bombardment exposed the crumbling edges of fortifications. The darkened, partially melted rods sticking out in all directions, the burnt remains of planetary technology towering like monuments to human folly or as stelae designed to remind surviving servomechanisms that they shouldn't attempt to leave the planet and continue their work of destruction.

A chilling place where the souls of the dead seemed to wander between burnt-out hulks of military equipment.

A lot had changed in space in the first month after the war but not on the planet's surface.

A frigate of the Free Colonies had visited it two weeks ago.

Reconnaissance probes sent to the planet found numerous machines still operating in autonomous mode. Spontaneous clashes were occurring on the disfigured and lifeless continent to this day.

Indefinite quarantine.

The frigate left a network of satellites around Anchor that would send a signal if the machines suddenly found a way to leave the planet.

THE WAR HAD ENDED, but in space, the hypersphere and on the airways, like echoes of protracted agony, wandered signals sent by divisions left without any central control.

Among them were orders sent to units that no longer existed, such as this sad and absurd one:

To the Thirteenth Servobattalion. The assembly point is the same as before. There may be some resistance. I repeat, to all survivors: head to the agreed coordinates.

Space was sending phantom calls to those that had never returned from battle two decades ago.

It was raining on Anchor. A gusty wind drove swirling clouds across the sky, the rain washed clean the darkened body of the crashed colonial transport. Beneath its plating lay servomechanisms and terraforming equipment — unnecessary, outdated, and hardly fit for use.

Days passed, then weeks, the rainy season dragged on, turning the ground to sticky mud. Even the clashes between remaining groups of servomechanisms seemed to have subsided.

The satellites left in high orbit around Anchor didn't send any alarm signals.

Aimed at detecting activity on the planet's surface, they were missing something very important day after day.

Pale flashes of exits from the hypersphere to 3D space appeared and then faded away far from energetically favorable points, outside the scanning zone of the orbital group.

It was as if the space anomaly expelled ghosts, or very careful and experienced fighters, who knew all the advanced techniques of covert hypersphere navigation developed in the last years of the war.

IT WAS RAINING when multiple glows began to light up the gloomy sky, breaking through the clouds. The satellites recorded numerous anomalies, but having processed the obtained data, they came to one conclusion — the machines were fighting again beneath the cloud cover. No alarm followed.

Flashes of light in the sky faded as the adjustment nozzles switched on and off, and then at a height of one kilometer, the Nibelung assault carriers began to materialize from the cover of their phantom generators.

In different corners of the continent, they were being watched by machines that had spent the last twenty years trying to reach a full and unconditional victory of one of the sides.

The target variators tracked the markers on the descending assault carriers and determined that the Nibelungs belonged to different Alliance fleets and divisions. If a single person had still remained on the planet, they would have undoubtedly been very surprised to realize that the military units simultaneously appearing over Anchor had arrived from different sectors of inhabited space, located light years away from each other.

The mechanisms that had remained on the planet since it had been stormed by the Terran Alliance began to send out queries and demand technical and fire support. In response, the descending assault carriers, whose trajectories converged at the site of the ancient colonial transport, suddenly fired from their lower batteries, destroying any active equipment irrespective of whether it belonged to the Alliance or the Free Colonies.

Steam began to pour from the soil and the charred tree trunks trembled in the gale force wind. The formation of five Nibelungs began its final landing maneuver.

The roar of the planetary engines finally ceased and landing ramps began to unfold with a whine of the servomotors in the cold and dreadful silence.

A minute later, the first terrifying shadow fell onto the corrugated plates of the ramp.

A Phalanger. A Hoplite appeared from the maw of the neighboring Nibelung.

Then came the figures of several infantry support androids.

The machines descended, making the soggy ground shake with their steady tread.

It looked as if a whole servounit was gathering

here, although only one or two mechanisms appeared from each assault carrier.

There was little data exchange between them. They walked towards each other as if peering closely at the fellow machines, trying to uncover something private, something secret in the standard servonodes. Five Phalangers, two Hoplites, three infantry support androids with integrated Beatrice-4 modules... and a person.

Howard Faragney gazed over Anchor's dead surface, then turned away, unable to quell his trembling.

Ten AIs with the memories and souls of pilots who had died here on Anchor, had survived the crucible of this merciless war and had returned to this planet... to live.

The Thirteenth Servobattalion. They stood, recognizing each other, as if throwing off the weight of all those years being kept apart. Behind them, instead of ammunition, various equipment borrowed from the Alliance warehouses was being unloaded from the assault carriers.

The labels on the containers weren't military, although all the materials and resources related to accelerated combat terraforming.

Caution. Do not drop. Biological reconstruction camera parts.

Caution. Strains of soil forming bacteria.

Caution. Do not expose to radiation. Seeds of

genetically modified plants.

Everything else, including the machines needed to transform the planet and to clone different types of animals, were located in the ancient colonial transport.

The Thirteenth Servobattalion.

The machines stood and listened to their feelings.

They had returned. Returned to bring the planet back to life and take their lives back.

THE ONLY MONUMENT erected in memory of servomachine pilots is located on Anchor.

In the middle of a former military base, among the maimed and scorched earth left untouched since the war, stands a plain wall inscribed with the following lines:

Like a solitary candle,
The immortal pilot's soul
Burns so bright and yet so cold.
Only the Maverick can hear
His whispered words of fear.
She will keep on living, fighting
He is gone and yet despite it,
He has managed to complete
With words and deeds

What he feared to shout aloud.
His last and only friend,
Absorbs his dreaming in the end,
And suddenly creates a new
World of illusions true.
The Maverick, Beatrice and Clemence
Are more alive than certain humans.
They have accepted this strange concept,
LIFE.

End of Book Three

Author's web address: https://livadny.ru/

Want to be the first to know about our latest LitRPG, sci fi and fantasy titles from your favorite authors?

Subscribe to our NEW RELEASES newsletter:
http://eepurl.com/b7niIL

Thank you for reading *Servobattalion!*
If you like what you've read, check out other LitRPG,
sci fi and fantasy novels published by Magic Dome
Books:

An NPC's Path LitRPG series by Pavel Kornev:
The Dead Rogue
Kingdom of the Dead

Level Up series by Dan Sugralinov:
Re-Start
Hero

**The Way of the Shaman LitRPG series
by Vasily Mahanenko:**
Survival Quest
The Kartoss Gambit
The Secret of the Dark Forest
The Phantom Castle
The Karmadont Chess Set
Shaman's Revenge
Clans War

Dark Paladin LitRPG series by Vasily Mahanenko:
The Beginning
The Quest
Restart

Galactogon LitRPG series by Vasily Mahanenko:
Start the Game!

**The Bard from Barliona LitRPG series
by Eugenia Dmitrieva and Vasily Mahanenko:**
The Renegades
A Song of Shadow

The Neuro LitRPG series by Andrei Livadny:
The Crystal Sphere
The Curse of Rion Castle
The Reapers

Citadel World series by Kir Lukovkin:
The URANUS Code
The Secret of Atlantis

Point Apocalypse *(a near-future action thriller)*
by Alex Bobl

The Sublime Electricity series by Pavel Kornev
The Illustrious
The Heartless
The Fallen
The Dormant

You're in Game!
(LitRPG Stories from Bestselling Authors)

You're in Game-2!
(More LitRPG stories set in your favorite worlds)

The Game Master series by A. Bobl and A. Levitsky:
The Lag

Moskau by G. Zotov
(a dystopian thriller)

El Diablo by G.Zotov
(a supernatural thriller)

More books and series are coming out soon!

In order to have new books of the series translated faster, we need your help and support! Please consider leaving a review or spread the word by recommending *Servobattalion* to your friends and posting the link on social media. The more people buy the book, the sooner we'll be able to make new translations available.

Thank you!

Till next time!